OTTERS IN SPACE 2

JUPITER, DEADLY

MARY E. LOWD

Copyright © 2013 by Mary E. Lowd

All rights reserved.

No part of this book may be reproduced in any form or by any electronic or mechanical means, including information storage and retrieval systems, without written permission from the author, except for the use of brief quotations in a book review.

For all the animals who inspire me. Including but not limited to: Trudy, Quinn, Wendy, Heidi, Theresa, Kelly, Peter, and Ray; Patrick; Tom, Peter, and Henry; Dale and Kira; June, Keegan, Winston, and Egon; Eliot, Kitsa, and George; Cassi, Toby, and their ever-changing foster sibling; Alistair, Oliver, Jeeves, Marlow, d'Artagnan, and all the others; the original Kipper Brighton who wandered through my backyard one day many years ago and all the other neighborhood cats for whom I make up names but whose real names I never know.

CONTENTS

1.	Earth	1
2.	The Asteroid Belt	7
3.	Earth	12
4.	Trailside	20
5.	Earth	27
6.	Trailside	35
7.	Earth	47
8.	Trailside	57
9.	Earth	65
10.	The Asteroid Belt	70
11.	Earth	77
12.	Jupiter System	89
13.	Earth	97
14.	Jupiter	105
15.	Earth	111
16.	The Great Red Spot	118
17.	Earth	125
18.	The Great Red Spot	130
19.	The Great Red Spot	136
20.	The Great Red Spot	150
21.	Earth	164
22.	The Great Red Spot	165
23.	Earth	178
24.	Earth	189
25.	Jupiter	196
26.	Earth	205
27.	Jupiter System	213
28.	Europa	221
29.	Earth	228
30.	Europa	230
31.	The Solar System	238
32.	Earth	243
33.	Papa Fido's T-Bone Steakery	248
	About the Author	255
	Also by Mary E. Lowd	257

CHAPTER 1
EARTH

Trudith watched the orange cats nervously. Although she was larger than them and undeniably stronger, Trudith saw Alistair—a skinny, ginger tabby—as her alpha dog, and Alistair's sister Petra was a complete wildcard. Petra wreaked havoc on any sane sense of hierarchy that Trudith could work out. Yesterday, Petra took orders like the rest of them, but, now, when Alistair needed their support the most, Petra had turned on him.

Trudith edged her black, Labrador bulk towards Alistair, trying to get herself between the two orange tabbies. She didn't think his sister would actually attack him, but, with Petra, she could never be sure.

"Right," Petra snarled, sarcasm dripping from her whiskers. "You believe all those cats turned up on election day... to vote for a dog?"

Alistair shrugged. His new, tailored suit looked loose on him. Trudith could see he was thinking about the night-shift forklift operator he used to be.

Petra spat. "We've *never* had a feline turn-out like this before. There's *no way* all those cats stood in line for hours to vote for the same old dog who would have won without them."

"Maybe it wasn't as many cats as it looked like, Pet," Alistair said to his sister. "It's not like we actually counted them."

Petra grumbled, and her voice lowered. "*No one* counted them. Someone made up the numbers and said…" Petra's voice went all goofy. She fluttered her paws in the air and said, "'Hey look! Big surprise! The *incumbent Sheltie* won.'"

Trudith snorted in spite of herself. "Was that your dog imitation?" she asked.

Petra merely frowned at her, as if to suggest that her brother's *dog* bodyguard wasn't worth actual words. "I think we should ask for a recount," she said to Alistair.

"I think I should concede gracefully."

The two orange cats were at a standoff. Trudith thought about her months working with Alistair. She'd never known a better cat—*no*, a better *person*—than Alistair. He saw right through the masks and walls that dogs and cats put between each other. Trudith had been a dog working for cats for a long time, and she knew cats had the short end of the stick in this world. There wasn't a glass ceiling keeping them down; no, the ceiling above cats was plenty visible with lovely murals drawn all over it. Yet, not just any cat could break that ceiling down.

Trudith's first cat boss, a half-Siamese tabby, had employed her to rough up other cats. That's how Trudith met Alistair. His sister—the *other* sister—Kipper was a target. That's when Trudith realized supporting cats' rights wasn't as simple as picking a cat, any cat, and following orders.

But following orders was most of what Trudith was good at. And she liked following *Alistair's* orders.

"I don't think you should step down," Trudith said.

Alistair looked surprised. Petra did too, for that matter.

"Not yet," Trudith said, smiling her nervous smile. "I mean…" She didn't know what to say, especially not with both cats looking at her. So, she harrumphed, importantly, clearing her throat as if there was more to follow. When she hesitated afterwards, Petra rolled her eyes and jumped in. Trudith was secretly relieved.

"Look," Petra said, "even the *dog* agrees with me. You need to ask for a recount."

Alistair leaned against a desk in their improvised campaign office. "Senator Morrison beat me by a thirty percent margin," he said. "A few miscounted votes wouldn't make that kind of difference."

"It would buy us time," Trudith said. What she needed was time to think. Time to think of a way to keep Alistair from giving up, from going back to operating forklifts at night.

"Yes!" Petra agreed. "Then we can figure out who's behind this!"

"Conspiracies?" Alistair said. He looked skeptical. Another beat and he'd be talking about saving their dignity.

"Kipper!" Trudith exclaimed. If only Kipper were there, she'd know how to keep Alistair in the running. But she was still in space, on that otter spaceship.

"Kipper?" Petra asked. "I thought she was en route to the asteroid belt."

"Yes," Trudith said, thinking about Kipper's last vid-letter. Her ship, the *Jolly Barracuda*, had a trade route to follow, but Kipper expected they'd cross paths with enough other ships in the asteroid belt that she'd be able to catch a lift back to Earth. "It'll be weeks, maybe months, before she gets back."

"Makes her kind of irrelevant, doesn't it, *Trudith*?"

Trudith could hear Petra wanting to hang a derogatory, "*dog*," at the end of her question, but she kept her verbal claws sheathed. Though, in Petra's mouth, even Trudith's own name sounded like an insult.

"Be nice, Pet," Alistair said. "Trudith has a point."

"I do?" Trudith asked. Her mind raced, trying to imagine what it was. Alistair saved her brain from overheating.

He said, "Kipper sounded very mysterious in her vid-mail. I

think she found something flying around with those otters. Something that might affect elections here." He pondered.

Petra looked ready to jump in, start arguing her point, but Trudith put a heavy paw, lightly, on the little cat's shoulder. Trudith knew when to wait.

"Okay," Alistair said. "We'll ask for a recount. We'll wait. See what Kipper has to say."

Trudith let out a slow breath of relief. She liked Alistair's plan. She was good at waiting.

Petra felt differently, of course.

She shook Trudith's paw away from her shoulder and said to her brother, "That's more like it. Now, how are we going to figure out who's behind this?" Her ears perked up, particularly tall, rotating and scanning as she thought. "And how did they manage to stack the votes? Or better yet..." Her voice rumbled into the lower register of a purr. "How can we *restack* them, in your favor?"

Trudith felt a familiar flash of guilt and confusion, the nervous feeling she used to get whenever her old employer told her to go rough some poor cat up.

"Petra," Alistair said. "I don't want to hear about that. If you want to investigate your conspiracy theories, you go right ahead. But don't expect me to get caught up in them."

There was an unhappy rumbling from Petra's throat. Before it could articulate itself into more poisonous words, Alistair added, "And whether the incumbent Sheltie is cheating or not..." He looked Petra levelly in her green cat's eyes. "*You're better than that.*"

Good old Alistair! Trudith knew she was on the winning side. Well, okay, maybe not the winning side. Not yet. But the *right* one.

"Fine," Petra said. "I won't *do* anything, but I will find out who's sabotaged you." She turned on her toes and walked out of the office, striped tail swishing behind her.

"She'll forget all about it in half an hour," Alistair said, now that they were alone in the room. "She'll have some other project taking up all of her attention. Writing a speech about the unfairness of Senator Morrison's space laws or adopting some orphan from a cattery."

Trudith's brown eyebrows furrowed in the midnight black of the rest of her face. She knew better than to say so, but Petra would be a terrible mother. Alistair probably knew it anyway. Hopefully he was being facetious about the idea of Petra adopting an orphaned kitten.

Trudith could much more easily picture Petra abandoning a basket of kittens on a cattery doorstep than taking even one kitten home. Perhaps that was why there were so many orphan kittens and so few orphan puppies.

No. Trudith shook her head, flopping her folded ears and jowls. One violent shake to knock that idea out. That was the kind of thinking that created these sorts of messes. Cats weren't more reckless than dogs. They were poorer. *Think of Kipper*, Trudith told herself. Now, there was a cat who would be a fantastic mother. Or senator like her brother Alistair would soon be. Or a space trader like the otters. Why, Kipper could probably do anything.

"I wonder what she found," Trudith said to herself.

Alistair flicked an ear and said, "Kipper?"

Trudith nodded, her jowls in a serious set.

"I don't know, but let's hope it's good."

Behind Trudith's brown eyes, she was thinking, *Let's hope she gets it to us soon. Before Petra does anything rash.*

"Well, I'm going to call the Election Office back and get the gears moving on a recount," Alistair said, hinting that he'd like Trudith to leave him in the room. However, since Trudith wasn't good at catching hints, and Alistair knew it, he added, "Why don't you go record a vid to send to Kipper? Let her know what's happening."

Trudith nodded another serious nod and left Alistair in his privacy. As she closed the door behind her, Trudith started planning what she would say in the vid. *"Come home soon"* was what she felt, but she knew those weren't the words she'd actually send bouncing from satellite to satellite, through the otters' central space station, and then out to space and Kipper.

CHAPTER 2
THE ASTEROID BELT

Although it only took Trudith's message seconds to reach the Deep Sky Anchor station in Earth orbit and would take another ten minutes to cross the space between there and the *Jolly Barracuda*, Kipper wouldn't receive it for two weeks. The *Jolly Barracuda* flew incommunicado, her flight plans unlogged. Captain Cod felt it was more *piratical* that way.

Every week or two, the *Jolly Barracuda* sent its location, speed, and direction back to Deep Sky Anchor, requesting that any messages for the crew be forwarded. After receiving them, Captain Cod ordered a slight change of course, and his ship slipped into the vastness of deep space.

Trudith's message had poor timing. It arrived at the Deep Sky Anchor communication hub mere minutes after a packet of messages was beamed to the *Jolly Barracuda*. The ship had already changed course, slipping off the station's radar as it approached the asteroid belt from a slightly different angle.

More than a hundred million miles away, Kipper watched a video of Alistair tell her how nervous and excited he was about the impending election, but she did not hear Trudith say "Alistair needs you. *Come home soon.*" (Despite her best intentions, Trudith did record those exact words in her vid.)

Kipper flexed her claws, sighed, and turned off the vidscreen. She gave a slight shove against the com-console and drifted backward and up. She floated through the room, buoyed in the foreign, weightless atmosphere. The *Jolly Barracuda*, from stem to stern, was flooded in a substance called oxo-agua: a highly oxygenated, breathable liquid; barely breathable from Kipper's perspective. The otters loved it. They could swim full-time, never surfacing to breathe, and it cushioned their delicate, earthly frames against the extreme accelerations of rapid space travel.

And the space travel *was* rapid. No ship could match the *Jolly Barracuda*. No other ship came close.

And yet, in true whimsical otter fashion, Captain Cod used his ultra-fast, proto-type spaceship to deal *in art*. Perfectly legal, heartwarming paintings of otters and other animals sailing the sky like sailors at sea. At least, he had dealt legally until a misunderstanding got him and his ship blacklisted by the asteroid art community.

Instead of selling his precious cargo, Captain Cod hung it on his spaceship's walls, protected from the oxo-agua under clear plastic. He wouldn't pay for it, on the theory that it was still in transit. But he wouldn't deliver it to paying customers either.

That's where the *Jolly Barracuda* had stood when Kipper found it. Impeccably decorated with an empty cargo hold.

Meanwhile, Kipper was a cat with a mission. She and her sister, back on Earth, had tripped onto the trail of a conspiracy. Captain Cod and his merry bandits had turned out to be the perfect otters to help her unravel it. But, now, Kipper felt like a kitten in a knitting basket. Her mystery had unraveled all over her, and she was completely tangled up in its threads.

"Any exciting messages?" Jenny, the river otter pilot, asked Kipper, speaking words by signing them with her paws as she swam a curlicue past the drifting cat.

Weeks upon weeks aboard the *Jolly Barracuda* had taught

Kipper to repress the reflex to answer questions with spoken words. Voices came out unintelligible in the liquid atmosphere, and she would invariably end up choking and sputtering on a gulp of oxo-agua. It was bad enough breathing the stuff; she didn't need the extra frustration of trying to force her vocal cords to manipulate it.

Instead, Kipper swung a clumsy paw, barely managing to snag the corner of her mattress. Her claws stuck, and Kipper pulled herself to the bunk. She could float comfortably there framed by the bed's legs and upper bunk. Fewer otters would have to swim curlicues around her while she talked with Jenny that way. Not only would that make her less of an inconvenience —a random obstacle floating in the middle of the barracks—but it also made Kipper much less nervous. The otters onboard swam closer to her than she liked; a clumsy person likes her space, and underwater—or *oxo-agua*—Kipper was a clumsy, clumsy cat.

"So?" Jenny signed, impatience in the quickness of her paws and the curve of her long back. "Did Josh message you?"

Kipper rolled her eyes. Jenny had completely romanticized the messages from Josh. "You don't have enough excitement in your own life?" Kipper signed.

Jenny loop-de-looped in response. Coming out of the loop, she signed, "I take it that's a yes." She treaded over to the com-console and asked, "Can I see?"

Kipper shrugged. Though she felt a secret thrill at the idea of seeing Josh's clear blue Siamese eyes again. Jenny turned on the vid and slid the earphones over her head. Kipper watched the image of Josh, speaking in silence. Josh didn't send vids in sign. He didn't know about the oxo-agua, and he probably didn't know sign language. There wouldn't be much call for it in his perfect little world. Kipper turned away.

The vid continued; Josh's purring voice spoke into Jenny's ears. His resonating tones didn't have the same effect on Jenny as on Kipper. She didn't find herself going all weak and quivery, but she knew enough about cats—and one cat in particular—to guess his message's effect on Kipper.

Kipper knew when the vid ended because she felt the oxo-agua shift as Jenny swam over beside her. Kipper reached out and caught Jenny's flippered paws in her own without looking at her, effectively silencing the otter. Jenny flexed her paws, clearly wanting to sign something, but Kipper gave her paws a squeeze. Jenny understood, and she let her paws go limp.

"Don't encourage me," Kipper signed. She could see Jenny tense, readying her paws to respond. Kipper rushed on: "He's only interested in me because I'm... *exotic*."

Jenny looked at her skeptically. It didn't need saying that Kipper was the plainest, garden variety, gray tabby there could be.

"It's true, though," she signed, earnest in the pain she felt. "He's..." Kipper's paws floated, stalled mid-sign. "Just leave it be." Her face turned down. "I can't explain."

Jenny hugged Kipper. Her short but strong river otter arms wrapped around Kipper's bony shoulders. Dense brown otter fur and fine gray cat fur pressed against each other as the two creatures wobbled slightly in the buoyancy of oxo-agua.

"Did Alistair message you?" Jenny signed when Kipper pulled away.

"The election happened today," Kipper answered. Her spirits lifted as she thought about the exciting things happening on Earth. "But his last message was from two days ago." For all Kipper knew, her brother was a senator-elect by now. She sighed, "I wish I could be there." With a hopeful look, she added, "Any word from Trailside?"

The busiest asteroid in the asteroid belt was called Trailside. That's where the *Jolly Barracuda* planned her next stop and where Kipper hoped to cross paths with enough other ships to find one headed home.

"There're a few ships listed on their registry that I recognize," Jenny signed. "But the cheapest and fastest ships don't usually advertise their whereabouts. Don't worry. We'll find someone the captain trusts to get you home."

Now that Kipper had finished her mission, she could hardly get home fast enough. However, since her body couldn't fly home to her brother, zipping through space on careless wings in the effortless way her imagination could, Kipper had to accept the reality of her situation. She was stuck on this waterlogged bottle of *oxo-agua* that passed for a spaceship.

If Kipper couldn't get herself home as fast as she'd like, there were other things that could precede her, specifically, the findings of her mission. Kipper may have satisfied her own catly curiosity, but there was a whole planet full of cats—and dogs—at home who had no idea about the secret she'd uncovered.

"Let's get back to work on editing that video," she signed to Jenny. "You said the ship picked up some aerial footage?"

"Indeed," Jenny answered. The two of them swam back to the com-console, Kipper lagging woefully behind Jenny.

"I'm so glad you thought to bring that camera with you," Kipper signed when she caught up.

Jenny smiled and signed, "I can't believe you *didn't* bring a camera with you."

Kipper conceded the point. "Regardless," she signed, "I'm glad you got all that footage. A few aerial shots will finish the film off perfectly."

Jenny punched up the record of the *Jolly Barracuda's* external sensors from their last stop. Kipper found herself looking at a grainy image of Mars. As the ship approached, the planet grew larger. Round, red, and exactly the same as it always had been. Then Jenny sped up to the good bits.

Kipper smiled behind her whiskers. It was time to change the world.

CHAPTER 3
EARTH

Trudith waited in the outer office of the campaign headquarters. She expected that when Alistair finished his conversation with the Election Office, he would come out and tell her the plan, but it didn't work that way. Instead, Alistair slinked out, his tail dragging almost on the floor. He was already wearing his jacket as if ready to leave, and he looked completely dispirited. Trudith knew better than to ask, *"What's the plan?"* but, she did ask, "How'd the request for a recount go?"

Alistair shrugged. "They'll do it. But I feel like I'm losing face."

"Better to lose face than lose the election," Petra sang from the corner where she'd been huddled over a com-console for the last hour.

Alistair didn't respond. He didn't say if he'd be in tomorrow either. He just said, "Good night, guys," and headed out into the chill, desert air of New LA. The door thwacked shut behind him, and Trudith let out a jowly sigh. It was frustrating working for cats. They never told her quite what was going on, and she was left to guess for herself. Trudith wasn't great at that. She was great at taking orders.

With a vacuum of command coming from Alistair, Trudith risked glancing nervously at Petra.

"What do you want, *dog*?" Petra asked without looking up.

"What're you working on?" Trudith asked.

Petra looked up at that and narrowed her eyes. "Why do you want to know?"

"Do you need help?" Trudith asked. "I could help you."

"Oh, I see," Petra said, losing interest in Trudith and turning back to her com-console. "The dog needs an order to obey."

"I'm just trying to help." Trudith harrumphed in a growly woof. "So, I guess you don't need help?" An ingratiating whine snuck in at the end of Trudith's sentence, despite her best attempts to quash it.

"No," Petra said. After a beat, Petra punched her com-console off and began gathering up all the papers from her desk. "Don't need it. Don't want it," she said. "Besides, I don't think it would help much to have some *follow-the-rules* dog reporting everything I do back to my *goody-two-shoes* brother. Kind of counter-productive, if you know what I mean." Petra shot Trudith a green-eyed glare, and then she swept out of the office, as quickly as only a cat could.

"Well!" Trudith woofed to herself in the aftermath of Petra's slammed door. There wasn't much point in pursuing an avoidant cat, and Trudith didn't have any other work to do. She guessed it was time to go home.

All their plans had been geared toward Alistair winning. They had lots of plans for pro-cat reforms to introduce to the legislature. Trudith sighed a jowly sigh, as she closed and locked the office.

Right now, fighting for the rights of cats felt highly unsatisfying, but Trudith didn't like to make any important decisions without sleeping on them first. In fact, she wasn't sure it was a good idea to even lay out her options until she'd slept on the facts. So, Trudith headed home for a good night of sleep.

When she woke up in the morning, a little groggy and bleary eyed, the facts didn't feel any clearer, and the idea of examining her options felt overwhelming. Trudith went into work at the campaign headquarters as if it were a normal day.

The whole drive over, Trudith kept worrying. She knew she'd arrive at an empty office and have to face the facts for real. None of the volunteers planned to come in after the election was over. In fact, Alistair might have stopped renting the office. Could it happen that quickly? Would she get there and find the Campaign Headquarters of *Alistair Brighton for Senator* replaced with... a daytime casino? A lot of dogs hanging around, placing bets, playing poker, and wearing green visors?

No, no, no. Trudith couldn't handle the world changing that fast. Fortunately for her, when she arrived at the Campaign Headquarters of *Alistair Brighton for Senator*, they were exactly as they had been, only empty of cat volunteers. Completely unchanged. Trudith unlocked the offices and opened the window blinds. She sat at the front desk. An uneasy grin turned up her jowls. Anyone who showed up would have been impressed by her friendly, welcoming demeanor.

No one showed up. But, sitting there in a familiar environment, waiting and waiting, as Petra and Alistair grew more and more tardy, Trudith found the wheels in her brain turning. Gears churned through the facts of yesterday, and Trudith wondered again and again what devious plans Petra was enacting. If she wasn't here at the office, she had to be somewhere. She'd made it clear that she hadn't given up on the campaign.

Where was she?

The more Trudith thought it over, the more ominous Petra's words from the night before became. If Petra didn't want Trudith reporting on everything that she did to Alistair, then Petra must be planning to do something she didn't want Alistair to know about. Something Alistair wouldn't have approved. Something *unethical*.

By midmorning, when Alistair arrived, looking harried and hassled, Trudith had made up her mind.

"Good morning, Trudith," Alistair said, hanging up his coat on the corner coat rack.

Trudith didn't want to add to Alistair's burdens. She wouldn't tell Alistair what Petra had said to her. Whatever personal problems Trudith and Petra had with each other, Trudith couldn't deny that Petra was on Alistair's side. So, if she didn't want Alistair to know what she was doing, maybe it was better that he didn't.

"Have you seen this?" Alistair asked. He sat at the com-console Petra had been using the night before.

Trudith's heart leapt to her throat. Was it too late to protect Alistair from Petra's nefarious, underpawed, unethical doings?

"Kipper's sent us a video. Want to watch it?"

Trudith's heart settled back in her chest, though it was still beating fast. Petra would know better than to leave her tracks uncovered.

"Huh," Alistair said. "There's a text message with the video." Alistair skimmed the text. "Apparently she hasn't got our message about me losing yet." He looked up at Trudith as he spoke. "She wishes me luck in tomorrow's election. Hmmph."

Trudith's troubled look and generally tense demeanor must have struck Alistair then, because his orange ears started wandering forward and back in a classic cat gesture of confusion. "You okay?" he asked.

Trudith pursed her jowls. "Yes," she answered. It wasn't entirely true, but it was the right answer nonetheless. As she realized that, Trudith finally understood what she had to do. Just as Alistair needed to be protected from her uncertainties and unhappiness right now, his career needed to be protected from whatever unseemly thing Petra might do. In order to protect him, Trudith had to find out what Petra was doing, and she had to do it alone. Trudith felt resolved.

"Well," Alistair said. Trudith read his uncertainty in the way he flattened his ears. "Kipper says I should use my new influence to make people watch this video."

Trudith flashed him a jowly smile to reassure him. It was completely fake, but she didn't think Alistair could tell. "Your influence is good enough for me. I'll watch it!"

Alistair did look reassured. His ears turned back to their normal, forward position. He swiveled the com-console around so that Trudith could see too, and he started the video.

Mars appeared center screen, growing until it filled the field of vision. Desolate. A cut zoomed closer, and both viewers drew in a sharp breath.

"I didn't know the otters were building on Mars," Trudith said.

"They aren't." Alistair sounded as confused as Trudith.

The structure was a giant, clear, bubble dome planted like a bead of sweat on Mars' red face. The video was grainy, but, inside the dome there seemed to be buildings. The video cut again, and a round river otter face filled the screen. The image wobbled; the otter seemed to be holding her own camera out to film herself. "I'm about to visit the first city on Mars!" she said. Her fur looked slick and damp. "Who knew that cats had their own space station? Well, planet station," she amended. "Mars station. I wonder what a cat city is like." The view zoomed out and around, bobbling about. The otter must have been turning the camera away from herself. Possibly, she clipped it on her jerkin, because the next shot was at shoulder height. It bumped up and down, like the camera was walking.

From behind the camera, a muffled voice came through. This one was male, and the accent sounded like an otter's: "*Singing seagulls! Let's get going. I've got to see what kind of a place you cats have whipped up for yourselves here on this red space rock.*"

Alistair and Trudith stared transfixed. "I can't believe it," Alistair said.

Alistair and his sisters had speculated together about the nature of a theoretical world peopled by, designed for, and *run by* cats. Undogged. *Free.* Alistair hadn't believed it existed. That's why he was on Earth, in politics, running for senator. Alistair sighed. Right now he wished he were up in the sky instead, having adventures like Kipper. In awe, he said, "She really found it. Cat Haven."

On screen, the camera bounced and wiggled toward the center of the town. Cats passed the camera left and right. Siamese. Burmese. Abyssinians. Egyptian Maus. Cats, cats, cats. Cats don't vary in size and shape nearly as much as dogs. It was completely foreign, from the perspective of the varied and diverse population of Earth. And yet... completely familiar. To Alistair. To a *cat.*

"Kipper can do anything," Trudith said, as though she thought Kipper had built this cat haven with her own two paws, rather than merely finding it.

As if on cue, Kipper came onscreen. At first, Trudith and Alistair didn't recognize her. The image was bouncy, and Kipper had spots. Apparently, Alistair's plain old tabby of a sister had dyed her fur up like a fancy Egyptian Mau.

"Scandalous," said a voice to the left of the picture. The camera swerved around, and a fluffy white Birman came onscreen. She must have been shorter than the otter wearing the camera; her face fell toward the side and center of the image, meaning she probably came to the otter's shoulder height.

"What's scandalous?" the male otter voice asked.

"I don't know what your Kipper is used to on Earth, but here...." The Birman hissed through her whiskers, "She's being awfully flirtatious with a cat who is *not* her breed."

The camera swung back around, and, sure enough, Kipper was standing very close to an extremely handsome Siamese cat.

"He's good looking, right?" Trudith asked. "I have trouble judging with cats."

"Oh, yes," Alistair said. His tail twitched protectively.

In the video, the female otter's voice asked, "What's wrong with that?"

"I wouldn't expect an otter to understand. You don't have breeds." The Birman's white face careened back on screen.

"Sure we do!" said the male otter from off-screen. "Why, Jenny here is an Asian small-clawed otter. And I'm a Neotropical. Not to mention the difference between sea and river!"

The Birman sniffed and then smoothed her whiskers with a paw. "That's not the same," she said. "We have a legacy left behind from the time of the First Race."

"She's a First-Racer?" Alistair whispered. "A First-Racer *cat*? That's unusual." It took a certain amount of devoted fanaticism to believe that the First Race—humans, who had vanished from Earth centuries ago—would return some day and had plans for the species they'd left behind. By and large, that level of devotion was much more common among canines.

"Guess so," Trudith said.

"Do you think they all are? The whole colony?" Alistair asked.

Trudith didn't answer. She hadn't the slightest idea. Fortunately, Alistair didn't notice. He was too absorbed watching the video and thinking about its implications. Trudith wasn't as good at thinking through those implications, but she knew better than to interrupt Alistair again when he looked so deep in thought.

Ten minutes later, when the video ended, Alistair looked at Trudith. "Cat politics will never be the same," he said.

"Is that good?" Trudith asked. She really had no idea what to make of this foreign land Kipper had found. *Siamhalla*, it was called. Learning about it was like watching a travel vid about the dingo outreach programs in Australia or the Antarctic Husky commune. But those were places that had fit into her concept of her world for years. She had no idea how Siamhalla related to, well, *anything*.

"Good?" Alistair puffed through his whiskers. Dumbfounded. "I don't know." His ears wandered nervously forward and back. The tip of his tail twitched three times. "You mean for me?" he asked. "For the election?"

Trudith nodded, a solemn nod. Though, she was really looking for any answer at all.

"Hard to say," Alistair said. "I feel like I'm playing a whole new game." He flattened his ears. "And I don't know the rules yet. Petra would probably tell me not to go public with this."

Trudith eagerly pointed out the obvious: "Petra's not here."

"Good point," Alistair said. He swished his tail and flexed his claws. "Truth's truth," he said. After another moment, he added, decisively, "Let's get this to the press. We'll figure out how it impacts my own election later."

Trudith's tail wagged, thumping the leg of the com-console desk. "Can do," she said. "I'll start calling all our contacts." Whatever Petra might or might not be up to, Alistair was back to his old self.

Trudith felt better already!

CHAPTER 4
TRAILSIDE

Kipper stared at the ceiling for an hour. She was so intent, she didn't notice the swell of current as Trugger, another one of her otter shipmates, swam up to her. He tapped on her shoulder to get her attention, and when Kipper looked around, the river otter signed, "Didn't Jenny tell you? Even though we're stopped, we won't be draining the oxo-agua until Trailside clears us for docking."

Kipper's ears flattened, and her whiskers lay flat against her face from every muscle being tensed. Kipper mouthed, "*Air.*" She was careful not to use her throat, so she didn't double over sputtering. No, she kept breathing the oxo-agua, nice and smooth, but she wouldn't sign. It was her last minute rebellion, small and pointless, against the atmosphere she hated.

Trugger had explained to Kipper before how the oxo-agua cushioned the *Jolly Barracuda's* inhabitants against outrageously high acceleration and decelerations. She knew they didn't need it to orbit an asteroid.

"What?" Trugger asked.

"Air." Kipper whispered it this time. The oxo-agua tickled her throat. Too thick for anything but drinking. She hated the stuff.

Her eyes locked back on the ceiling. She would wait.

When she finally saw the first glimmer of silvery, sweet air, it would be heaven, floating above. Except, she knew that even when she saw the shimmering shine of wonderful, light air, it would still be too little to breathe. She would have to wait as the oxo-agua slowly lowered around her, draining into the external, expandable atmo-tanks. Heaven in sight but out of reach.

And, for now, still out of sight.

Trugger shrugged and left the *Jolly Barracuda's* most eccentric member (or *least*, depending on who was asked) to her vigil.

Ages later, Kipper felt Trugger's return in the tides of oxo-agua around her. She didn't know it was him, but she knew one of her otter shipmates had swum into the barracks with her. She had remained alert and focused as only a cat could. Her eyes had not moved. Hardly blinked.

"What's the delay?" she signed without looking down.

A slight flutter in the atmosphere told Kipper that the otter who'd come to see her was signing. She deigned to tear her eyes away from the painfully unchanged ceiling in time to see Trugger's round otter face look exasperated. He grumpily crossed his arms and, meaningfully, tucked his paws under them.

"I'm sorry," Kipper signed.

Luckily for her, Trugger was a big softy. "Jenny told me you meant to stare at the ceiling until we switched atmospheres," Trugger signed. "Neither of us thought you meant it. Do all cats have attention spans like that?"

Kipper shrugged and dipped her ears. She knew Trugger still wasn't good at reading feline body language, so she signed, "Most."

Trugger still looked interested.

"Not all," she added. "I knew a Turkish Van cat,"—she had to spell out the breed name *Turkish Van* with alphabet signs, because the otter sign language didn't have a separate word for it—"who wrote down what he was doing on a post-it anytime someone interrupted him. Otherwise he couldn't remember it five minutes later."

"So not all cats," Trugger signed.

Kipper was pensive. "Some herd dogs are pretty patient." She thought a little more. "President Chiyoko could beat any cat, dog, or otter in a test of patience and focus. She's an Akita. That's a kind of dog." Kipper had to spell that breed name out too.

"I've seen her on the news vids."

"Speaking of news?" Kipper signed.

"Yes, I have some." Trugger paddled his tail, causing him to bob in the oxo-agua before her.

It made Kipper sea-sick when the otters bobbed like that. Why couldn't they just float in place? Like drowned rats... "What?" she signed. She hated being underwater, and she just knew Trugger was going tell her it wouldn't be over any time soon.

"There's been a delay."

Kipper felt her stomach knotting up. Even though she knew it was coming, she couldn't stand to see him sign it. Her ears flattened again. Her eyes closed tight. The world shut down in darkness around her, until all that was left was her breathing. Her infernal, hated, watery, oxo-agua lungfuls of breathing.

She felt Trugger's flippered paws grip her shoulders. He firmly held and lightly shook her. She swayed, and, because he was good to her and deserved better than her wrath, Kipper opened her eyes for Trugger.

He took a paw off her shoulder and pointed up.

Sweet, sweet air! Kipper could hardly take her eyes off it. A whole inch at the top of the room had filled with true gaseous air.

"There's *been* a delay," Trugger signed again when she looked down, "but they've dealt with it now." He swished his tail lazily until he was floating on his side. It made his signs harder for

Kipper to read, but she took comfort in the fact that they'd be *talking* with *airwaves* again soon.

"There's a huge influx of ships from the Jupiter area," he continued to sign from his sideways position. "Something about unidentified attacks."

"Pirates?" Kipper signed. It was a light jab. She knew the Jolly Barracuders thought of themselves as pirates, but aside from their misunderstanding with the Asteroid Artist Alliance over Captain Cod's interior decorating, she hadn't seen them do anything terribly piratey.

"Pirates would steal something, surely?" Trugger paddled his back paws, rotating himself even further, until he floated upside down.

"Are you trying to make me dizzy?" Kipper signed.

"Sorry." Trugger flipped himself around in a double summersault. "I'm just trying to take full advantage of our last few minutes."

Trugger and Kipper both glanced up. The air was a foot deep from the ceiling now. Kipper couldn't wait. She launched herself upward. One firm kick off the floor, an infinite moment of waiting as she glided upward, and, finally, Kipper burst into air.

She spent the next few minutes hacking and coughing as the oxo-agua worked its way out of her lungs. It was like the worst hairball ever.

By the time her lungs cleared out, Kipper found herself treading water in a room still half filled with oxo-agua. The dry air stung in her eyes, but she saw Trugger swimming loop de loops in the liquid half of the room under her. His long, dark body twisted and curled. He swam much faster than Kipper ever could. If she could swim like that, Kipper supposed she might understand wanting to be in a liquid atmosphere. As it was, though, she wasn't built for swimming, and she felt huge relief when the oxo-agua drained low enough for her hind paws to touch the floor.

"Come on in! The water's fine!" Trugger signed to her with a huge grin. His gestures looked wavey and stretched under the oxo-agua, but Kipper could still make them out.

"You're looking a little cramped down there," Kipper said, trying out her voice. It felt weird after weeks of disuse. And abuse. Breathing liquid wasn't good for the vocal cords. It didn't matter; Trugger's ears were still submerged with the rest of him, so Kipper echoed her words with paw signs.

She wasn't sure if he caught them, what with all his circling. Trugger kept swimming around her until the oxo-agua was barely deep enough for him to steer with his tail. As his broad rudder of a tail swayed to turn him, the oily brown fur broke the surface. While he continued to swim tight circles around her, the fur along his side emerged. Fuzzy and wet. Finally, Trugger gave up the game. He stood up, dripping, coughing, and sneezing. Even so, Kipper thought he recovered from the liquid to gaseous atmosphere transition much quicker than she had. Of course, he had much more experience, being a seasoned Barracuder.

Kipper was only on her second flight. First, she flew from Earth to Mars—where she discovered Siamhalla and all its *catly joys*. Now, from Mars to the asteroids. And what, she wondered, would she find here?

"Seriously," Trugger said, interrupting her reverie. His voice was growly with the adjustment back to real air. "The Captain wants you to find out what's going on with all these ships from Jupiter."

"Right..." Kipper said, startled by Trugger's indirect reminder of her official position on the *Jolly Barracuda*: ship's spy. Why exactly Captain Cod felt that his ship needed a spy and how he got the idea that the only cat in outer space was the right animal for the job, well, that was anyone's guess.

"I was—" Kipper coughed. Her voice startled at speaking again. "I was planning to find a ship that could take me home."

Trugger stared blankly at her. If anything, his whiskers turned down. Kipper wasn't sure, but she thought he looked a little more serious than usual.

"Jenny knew that," Kipper added, hoping to make the serious look go away.

Instead, it got worse. "You'd better talk to the captain," Trugger said. But then he brightened, "You'll find him at the Foghorn. It's the best bar in the solar system." Trugger gave his long body a twisty shake, ruffling all his oily-wet brown fur. Droplets of oxo-agua sparkled as they flew off him, leaving his fur bushy and sticking out. "I'll take you there."

"You mean he's not on the ship?" Kipper asked.

"When we hit Trailside," Trugger said, wringing out soggy folds of his trousers. "The captain doesn't waste two shakes of a titmouse's tail. Why, he'll be sucking down rum spiked clam juice at the Foghorn before we can get changed into dry clothes."

The clingy, soaked fabric of her vest and pants felt unbearable to Kipper. "Maybe before *you* can," she said, turning and slogging her way toward the hall down to the barracks. The oxo-agua was still a foot deep, but she felt more agile splashing her way through that than she had in weeks. "No otter is going to beat this cat into dry clothes!" She yelled over her shoulder as she ran. "Let alone off of this soggy puddle of a spaceship!"

Of course, Kipper would have been right, except that one otter, namely Captain Cod, had his own quarters in the *Jolly Barracuda's* nose, nestled only one level below the bridge. Kipper had a bottom bunk in the barracks, and the barracks were two levels lower. When Kipper got to the stairs down, the importance of that difference finally sunk in. Up and down hadn't mattered much in the oxo-agua. Now they did.

"Rats!" she cried, staring in dismay at an oxo-agua filled staircase. She stamped her foot on the slick but drying floor. It would take another twenty minutes for the oxo-agua to drain all the way down to the barracks. She was still staring intently at the insidious liquid filling the staircase when Trugger approached from behind.

"Don't even think about it," he said.

"What?" she asked, flattening her ears. Certainly, there could be nothing wrong with heading straight to the bar. "If the outpost on this asteroid is anything like Deep Sky Anchor," she referred to the otter space station in geosynchronous Earth orbit, "then, my clothes and fur will be getting wet again all over the place out there."

"Well, that's true," Trugger admitted.

Kipper shuddered out to her whiskers. She'd been downright creeped out when she first saw the artificial rivers that otters treated like freeways flowing through the center of Deep Sky Anchor. Otter architecture took a lot of getting used to.

"So what's the point in waiting for the barracks to drain out, waiting my turn for a chemical brush, and then digging out the one set of dry-packed clothes from the back of my bunk drawer?" Kipper's nose wrinkled remembering which vest and pants she'd shoved in the dry-bag as they'd been leaving Mars. It was what was clean... And she'd been in a hurry. "Well?"

"Let's just say that oxo-agua doesn't dry so nicely."

Kipper gave Trugger a quizzical stare; one ear flattened, the other held high.

"It'll make your fur all gummy."

Kipper sighed. If an otter who'd had his fur dyed and sculpted into purple spikes when she'd first met him was concerned about dry oxo-agua messing up his fur, then it was definitely something to worry about. She sat down on the top step of the staircase, her feet dangled over the next two, recently air-exposed steps. She could wait.

CHAPTER 5
EARTH

"You couldn't wait?!?" Petra exploded. "This dumb-as-charcoal dog said, *oh yeah, let's go to the press*, and you thought that was a good idea?!"

Alistair's ears were flat and his brow drawn. "Are you finished?" he asked.

"Never listen to a dog." Petra glared at Trudith. "*Now* I'm done."

"First of all," Alistair said. "Trudith and I decided to go to the press together. It wasn't only her idea. Not to mention," he mentioned, "that it's what Kipper wanted. Secondly, I know you're not crazy about Trudith," Alistair gave Trudith an apologetic shrug. They both knew it was true. "But you spend an awful lot of time insulting dogs for someone who's married to one."

"Hey, I hadn't thought of that," Trudith said. Her tail wagged from nervousness and also her irrepressible need to be liked, even by a cat like Petra. "If you're down on dogs so much—"

Trudith didn't get a chance to finish. Petra cut her off with a swishing tail and then spat words. "Lucky doesn't count. Besides, this isn't about me and Lucky."

"It's about the campaign," Alistair said.

"Yes."

"Well, we don't need to worry about that, do we?"

"We got scooped," Trudith woofed. She was still a little in shock from the day's stupefying events.

"Getting *scooped* means that someone beat you to a story," Petra said scornfully. "You didn't get *scooped.*"

"More like eclipsed," Alistair said. "No one cares about a bunch of cats and their lifestyle choices right now. On Mars *or* Earth."

"That's not true," Trudith said. She knew it wasn't true, because she cared. She wished everything wasn't moving so fast. She wished the world would give her time to assimilate the meaning of one event before throwing a new one at her.

Jingle, thwack! The front door flew open, ringing the ceiling bell, and slammed against the wall. Two figures stood framed in the streaming sunlight from outside. At first, Trudith assumed from their height that the two silhouetted figures were two cats, but as they stepped forward, Trudith could see that the second figure was a small mixed breed dog.

"Lucky!" Petra said. She looked confused and startled, but after a wild glance around the office, finally settling her eyes on the wall clock, she said, "I'm not late for our meeting yet."

"Yet?" the dog quipped. "You were *planning* to be late?" He was a classic mutt: a lean but stocky figure, a few wiry wisps of beard around his chin, triangular ears that drooped at the top, and a big, round spot covering one eye. Combined with his ultra-traditional name and a dull-brown sweater vest—he was the perfect picture of a First-Racer, waiting for humans to come home. Why, he should have had his head tilted over a Victrola.

"There's a rally," said the cat beside Lucky.

"Yeah, a bunch of crazy First-Racers are making complete fools of themselves," Lucky said. Apparently, looks could be deceiving. If one were to go by looks, one would never guess that Lucky and Petra were a couple. Clearly, each of them had a few surprises up their sleeves.

"I don't think it's just First-Racers," the cat, who had mottled orange and black fur, said to Lucky. If she'd had white fur too, she would have been a calico cat. If she were a dog, her coloring would be called brindle. Trudith wasn't sure of the word for that coloring in cats.

"This is big," the brindle cat said. "We thought you should know, right away."

Trudith went to the window and peeked through the blinds that were drawn. Cats and dogs filled the streets. Some carried signs. A lot of them were running. "Where are they heading?" Trudith asked.

Alistair came up behind her. Like all cats, he was shorter than Trudith, barely coming up to her shoulder, so Trudith stepped away to let him see out the window.

"The crowds started all the way back at the cattery," Lucky said. "I'm surprised you didn't hear them."

Trudith, Alistair, and Petra looked at each other, each of them blaming one (or two) of the others for causing such a tempest in a teapot that they'd missed the full-size tempest outside.

"I know one way to find out where they're going," Petra said, punching off the display on her com-console and sweeping all the papers on her desk into a drawer that she pointedly locked. "Let's get going," she said.

"That's my girl," Lucky said. Petra looked like she wanted to hiss at him in answer, but she contained the sentiment down to a rolling of her emerald green eyes.

In short order, Lucky, Petra, and the stranger cat were out the door. Alistair paused before following them. With his paw on the door and his keys ready to lock it behind him, he asked Trudith, "Aren't you coming?"

Trudith wagged her tail reflexively, but she couldn't help wondering about that locked drawer. Petra didn't usually leave her papers in the office, but, when she did, she didn't lock the drawer. Something was up, and the clues were in that drawer.

Alistair stared at her expectantly, waiting for an answer. Trudith couldn't think under these conditions. All this pressure.

"Well?" he said.

Trudith's tail wagged some more, her mind failing to come up with any words to answer him.

"Tell you what," Alistair said, putting his keys away. He pulled something else out of his pocket and tossed it to Trudith who caught it with ease. Even under pressure, she had excellent reflexes.

"After the fiasco with Petra and Lucky's elopement," Alistair said, "I got us both cell phones. Give me a call on Petra's cell— the number's in there—when you're ready to catch up with us. Okay?"

Trudith looked down at the delicate square of metal and plastic, barely the size of a single one of her paw pads. She felt like she could have crushed it easily between two pads, let alone between two paws while trying to operate it. It was clearly designed for a cat.

"Lock up behind you," Alistair said. By the time Trudith looked up, he was already gone, leaving her alone with a moral quandary. Trudith may have been big and tough—covered in sinewy muscles under her smooth black fur from head to paw— but she didn't like being left alone with a moral quandary. Those beat her up from the inside, and her brain was a bit of a wimp, or at least a coward.

Trudith eyed Petra's desk. The faux-mahogany top was mockingly blank, and the brass keyhole looked tauntingly easy to pick.

There was nothing else for it. Trudith's brain would have to tackle the big scary, desk-shaped moral quandary staring at her from the corner.

She wondered if she should do some warm-ups first. Some

brain exercises. *Five times five is twenty-five. Nine times nine is eighty-one.* This wasn't helping. *No, no,* Trudith scolded herself. She would never bother with pushups or her morning run if she tried to measure their effects immediately after. Although, she also couldn't get into the kind of shape she was in by going on a quick run right before an important scramball game.

She would have to work with what she already had. And, maybe tomorrow, she'd pick up a book of brainteasers and add a brain workout to her morning routine.

If only she'd done that a month ago.

The problem was deceptively simple. Petra was hiding something, and the clues were locked in that drawer. Trudith could break into the drawer. She'd had plenty of practice back in her thug days. She could do it without leaving a trace. And, if no one ever knew, then it was like it hadn't happened, right? *So,* Trudith thought, she *should* break into that drawer. The clues inside could lead to protecting Alistair from Petra's nefarious plans, whatever they were.

Boy, would Alistair be happy with her, Trudith thought, when she told him all about what Petra was up to so that he could put a stop to it! Why, he'd probably tell her just what a good job she was doing. Trudith grinned. It would be great.

Oh....

Wait....

Alistair would want to know how she'd found out whatever it was she found out. Trudith shook her head, flapping her ears.

Alistair would *not* be happy with her if he knew that she'd broken into Petra's desk. She could lie to him and tell him that she'd made her discoveries... um... some other way. For instance, Petra might have left the papers sitting out. Or maybe she hadn't locked the drawer. It would be Trudith's word against Petra's, and who would Alistair believe?

A good, loyal, trustworthy dog, who just happened to have worked as a thug in the past. *Hmm.*

Or his sister. Alistair would believe his sister. Trudith could picture the scene. Petra would spit and swear and call Trudith a thieving *dog*. It would be very unpleasant, but it would be worth it to save Alistair from...

From what exactly?

And therein lay the problem. Trudith didn't know. There could be anything locked in that drawer. Petra was an extremely unpredictable cat, and that was saying a lot. Trudith wasn't good at predicting normal cats.

Petra could be hiding evidence of charity work in that drawer, or conspiracy theories about humans having gone literally underground and living in a giant subterranean cave for the last two centuries. Or love poems for Lucky.

Ugh.

Trudith shook her head, flapping her ears again. She gave her head an extra hard shake, flopping her jowls even, to get the idea of Petra writing love poems out of her head. It was like hitting reset on her brain. All that arduous, complicated thinking, and where was she at? Nothing was any clearer than when she started.

Except for the image of on Alistair's face of quietly disappointed disapproval when Trudith imagined Petra ratting on her for breaking into the drawer. That image was very clear.

Trudith didn't know what was right, but she knew she didn't like that look at all. Not one bit. She had to find a way to uncover Petra's schemes without risking that look from Alistair.

With a final wistful but determined (and still confused) look at her nemesis—the locked drawer—Trudith gathered up her own keys to the office and prepared to follow her cats.

Standing in the sunlight outside, Trudith locked the office, and then pulled Alistair's cell phone out of the pocket where she'd stowed it. She grimaced. *So small.* The blunt claws tipping her paws felt comically clumsy scrabbling against buttons designed for the tiny, delicate, retractable claws of a cat.

"Pfff," Trudith snort-sighed through her jowls. She shoved the cell phone back in her pocket. Alistair and Petra's group couldn't have got far. She'd follow the crowd like they had, and surely they'd show up.

Trudith took off down the sidewalk. As she loped along, the currents of the crowd caught Trudith up, and she let herself be swept into the middle of the roadway. No cars would be driving there anytime soon. The few cars that Trudith did see were stuck, inching along, nosing between pedestrians. If they were smart, the drivers would give up and park as soon as possible. Most of them would probably join in the crowds after that.

Another few blocks brought Trudith to Central Square, the brick and concrete meeting space in front of City Hall. Looking around, the enormousness of it all started to dawn on Trudith. She wouldn't be able to find Alistair and Petra in this crowd.

Dogs with picket signs, reading "FIRST RACE RETURNS!" or "HUMANS COME HOME!" paced about the Square, moving together in large groups. Probably church groups. The cats in the crowd were more intermingled, moving singularly or in small cliques, but there were lots of them.

In the far corner, beside the brick planters of marigolds, a group of Greyhounds stood together, head and shoulders taller than most everyone else. They were dressed in very nice suits, and Trudith noticed wires running from their collars to the insides of their ears.

Moving closer, Trudith managed to see between them. Their long bodies and long limbs obscured a short, bushy dog with a thick, gold-orange mane. His long-nosed face was that of a Collie; except, a Collie would be nearly the Greyhounds' height. This dog looked laughably short and stubby in their midst. He was a Sheltie, Alistair's rival Senator Morrison, and the Greyhounds were clearly his security detail.

Trudith, still drifting with the various currents of the crowd as it milled about Central Square, made a point of drifting closer to the senator.

Even to a big dog like Trudith, the Greyhound guards were imposing. Nonetheless, they seemed relatively at ease with the crowd—checking their watches, answering cell phones, looking around. None of them exuded the kind of prickly, porcupine tension that warned, "*Stay away at all costs!*"

Trudith drifted within earshot.

"Is it time?" a Greyhound asked.

"Not yet," Senator Morrison answered. "Let them get more riled up first." He looked around, as if gauging the temperature of the crowd around him, perhaps counting the cats and dogs who looked riled up *enough*. By the wolfish grin on his thin, orange face, Trudith judged that he liked what he saw.

"Let's wait until they're almost boiling over," he said. "Then we call for *war*."

Trudith gulped. Her heart raced, and her ears rang.

CHAPTER 6
TRAILSIDE

Trailside was smaller and more cramped than Deep Sky Anchor, that giant outpost of Otterdom in geosynchronous orbit with Earth, anchored to the land of dogs and dog-oppressed cats by the slender thread of the space elevator.

Kipper had taken the space elevator to Deep Sky Anchor, where she met up with Captain Cod and his ragtag Barracuders. Before Trailside, their only stop had been at the disappointingly exclusive cat colony on Mars. So, Trailside was the second-ever otter outpost that Kipper had set paw on.

She was not disappointed.

Despite Trailside's smaller size, Kipper felt more like she was *in space* than she ever had on Deep Sky Anchor or the *Jolly Barracuda*. Both Deep Sky Anchor and the *Jolly Barracuda* were uniquely, and bizarrely, *otter* in nature. Beyond the sickening oxo-agua that Captain Cod flooded his ship with while in flight, there was the hideous, tacky decorating. The whole ship felt like —*a sailing ship*. Except in the tawdry, themed, shore side seafood-joint kind of way. All it was missing was a few buoys and life preservers on the walls.

Deep Sky Anchor was better, yet Kipper couldn't help feeling creeped out by the artificial rivers that ran down the center of the station which the otters jumped in and out of like personal freeways. Kipper shuddered merely thinking about it.

Now Trailside was Kipper's idea of a space station. Every way she looked *she saw space*. Vast, gaping windows of blackness, starlight, and asteroid dust. The gravity was low, because the asteroid was small. For a cat who'd dreamed her whole kitten-hood of floating among the stars, this was close to heaven.

"You like," Trugger said. It wasn't a question, because it didn't have to be. Kipper's round eyes, perked ears, and swishing tail were easy to read, even for an otter.

"Come on, let's get her to the Foghorn," Jenny said, taking Kipper by the paw. They stepped out from the arch of the airlock that connected the *Jolly Barracuda* to Trailside, floating lightly on their paws.

"It's not that much more impressive than the *Barracuda*." Trugger grumbled at Kipper's obvious, continued awe. "Is it?"

Kipper looked at her friend. She'd grown very close to Jenny and Trugger on their journey. Though she had to seriously question Trugger's taste sometimes, like when he'd chosen to have his fur dyed purple with spikes. She wasn't at all sorry that both of their fur jobs—his spikes and her spots—had faded away over the last few months.

"Are you kidding?" Kipper said. "The entire ceiling here is the yawning emptiness of space."

"So?" Trugger said. "That's true on Earth too. And it's not like the *Barracuda* doesn't have windows!"

Kipper opened her mouth to retort that the windows on the *Jolly Barracuda* were the equivalent of a few dingy portholes, but she stopped herself in time. Trugger was nothing if not loyal, and she didn't think he'd take that well. Instead she said, "We don't have the weightlessness on Earth."

"Weightless?" Trugger snorted. "You call this weightless? There's got to be a full sixteenth gravity here. Now, weightless is oxo-agua. Weightless is swimming."

Kipper hacked like she had a hairball. "Don't remind me."

"Look over there," Jenny said in a less than subtle attempt to redirect the conversation. Kipper didn't mind the diversion.

It took Kipper a moment to see what Jenny was talking about. Crawling along the far wall of the crowded docking bay, just above otter head height, were two ashen gray octopuses. The chef on the *Jolly Barracuda* was an octopus, so Kipper had met one before. However, Emily could only roam the ship freely while it was flooded with oxo-agua. At other times, she was confined to the glassed in, submerged kitchen.

"How?" Kipper asked, but then she noticed their equipment. "Is that scuba gear?"

Each octopus had a dull metal tank strapped to the side of its bulbous mantle with a nexus of tubes congregated where the mantle met the arms, completely covering their tube-like breathing siphons.

"Pretty much," Jenny said.

"Or kind of the opposite," Trugger added.

"Huh." Kipper hadn't thought about how Emily, the *Jolly Barracuda's* chef, had traveled from her native home under the ocean, up the space elevator, through Deep Sky Anchor, and into her cozy little oxo-agua flooded kitchen. It was a simple enough trip for Kipper, but Kipper breathed the same as the otter architects who had built the space elevator, Deep Sky Anchor, and the *Jolly Barracuda*. An octopus could survive outside of water for hours at a time, but not *that* long.

Kipper knew that Emily had once lived under the ocean. She hadn't always been behind the acrylic glass shielding around the *Jolly Barracuda's* permanently submerged kitchen. It was like a personal fish tank for Emily. Kipper realized that she must have pictured Emily traveling from the ocean in an actual fish tank, wheeled about on a dolly by muscular, hired otters.

Inverse scuba gear made a lot more sense.

"How come Emily doesn't use it?" Kipper asked. "She could come out to the Foghorn with us."

Jenny shrugged. "After Captain Cod hired her, she convinced him to wall in the kitchen like that. She never leaves it."

Kipper realized that in all her time on the *Jolly Barracuda*, she'd never seen Emily venture farther away from the kitchen than to the galley even when she could have. Sure, the ship was drained now, but, for weeks, the entire ship had been a much more comfortable environment for Emily than for Kipper. Still, Emily had stayed in that one, confined area. *Could it be agoraphobia?*

The three companions walked past the scuba-suited octopi, and Kipper saw a cursive, neon green sign reading "The Foghorn" looming ahead. When they reached that bar, Captain Cod would have work for her, and she would have to explain that, after all his kindness, she didn't want to do it. She wanted to be released from her contract and freed to return home.

Kipper's tail tip twitched in trepidation. Captain Cod could be a bewildering and enigmatic otter. She wasn't sure how far his power over her extended, as she had only skimmed the lengthy contract, and she wasn't sure how whimsically he would use it. So far, he'd been... not reasonable, but good natured. She didn't know if he had any other nature, but she hoped not to see it if he did.

The captain sat at the bar. A monitor in the corner showed a sports scene—it must have been an Earth broadcast, because the game was clearly scramball and the three teams were composed of Golden Retrievers, Boxers, and Airedales. The Airedales were winning.

The captain wasn't watching the game. He was talking to the bartender, a bulky sea otter wearing a frilly apron. The bartender was short for an otter, but that still made him more than a whisker taller than most cats, including Kipper.

"Trugger! Jenny!" the captain called out. When Kipper

stepped out from between them, Captain Cod jumped off his barstool. "Just the cat I've been waiting for!" he exclaimed. "Why, I've been telling Gus here all about you."

Gus, the bartender, grinned a whiskery grin and would've agreed, except the captain didn't give him a chance. Instead, the captain launched into a dramatic retelling of how Kipper, disguised as a leopard, had sneaked onto the *Jolly Barracuda*, and only through his own brilliant cunning had Captain Cod apprehended her, regained control of his ship (which, apparently, she'd somehow stolen), and then through the largesse of his kindly heart offered her the position of ship's spy so that she could work off her debt to society on the great and grand *Jolly Barracuda* rather than while rotting away in a cell on Deep Sky Anchor.

It was an interesting story, bearing little relation to reality, of course.

Gus, the bartender, waggled his furry brow at Kipper when the story was done in a way that suggested he understood the proper tone of levity to apply to Captain Cod's tales. Clearly, the captain had been chewing his ear off. Gus probably hadn't gotten a word in the whole time.

"Now," said the captain, reaching a proprietary paw around Kipper's shoulders, "if you all don't mind giving us some privacy, I believe my crewmember and I have some spy business to attend."

Trugger saluted, and Jenny nodded. The bartender merely took a few steps sideways along the bar. Trugger and Jenny followed, ordered drinks from him, and then made their way to a pinball table under the corner news monitor.

"Sit down." The captain gestured at the stool beside him. Kipper perched on it lightly. Without the oxo-agua, low gravity was quite pleasant. "All right," the captain continued, hunching conspiratorially toward Kipper. "Let's get down to business. *Spy business,*" he said in a conspicuous hush. He darted a few equally conspicuous and corny glances around the bar. No one was paying any attention to them, except Gus who politely looked away and ambled farther down the bar after Captain Cod shot him a glare.

Satisfied that it was now safe, Captain Cod began: "You know about the crowd of ships from Jupiter?"

Kipper nodded, thinking about how those ships had kept her breathing a liquid longer than she otherwise would have had to. Ugh.

"You do?" he asked, his voice rising in surprise.

"Well, yeah, Trugger told me that was—" Kipper faltered under the intensity of Captain Cod's stare. "—um, you know, why we weren't able to dock for so long."

"Oh," Captain Cod looked disappointed. "So you only know what I know." He shot her a suspicious look, as if he thought she were holding out on him. Clearly, as ship's spy, she should have deduced what he'd want her to know about and have already studied out the answer for him. "Well, I wish you'd get on it," he said. "Whatever's going on, causing so many ships to flee the Jupiter system and run Earthwards like wrens with their tail feathers on fire, we need to know about it!" He slammed the bar with a fisted paw.

Gus gave the captain a look that said, "*You dent it, you pay for it.*" The captain mumbled an apology. Then, promising to return and discuss Kipper's spy plans with her in a few minutes, Captain Cod explained that he had important business to attend to at the establishment next door, a sweets shop. She strongly suspected that the captain's "*important business*" was with a bag of saltwater taffy.

She wondered if they made catnip flavor?

Kipper shook the image from her head. She had more important things to worry about. The whole "ship's spy" thing was cute onboard the *Jolly Barracuda,* but she wasn't sure what the captain expected of her. She was the only member of his crew who'd never been to Trailside before. She was also the only member of his crew who stuck out like a sore thumb, since, apparently, there were even other octopi around, whereas she was the only cat in the solar system whose paws weren't firmly rooted to a planet.

Kipper sighed, and the bartender came her way. "Need a drink?" he asked.

Kipper nodded, and before she could give him her order, Gus whipped out a glass, a bottle, a stirring rod, and a tiny, metal canister.

"You wouldn't expect me to have this," he said, waggling the canister. "But I like to be ready for any customer."

The spicy, tangy, weedy smell intoxicated Kipper the moment he opened the canister. Her eyes dilated as he sprinkled flecks of leaf over her drink. "You're the first cat I've ever had the honor to serve," he said. "One catnip froth. On the house."

Gus slid the frothy glass her way.

But Kipper sighed and slid it back. "I was just craving catnip," she said, wistful.

"Is there something wrong?" Gus looked at the drink, holding his stirring rod ready, as if he hoped to perform emergency surgery and re-fix the drink however was necessary to make it to his customer's liking.

"No, no," Kipper said. "The drink is fine. The drink looks great." In fact, she couldn't take her eyes off it. Another sigh. "But I have a job to do."

"Ah," Gus said, knowingly. "Spy business."

"Right," Kipper grimly agreed.

If she were a real spy, she'd probably infiltrate one of the other ships somehow, gain confidences, and overhear privileged conversations. Even if she were a real spy, being the only cat in all of space—except for the xenophobes on Mars—would be a real hindrance. She had no idea how she was going to surreptitiously uncover secrets from the otters fleeing Jupiter.

"If you change your mind," Gus said, "the drink's here. Until then..." The pudgy sea otter looked about surreptitiously—Kipper couldn't tell if he was mocking Captain Cod's earlier behavior or if he'd really been sucked into the whole spy mythos. "Don't suppose you can drop a hint?" He winked. "You know, about who you're spying on?"

It was amazing. Were all otters fools? Or just the ones Kipper ran into?

There was a thought. Perhaps the only otters who had time for a penniless tabby *were* the fools. "Gah," Kipper said. She raked her paws over her face, flattening her whiskers uncomfortably. "Can you just point me toward an otter who recently got here from Jupiter?" She peered from behind her clawful paws.

Kipper had a feeling that Captain Cod wouldn't like her asking that question. He might think it revealed too much. Though, since she didn't know anything, she wasn't sure what it could reveal. Besides, wasn't asking bartenders for leads a time-honored tradition among spies? Yes, Kipper decided. As far as Captain Cod was concerned, from now on, asking the bartender was rule number one in her spy book.

The Captain would probably believe her if she said she had a spy book. And he would believe her if she said it was too secret for him to see.

"Every otter in here, 'cept the ones you walked in with, just rolled in from Jupiter System."

Kipper looked around, one eye narrowed and one ear flattened.

"Oh, and if you're interested in that whole fiasco, I'd watch the news." Gus gestured with his dishrag toward the monitor suspended above the pinball machine. Since it was directly above Trugger and Jenny's heads, Kipper could tell they hadn't watched a lick of it. They hadn't talked to any other otters around the bar either, Kipper realized. In fact, Captain Cod hadn't been talking to anyone either—or, at any rate, *listening*.

Suddenly, Kipper wasn't sure if she had the stupidest job ever, or maybe, the best job?

"Yeah," Gus said, staring at the monitor, "They've been looping this story all day between the scramball. I must'a seen it ten times." Even so, the steady gaze Gus held on the monitor and the way his voice trailed off showed that he was already absorbed into watching it again. Kipper swiveled her barstool around, and they watched the newsfeed in silence.

Two ships had been confirmed destroyed. A dozen otters on each. Other ships had taken heavy damage with casualty numbers coming in. As the word spread, every other ship in the Jupiter system fled.

The attacking ship was sleek and fast. The newsfeed showed a grainy picture of it, taken by a fleeing ship's external cameras. It looked sinister to Kipper, but, then, anything would when compared to what she was used to: namely, the bizarre bulk of the *Jolly Barracuda*, which looked like a spaceship being strangled by inner tubes.

This was more like a rocket with missiles strapped on, and a few shotguns and pistols thrown in for good measure. The entire ship looked like a weapon, and it wasn't the only one. At least three had been spotted, and their attacks were, as far as anyone knew, utterly unprovoked.

One haggard and harried looking river otter explained to the extremely well-coiffed sea otter anchor woman on-screen that, "They appeared out of nowhere and started shooting us! Now, I'm no coward, but I had a ship full of crewmen I was responsible for."

"So you fled the system?" the anchor woman prompted.

"They gave us little choice," the river otter said. "I've never killed anyone. I have no quarrels with anyone!" He looked pensive and then sighed. "At least, I hadn't. But, that's neither here nor there. I don't know who was on that ship, and I wasn't about to start firing. Besides..." He looked ruffled. "My ship wouldn't have stood a chance."

The news program concluded with the chilling information that fleeing ships had been chased almost to the orbit of Sinope, one of Jupiter's outermost moons, before their attackers gave up pursuit. All ships were now advised to stay away from the Jupiter system until further notice.

"Are they otters?" Kipper asked Gus. If the attackers were otters, that would mean civil war.

Gus shrugged. He looked dispirited. "Not as far as anyone knows. But, then, who else could they be?"

Kipper suddenly flashed on those octopi wearing scuba gear. She'd have to talk to Emily about the state of octopus rocket technology when she got back to the *Jolly Barracuda*.

"Some dogs down on the dirtball,"—that's what some otters called Earth—"are claiming it's their 'First Race' come to bring salvation to the worthy."

"The *worthy* meaning First Race believing *dogs*," Kipper said.

Most First-Racers believed in a definite hierarchy to the races, and, despite otters being the *second race to develop space travel*, they usually didn't come second in that list. No, second was reserved for Man's Best Friend, and first were the humans who'd abandoned Earth long ago. Kipper got the sense that Gus was interested in her comment. She probably knew more about First Race doctrine and general canine culture than anyone he'd ever met out here in the asteroid belt, but a theological discussion would have to wait.

Captain Cod came swaggering back into the Foghorn, proudly holding a little bag to his chest. It was nearly bursting its seams with saltwater taffy. His whiskers looked sticky, and when he spoke, his voice was muffled and chewy.

"You should really try this stuff," he said. Seeing Kipper eye the bag, as if she actually might pick out a piece to try, Captain Cod clutched the bag closer. "They're quite cheap. As soon as we're done *stra-a-a-tegizing*,"—that last word sounded particularly sticky in his taffy filled mouth—"you should head next door and buy yourself a bag."

Gus rolled his eyes at the captain's lack of generosity, but he made sure the gesture was visible only to Kipper. In fact, he made a point of drifting away, politely out of earshot before Captain Cod made it all the way back to his barstool.

Captain Cod and his spy were safely secluded for continuing their spy shop-talk. Kipper figured she'd cut to the chase. "Anonymous spaceships are attacking innocent otter ships in the Jupiter system—" She was going to add, *"And you want me to figure out who they are?"*, but Captain Cod jumped up from his seat.

"Great hopping herons!" he exclaimed. "How did you do that? I was only out of the bar for a few minutes." He looked around suspiciously, then he buddied up to her and said, "No, don't tell me. Keep your secrets." Leaning back, making himself comfortable, he said, "Anonymous spaceships, eh?"

Kipper felt at a loss. Had he really been in this bar for the last two hours and not noticed the news?

"I thought it was some sort of gold rush. Clearly, this is much worse," he said.

Apparently so.

Looking around the room, Kipper noticed: every otter she recognized from the *Jolly Barracuda* socialized strictly with other otters from the *Jolly Barracuda*. None of them were watching the news. In addition to Jenny and Trugger at the pinball machine, there was a whole table of Barracuders. None of them seemed even slightly aware of the rest of the otters in the bar.

Captain Cod didn't need a spy. He needed a liaison to the outside world.

Kipper supposed it *would* be the ship full of outcasts that would accept her into their midst. Kipper tried not to think too hard about that. Right now, *outcast* was a word that conjured an image for her of a world sparkling with everything a cat could dream of, all of it out of her claws' grasp, simply because she had the wrong pattern on her fur.

"If that's all you wanted me to find out," Kipper said, "I was thinking of looking for a ship that could take me home."

Captain Cod looked surprised and then dismayed. His whiskers drooped, and his flat, black nose looked very large in his suddenly mournful face. "I was afraid of this." He held out his bag of taffies now, but Kipper politely demurred. She didn't think she could chew taffy with her heart in her throat.

"I was hoping you'd stay," the captain said. "But I guess I knew it was too good to be true. I'll have Jenny pull up your records, and transfer your pay into any account you specify. Boris can help you book passage with an appropriate freighter back to Earth."

"It's that easy?" Kipper asked, suddenly disappointed in herself for thinking Captain Cod would ever try to keep a crew member who didn't want to stay. He might be strange, but he was a good guy. "I suppose I'll go back to the ship and pack."

"As you will." Captain Cod stuffed several taffies in his mouth and gave her a friendly, albeit sticky, pat on the shoulder. Then, he looked away, quickly. She thought she saw a hint of moisture around his eyes. She felt really guilty, and didn't think she could face saying goodbye to Trugger and Jenny just yet.

She meant to hurry out of the Foghorn. But before she'd made it five bouncily weightless steps, the video on the monitor in the corner had her rooted to the ground. A different late-breaking news report interrupted the televised scramball game —and changed *everything*.

CHAPTER 7
EARTH

There was nothing for it, Trudith decided. She had to find a way to use this little, cat-paw-sized cell phone, because Alistair needed to know what she'd found out. Right now.

Trudith pulled the borrowed phone out of her pocket. She held it lightly between keratinous black claws, and an idea struck her. *She* couldn't operate this phone, but a cat could. *Any* cat.

Trudith backed away from Senator Morrison and his Greyhound posse. She made sure to put at least twenty paces between them before looking around for a likely cat to ask for help. She didn't want the Greyhounds to overhear her, and, even with the noise of the crowd, it was better to be safe.

There were a lot of cats dotting the crowd, mostly angry looking individuals or conspiratorial looking pairs. None of them looked likely to help a large dog, but Trudith's need was great. She chose a calico woman with a trio of kittens mewling over her shoulders from a back carrier to approach.

"Excuse me," Trudith said, leaning down as she approached so as to not look *too* large. "My friend lent me his cell phone and told me to call his sister on it when I want to find them."

The calico glared, her ears darting about nervously. She seemed to hope that Trudith was talking to someone else, but Trudith carried on gamely.

"I can't work it," she said. "My claws are too big, see?"

The calico peered curiously at the tiny phone cradled in the giant paws. She snickered at the sight, and her amusement softened her. She snatched the little phone away and asked, "What number do you need?"

"It should be listed under *Petra*."

One of the kittens swatted over her mother's shoulder as the calico searched the phone's memory. "Here," she said, handing the phone back. "It's ringing."

"Thank you! Oh, thank you!" Trudith said.

"Not a problem," the calico said graciously, her ears standing tall and her tail straightening with a clear sense of empowerment.

Trudith drifted into the crowd and anonymity—a simulation of privacy—as she settled the tiny phone against her head, under the flop of her ear. By the time she could hear it, the phone was practically inside her ear.

"Hello? Hello?" the phone said.

"Petra? It's Trudith!" she barked.

"Trudith?" Petra said in a disgusted voice, followed by some squabbling in the background. When next the phone spoke, it was Alistair's voice. "Trudith, where are you? It sounds like you're in the crowd?"

"Yeah... I thought I could find you." Trudith looked around the growing crowd, realizing how foolish that idea had been. "I couldn't."

"Right. Where are you?"

Trudith and Alistair walked around the crowd playing the complicated describe-things-you-see-over-the-phone-until-you-find-each-other game. Alistair, Petra, Lucky, and the brindle cat with them spotted Trudith before she spotted them. They may have been the larger group, but they were shorter and had more eyes.

"Trudith," Alistair said. "I think Senator Morrison is about to make a big move."

"That's what I was trying to call you about, and then the phone—" Trudith held out the tiny phone which Petra snatched away from her and handed demurely to Alistair. "But, a calico woman... And Morrison's Greyhounds!" Trudith was so tongue-tied by trying to squeeze all the experiences of the last quarter hour out of her brain and into coherent words that her breath gave out in a cross between a woof and a whine.

Three pairs of cat eyes and Lucky stared at her.

Fortunately, Trudith was spared the pressure of their gaze through redirection. "What's that?" Trudith said and pointed at the giant screen that Morrison's Greyhounds were erecting on the steps of the capital building. The cats and Lucky turned around.

Everyone in the crowd turned that way.

"Fellow citizens," an edgy voice boomed over a loudspeaker. It was Senator Morrison, standing to the side of the newly erected screen. He had a mic clipped to his collar, and speakers were being erected as part of the whole screen setup beside him.

"Fellow citizens," he repeated. The crowd began quieting down, and when it quieted enough, Morrison continued. "The video that we are about to play for you will hit the mainstream media by the end of the day. But I don't think that's soon enough."

There was an interrogative tone to the crowd's hush, but Senator Morrison's steely gaze kept the crowd under control.

"When it's over," the senator said, "I'm going to call for us to pull together and take action! An action that has been coming for a long time."

Trudith's tongue came untied all of a sudden, and she edged

over to Alistair. In her husky voice she whispered, "It's war. He's going to call for war."

Alistair turned and stared at her pointedly, his green eyes complex and mysterious.

"I overheard him talking to guards," Trudith said.

"Thank you," Alistair said.

"So what do we do?" Trudith asked, eager to please as always, and ready to do whatever Alistair commanded.

"We watch the video," Alistair said. "And think."

"Right," Trudith said. She was certainly willing to do at least one of those. She hoped Alistair would be okay carrying the weight of the second half on his own.

The video playing on the big screen, set up on the steps of the capital building, was an otter newscast. In fact, it was the same otter newscast that had rooted Kipper to the low gravity floor of Trailside a hundred million miles away.

"This is Minnow Miller, and I'm here with a late-breaking follow up to the Jupiter massacres," said the same sea otter woman with fluffy, well-coiffed fur. "As you know, all otter ships have fled Jupiter System, and we *thought* the entire area was evacuated. Then we received *this* from the surface of Europa, Jupiter's fourth largest moon." The video cut from Minnow Miller and her fluffy sienna pelt to a grainy, staticky image of a tomcat with an equally fluffy, snow-white pelt and an imperial pug face.

"We surrender," said the tom. "Stop your attacks! New Persia surrenders! Stop your attacks! *Stop your attacks!*"

The crowd watching the video around the capital building went silent. Utterly. Completely. Silent.

Crashes and explosions, however, continued to rock the image in the video. The tom, in a broken voice unbecoming the pride of a cat, especially an obviously pure-bred cat of such an old, respected breed as Persians, said in a whisper, "Help us. We have no way to evacuate. *Anyone.* Send help. *Please.*"

The silence in the crowd lasted three flicks of an agitated cat's tail before whispers of *"New Persia?"*, *"Another cat colony?"*, and *"On Europa?"* broke out everywhere.

Trudith looked at Alistair, her little alpha cat. The brown eyebrow spots above her eyes furrowed, giving her face a sad, worried look. She hoped Alistair had a plan.

On the steps, Senator Morrison cleared his throat into the mic, and the crowd started to quiet again. If Alistair had a plan, the time was now.

"He's going to call for war?" Alistair asked, looking up at Trudith. "Against the otters? Now?"

He asked, but the question was rhetorical. Senator Morrison had been nearly as anti-otter in his policies as he was anti-cat. "The *fool.*" Alistair spat and sprang into action.

The crowd was thick, but Alistair was lithe and quick. His dignified, orange-striped body ducked between crowd members until he was on the steps, not far below Morrison. A Greyhound guard moved to block Alistair, but the little cat gave the towering dog a steely gaze to match Morrison's own. Trudith could see Alistair speaking, and then the guard reluctantly let him pass. Trudith imagined it would not go well for that guard with Senator Morrison later.

The Sheltie senator, still unaware of Alistair's presence, said to the crowd, "I think it's obvious what our nation must do. No more can we be neutral!"

Moments later, Alistair leaned toward Morrison and said into his mic, "I couldn't agree more, dear Senator."

Morrison looked shocked to find his competitor beside him, and Alistair rushed on before Morrison could recover his composure. "We must make the otters our allies once and for all!"

"No!" Morrison shouted, but Alistair joined right in with him, turning it into a chant: "No more neutrality!"

Trudith, quick to take a cue from her alpha, picked the chant right up in her booming, barrel-chested voice: "No more neutrality!"

"Otters are allies!" Alistair added, and soon the two of them —orange cat on the stage and black dog in the crowd—had the entire crowd chanting with them: "No more *neutrality!* Otters are *allies!*"

Senator Morrison may have been an anti-cat, anti-otter extremist—a complete bigot, if you asked Petra—but he was also a politician and a herd dog. He knew the direction of a crowd, and he knew how to move with one in order to have a chance at making the crowd move with him later.

Morrison spread his white paws in a gesture that symbolically, and effectively, turned down the volume of the crowd a notch. Then, he put one paw on Alistair's shoulder and said, "When two opponents see eye to eye on an issue,"—Morrison, who was short for a dog, looked down at Alistair pointedly— "Then you know it must be right." He signaled to his Greyhound guards who circled around him briefly in a huddle and then disseminated into the crowd, carrying clipboards.

Speaking to the crowd again, Morrison said, "I want each and every one of you to sign this petition that my assistants are bringing around. I'll deliver it in the senate tomorrow."

Morrison covered his clip-on mic with a paw, and Trudith watched her alpha cat argue with the incumbent competition. Morrison and Alistair were much too far away for Trudith to make out their words, but their exchange looked heated. It ended with a wolfish grin on Morrison's side, and flattened ears on Alistair. However, despite the conflict apparent in their body language, the two opponents made a point of shaking paws, ceremoniously, before Alistair left the steps. They both knew the importance of keeping up appearances.

When Alistair made it back to his group, he said, "Can you grab hold of one of those Greyhounds? I want to see the petitions they're taking around."

With an eager swish of her tail and a malicious gleam in her eye, Petra said, "Sure thing, brother." But, as they watched Petra bob through the crowd, popping up in front of Greyhounds, it became clear she'd have no luck. Every Greyhound she found looked right past her, literally over her head. In fact, they seemed to be ignoring most cats as they wandered the crowd proffering their clipboards.

"They're being extremely selective," Lucky said.

"Yeah," Alistair agreed. "That's why I'd like to see what they have in those petitions. It's got to be something Morrison threw together *before* he knew I'd be here and would manage to derail him."

Without another word, Lucky drifted casually away. At first, Trudith thought he was being rude—something that wouldn't surprise her from someone so close to Petra. Then Trudith realized what he was doing.

Lucky had the *look* that the Greyhounds were searching for. As soon as he was away from Alistair and the brindle cat who'd come with him, a Greyhound with a petition spotted Lucky and came right up to him.

"Would you like to sign?" the Greyhound said.

"I don't know," Lucky answered. "I usually believe in everything the senator says, but making nice with otters?" Lucky shook his head disapprovingly. "That's not his usual party line."

The Greyhound glanced surreptitiously around, and Trudith belatedly realized that her cats were making a point of looking in other directions, as if they weren't paying attention to what was going on with the Greyhound and Lucky. Fortunately, Trudith didn't look like a threat to the Greyhound. Trudith wasn't sure if that was meant as a comment on her intelligence, or if the Greyhound simply didn't recognize her as Alistair's right-hand dog. Either way, she felt a little insulted.

"Don't worry," the Greyhound told Lucky, holding the petition down where Lucky, a much, much shorter dog could see it.

"As you can see, *this* doesn't stray quite so far from the party line."

While Lucky looked over the document, Petra popped up behind him and snapped a shot with a camera over his shoulder. "Ha!" she said.

The Greyhound snarled, *"Give me that camera!"*

"Fat chance!" Petra quipped and slipped back into the crowd.

The Greyhound could have outrun Petra, but not in a crowd. As thoroughly surrounded as they were, there was no chance of *running*. The Greyhound put a paw up to the wire in his ear and gave a laughably vague description to his cohorts: "A cat with a camera got a picture of the petition... No... I dunno... Orange? Sounded female... I think..." Finally, the Greyhound narrowed his eyes in anger and glared into the crowd.

Petra had bested him.

Lucky gave Trudith a goofy grin that said, *"I am so in love with my clever feline wife."*

Trudith gagged like a cat with a hairball.

When the Greyhound gave up glaring at the crowd, he re-approached Lucky about the petition. Lucky, however, politely declined to sign.

Once the Greyhound was a safe distance into the crowd, Lucky and Trudith rejoined their cats. Even Petra had managed to loop her way back through the crowd. She was staring intently at the viewer on her camera.

"I don't think you can zoom it in enough, Pet. We'll have to wait until you get it downloaded onto the computer," Alistair said.

"Is this the camera for taking pictures of the kittens?" the brindle cat asked.

Petra nodded.

"Kittens?" Trudith asked. Then, "Excuse me, but what *is* your coloring called?"

"I'm a torbie," the cat answered proudly. Most cats, no

matter how ordinary, seemed to be proud of their fur color. "That's short for *tortoiseshell tabby*."

Petra looked at the torbie appraisingly. "A torbie would be good," she said.

"Really?" Lucky asked, looking surprised. "Aren't torbies all girls? I was thinking—"

Petra spat at Lucky, shushing him right up so that no one got to hear what he'd been thinking. Petra shoved her camera in her pocket, grabbed Lucky with one arm and the torbie with another, and said, "We have to be going, but I'll download this picture as soon as we're done."

Alistair waved goodbye, then he turned to Trudith and said, "I wonder why they were talking about kittens. I know Petra had some idea for a publicity stunt, but the campaign has gotten a bit past that now."

Trudith wasn't at all sure that she liked the sound of a publicity stunt involving kittens, especially not one born out of Petra's scheming mind. She imagined kittens suspended over shark-infested waters or trapped inside burning houses. Sure, the intention would be for Alistair, amidst great fanfare, to rescue the kittens, but mostly Trudith imagined crying, mewling, endangered kittens.

"Never mind," Alistair said. "I need to come up with an idea for a stunt of my own. We may have turned the tide of *this* crowd for *today*. But, tomorrow, Morrison will be addressing the senate. And, you can bet that he *won't* be presenting a petition that says '*Otters Are Allies*.'"

"It might say '*No More Neutrality*,' though," Trudith said, feeling unusually clever. She was rewarded with an amused smile.

"We have a long day of scheming ahead of us," Alistair said. "Let's get back to the office, and figure out a way to prevent a war."

Trudith nodded, feeling worried. She believed in her little

alpha cat, but she'd seen the fire in Senator Morrison's eyes when he'd said the word *"war."* And she'd felt the fear throughout the crowd. She'd felt it herself. Someone was attacking otters, and now, that same *someone* was attacking cats. Right now, the attack was on cats she didn't know, up on a moon of Jupiter.

Next would it be *her* cats? *On Earth?* And *dogs*, even?

CHAPTER 8
TRAILSIDE

Kipper stood among the noisy patrons of the Foghorn, shocked by what she saw on the vid screen. *Did this change anything?* she wondered. She'd uncovered and visited one hidden cat colony on Mars. She'd *spoken* with the cats there. She'd made *friends* with one of them, or so he would have her think from his letters, anyway.

But he was keeping this *giant* secret. They all were. An entire other colony *in an entire other part of the solar system*. None of them, not even Josh, who was so seemingly smitten with her, had mentioned it.

Cats are good at keeping secrets.

Okay, so Josh *had* mentioned New Persia. But he had purposely let Kipper believe it was just another atmo-dome on Mars. Hadn't he?

Cats are also good at getting revenge, Kipper thought. The word *catty* does come from somewhere, but Kipper felt tired of cats and cattiness. She didn't want to be a cat.

That Persian cat had looked so scared.

"Kipper, Kipper!" Trugger was shaking Kipper by the shoulder. "Are you okay?"

Against every catty bone in her body, Kipper said, "I have

to help those cats." But she didn't know how. She was the only other cat in space. The only cat on a spaceship, but she was too far away. It would take weeks, at the least, to get from the asteroid belt to Jupiter. By then, it would surely be too late.

"Of course we have to help them," Captain Cod said. He and Jenny both stood beside Trugger, who still held Kipper by the shoulder. She was glad of the support. Without it, she might have fainted.

Looking around the Foghorn, Kipper realized the rest of the Barracuders had already left.

"I've ordered the rest of the crew back to the ship," Captain Cod said. "You're coming with us, right?"

"With you?" Kipper asked, still in a daze.

"To Jupiter," Captain Cod said. "To help the New Persians."

"That's weeks away," Kipper mewled, despair trembling in her voice.

"Well, sure," Trugger said, "Using the *normal* engines."

Kipper's eyes dilated. *The normal engines? There were faster engines? And the otters hadn't been using them?*

"You're coming?" Jenny asked.

Kipper nodded mutely.

She let Trugger and Jenny walk her back through Trailside toward the ship. The captain had to deal with the dock master before the *Jolly Barracuda* could disembark. Trailside kept a complex and busy docking schedule.

As she walked, Kipper felt the despair lifting. She was terrified of what these *non-normal* engines might be, and she didn't want to breathe oxo-agua again. But...

In a way, she was relieved. She'd been only a whisker's breadth from saying goodbye to her otter friends and starting her voyage back to Earth, but at some level she was glad of the discovery of the Europan cat colony and her clearly felt duty to come to their aid. She knew that was wrong. Those Persian cats were under fire, facing unimaginable horrors at the hands of an unknown foe. Kipper couldn't help it.

It wasn't that she didn't want to say goodbye, with all the sad awkwardness that came with that. She didn't want to leave the *Jolly Barracuda*.

Perhaps Kipper hadn't found what she'd come to space looking for, namely a *friendly* colony of cats with their arms wide, ready to welcome her. The cats had not welcomed her. But the otters had.

There were reasons she had left Earth. She was tired of living a dog-trodden life. There were good dogs like Trudith, sure, but, for every Trudith, there seemed to be a dozen Morrisons. Dogs aside, on Earth, Kipper had felt like nothing more than an interchangeable, unimportant cog.

Up here, she was the cat discovering giant Siamhalla-sized secrets. She was the cat coming to rescue New Persia. Perhaps it was the *Jolly Barracuda* insanity claiming her, but being the Ship's Spy for Captain Cod and his crew made Kipper feel *important*.

The feeling lasted until the moment she set paw on one of the grated iron drains in the floor of the chlorine-scented *Jolly Barracuda*.

Oh god, she thought. *I'm going to be breathing oxo-agua again.*

"You know, Kipster," Trugger said, slapping her on the back, "I'm glad you're staying."

"*Kipster*?" Kipper asked. Only Petra called Kipper that, and only because Petra was too much of a force of nature for Kipper to stop her.

"Yeah," Trugger said. "That's what I call you."

"Not to my knowledge," Kipper said snippily.

"See?" Trugger said, using the Standard Swimmer's Sign for a kippered herring which had become Kipper's name under oxo-agua.

"So?"

"You're not seeing it?" He made the sign a few more times; it involved wiggling his littlest paw pad. Apparently, however, he was wiggling it slightly differently than for the normal sign. Jenny shrugged at Kipper; she didn't get it either.

Trugger kept signing, however, and, eventually, Kipper figured it out: the rhythm of the wiggling pawpad was syncopated. In Trugger's mind, that must make it a nickname—one which it would be too late to object to now. Apparently, like Petra, Trugger was a force of nature. Only where Petra was a tsunami, Trugger was more like an ice age. He snuck up on you.

"Right," Kipper sighed with a sense of resignation. "I need to talk to Emily before we take off... about... some stuff." It wasn't the smoothest exit, but Trugger saluted, saying something about an errand he needed to run on Trailside, and Jenny gave her arm a friendly squeeze. More importantly, they let her escape. She must have seemed steady enough to convince them that she was all right. Kipper wasn't convinced. What she needed right now wasn't sympathetic otters.

As Kipper approached the kitchen, she could see Emily busy at work inside. Her tentacles flew, wielding knives, steadying cutting boards, sweeping chopped vegetables into bowls, and turning a crank on the top of a big pressure cooker. She must be fixing her traditional clam chowder.

Otters love clam chowder, and Kipper had to agree with them. However, soups of any sort don't fare well under oxo-agua, so Emily only ever fixed it while the *Jolly Barracuda* was drained and docked at a station. Personally, Kipper was surprised she made it at all. While being docked made eating clam chowder easier, Emily still had to cook it in oxo-agua. As Kipper understood it, the process was quite complex, involving a carefully sealed pressure-cooker. Somehow, Emily managed.

Kipper walked up to the kitchen and, with the sensation of breaking a taboo, knocked on the glass. Emily had said she didn't mind people getting her attention that way, but Kipper felt like a kitten on a visit to an aquarium, illicitly tapping on all the fish tanks despite clearly marked signs reading, "Do Not Tap on the Glass!"

Perhaps that said more about Kipper's kittenhood than anything else.

Emily looked up. Her eyes were yellow with rectangular pupils, and the rectangles narrowed in a smile when she saw Kipper. Her face—or what passed for it—was really just the gray expanse of skin under her eyes. Nonetheless, Kipper had learned to read the way that her skin stretched, and she knew Emily was happy to see her.

"You've come to say goodbye?" Emily signed with two of her free tentacles.

"I'm staying," Kipper signed.

Standard Swimmer's Sign was a dual language—for every word there was a sign designed for otter paws and another sign designed for octopus tentacles. Kipper used the otter signs since she was two-pawed like them, but she knew how to read octopus signs.

"What changed your mind?" Emily asked. It constantly amazed Kipper how Emily could easily communicate in sign language without even hesitating at her cooking. She worked the signs in fluidly with whichever tentacles were handy while all the others kept busy with knives, pots, and pans.

Otters—and Kipper—couldn't do that. With only two front paws, it took a person's every appendage to sign.

"There's been news," Kipper signed. "There's a second cat colony. On a moon of Jupiter."

It was momentary, and Kipper almost missed it; but all eight of Emily's tentacles froze. The skin around her eyes rearranged in surprise. Then, as quick as the blink of a cat's inner eyelid, six of the eight tentacles were back to cooking. The last two signed, "Which moon?"

"Europa," Kipper signed. She had to resort to spelling the

name out, letter by letter, as she didn't know the Swimmer's Sign for it. As she spelled, Kipper's brain buzzed. She tried to make sense of the reaction she'd just seen.

Had Emily really been that surprised to learn of another cat colony? It seemed like too much surprise for just that, and, if it was just that, why had Emily tried to cover her surprise?

Or had Emily been surprised to learn that *Kipper knew* about the second cat colony?

"I'm sorry," Kipper signed, realizing she hadn't been reading Emily's signs at all. "What were you saying?"

"Are you going to this other colony?" Emily repeated. "Do you think the cats there will be more accepting?"

"I don't know," Kipper signed. She hadn't really thought about it, but she supposed she couldn't help hoping a little that they'd be more accepting. Especially if she brought the only otter ship crazy enough to head *into* Jupiter System to their rescue.

Who was she kidding? These were *Persians.* On *New Persia.* "No," Kipper signed, "I don't think they'll be more accepting. But they need help, and they're cats. I have to go help them."

"Noble," Emily signed. "I wouldn't necessarily feel the same *empathy* for another member of my race." Emily had left her home under the ocean in disgrace, and Kipper knew that she felt a great deal of dissonance about the culture and society of her people.

"What if it was an octopus up here?" Kipper signed. "In space—*like you.*"

"There are other octopi in space," Emily signed. "They're not like me."

"They're all males," Kipper guessed.

"Yes."

From what Emily had said in the past, Kipper inferred that the octopi had a profoundly sexist society. Kipper wasn't clear on the details, but it seemed that women were expected to lay their eggs, watch over them until they hatched, and then die. Emily hadn't died.

Emily didn't know why—whether it was a biological quirk or, as it was seen in her society, some sort of mental weakness that caused her to fail in what was seen as her natural biological role. Either way, there simply hadn't been a place in octopus society for a female past egg-laying age.

Kipper sighed and felt some of the tension between her ears relax. She didn't know why she'd doubted Emily. If octopi were involved in this, Emily wouldn't be part of it. Perhaps Kipper was just in a paranoid, catty frame of mind. Being cast out by a society of your species-peers can do that to you.

"There are ships attacking this cat colony," Kipper signed. Even if Emily wouldn't be involved, she *might* know something. "These anonymous ships have been attacking otters, too. Do you think they could be octopus ships?"

This time, when all of Emily's tentacles stopped—mid-chop, mid-stir, and with a soggy baguette of Emily's special underwater bread held aloft—they stayed stopped. She held stock still for several heartbeats before all of her tentacles, still mainly motionless, started that almost imperceptible squiggling and squirming that meant Emily was thinking.

"No," she signed.

The signed word was simple, final, but Emily's tentacles hadn't stopped wriggling.

"Are you sure?" Kipper signed.

Green eyes and yellow eyes locked on each other across atmospheres and an acrylic glass barrier. Her yellow eyes narrowed, but when Emily spoke, her tentacles signed, completely nonchalantly, "I've almost finished this chowder. You should spread the word—it's best when it's hot."

Nonplussed, Kipper's ears danced forward and backward, finally settling, flattened against her skull. Emily did know something, and she wasn't talking.

Kipper sighed through her teeth. When it came down to it, she really couldn't tell. Emily was too foreign, and Kipper was too exhausted. She'd have to go round up the otters for their clam chowder feast and put her confusions and suspicions on hold. For now. Yes, for now, she would eat, drink, and be merry —for, tomorrow, she would be breathing oxo-agua.

CHAPTER 9
EARTH

etra, Alistair, and Trudith huddled around Petra's computer, reading the enlarged photo she'd taken of Morrison's petition. The petition didn't look good.

"Well," Alistair said, "that explains why Morrison's hench-hounds were so withholding with these."

"Indeed," Petra agreed, seeming unusually restrained, but her restraint didn't hold. She spat through her teeth, "Lying canine bully!"

"Hey now," Alistair said, looking at Trudith to see if she was hurt by the species-slur.

"That's okay," Trudith said. "Morrison *is* a lying canine bully." Petra looked like a little orange kitten who'd been caught with her paw in the fish tank, only to have her parents assume she'd been cleaning it. "Doesn't mean we all are," Trudith added. Petra nodded mutely, accepting her reprieve with grace.

"What do we do?" Trudith asked.

Morrison's petition didn't call for an alliance with otters, but it did call for an end to neutrality. Specifically, the petition called for an ultimatum: the otters were to stop attacking New Persia —although no one in their right mind really believed *the otters* were attacking New Persia—and turn over control of their space elevator. Or else war. It was an unprovoked grab for otter technology, designed to be delivered at the worst time.

Petra pulled out a calculator, and after a flurry of calculations said, "If it came to war, I think our government *could* take control of the space elevator by force."

Trudith's eyebrows raised in a worried look. She wasn't sure how Petra had arrived at that conclusion using a calculator, but the conclusion seemed right. And wrong. "That's the *otters'* elevator," Trudith said.

Petra looked at Trudith pityingly. Clearly, they were working with different definitions of ownership. Trudith felt that her definition was more moral somehow. Petra's, admittedly, might be more practical for understanding this situation.

"So," Alistair said, "I need to offer our government something better than the space elevator to keep them from declaring war on the otters."

"Like moral fortitude?" Petra asked mockingly.

"It does *feel* better when you do things that are right," Trudith said.

Petra cast her the pitying look again.

"Don't fight," Alistair said. Petra and Trudith both opened their mouths to defend themselves, but Alistair stared them down. "*Please*," he said. "Don't fight. I think,"—his eyes went dreamy and faraway—"I need to go for a walk. Get outside. See the stars."

Petra nodded, ears submissively lowered. Trudith could tell that both cats were thinking about Kipper, their missing sister. Trudith had never seen all three siblings together, but she could feel the space left behind where the third sibling was meant to be. Trudith couldn't fill that hole. It was Kipper shaped.

Trudith and Kipper had become close friends—almost sisters —on their long journey down the Pacific Coast, all the way to Ecuador and the space elevator. When they parted ways, Kipper sent Trudith home to look out for her wayward politician of a brother. Until Kipper returned, that's what Trudith would do.

Trudith went to the office's front window. She could see Alistair standing on the sidewalk, staring upward at the stars. Trudith stared at him, keeping him safely in her steady gaze. She would let no harm come to that little cat.

"Ali?" Petra said. She rolled her chair back from the computer and looked around. When she didn't see her brother, Petra said, "Trudith. Go fetch Alistair for me."

Trudith made it all the way out the door before realizing that she probably should have felt insulted by the way Petra ordered her around. It just came too naturally to her to fetch things. "Alistair." Trudith walked up to him. "Petra wants you."

Trudith flanked Alistair as they walked back inside. The sound of Kipper talking greeted them as they entered the office. Petra glanced at them over her shoulder and said, right over Kipper's voice, "Too slow. I couldn't wait." Kipper's image was on the screen in front of her. "But we can start it over when we reach the end."

Alistair's ears perked right up, and he leaned past his sister to crank up the volume.

"...and the ship won't be ready to fire up its Ryderian engines for another few hours. So, if you get this message in time... Well, I'll be hanging around hoping that one of you messages me back." Kipper smiled, her eyes full of warmth, and then looked away from the camera. "I miss you guys."

The image went to black, and Alistair immediately snaked his paw over Petra's shoulder toward the keyboard. Before he reached a single key, though, Petra slapped his paw away. "I know, you want to watch the beginning," she said, switching programs on her computer, "but this is more important."

Any given change in Alistair's stance was imperceptible, but his entire demeanor changed. He was furious. And it was menacing. Trudith felt like whimpering, but Petra completely ignored him.

"Hi Sis," she said to the tiny camera embedded at the top of her computer screen. "We're all here. Alistair and your watch dog walked in late, so I have to replay your video from the beginning. But we'll be here as long as you're available and want to talk. Swap messages. Whatever." Petra cast a querying glance over her shoulder at Alistair who had begun to visibly relax when he realized what Petra was doing. "At least, I will be."

Petra sent the message and switched back to the other program, then stood up and offered Alistair her seat. He immediately sat down and restarted the video.

"Her time lag should be something like ten minutes." Petra moved to the other side of the room and began poking at Trudith's desk. "So, think quick about what you want to say to her."

Alistair swished his tail in irritation at Petra speaking over Kipper's video, but he didn't deign to turn either ear in her direction.

Trudith tried to listen to the recording of Kipper, but she felt overwhelmed by the subtle interplay of aggression and dominance that had happened in front of her. She always felt wibbly inside when Petra challenged Alistair like that. And was Petra poking at Trudith's desk just to *bother her* or was she really interested in the notes Trudith had jotted down on how to get to her cousin's apartment to babysit his puppies next week?

Even when Trudith did manage to focus on Kipper's words, they were all sorts of confusing. She seemed to be describing the physics behind some super fast engines on the otters' spaceship. Trudith couldn't keep up, but Kipper seemed excited about it.

The video looped back around to the part where Trudith and Alistair had come in. Alistair didn't wait for the end. He whipped around to look at his companions, eyes glittering. "Well, that's that, then!"

"Wait," Trudith said, "what's what, when?"

"They're never going to succeed." Petra scowled. "Have you listened to Kipper's other videos? Those otters she's hanging out with are complete loons." Petra took a moment just then to eye Trudith, but she pointedly *didn't* say anything more *general* about the kind of company her sister kept.

Alistair wasn't watching them, or listening. He'd switched to the recording software on Petra's computer. "Kipper," he said to the pinhole video camera hidden in the monitor, "I'm going to address the senate tomorrow, and I need you to record a video message for me."

CHAPTER 10
THE ASTEROID BELT

Kipper recorded the video. It took a few takes to get just right. She wasn't much for public speaking. At least, she wouldn't have to be there in the senate assembly when Alistair played the video. She hoped it would give him what he needed.

She wouldn't find out until his coup was all over.

For now—and the next week—Kipper would have her own concerns, and very few of them had to do with planetary-bound politics, canine rulers, or even gravity.

When Trugger first explained the way Ryderian engines worked to her, Kipper had been excited. She liked the idea of riding to Jupiter in stasis and skipping all that unpleasantness with oxo-agua. Then Trugger explained how the stasis worked.

First, the *Jolly Barracuda* would be flooded with oxo-agua, like normal, which would be bad enough. But, *then*, a Tesla helix embedded in the ship's hull would create an electro-magnetic field that would *gel* the oxo-agua into a colloid *right inside their bodies*. The worst part was that they would remain conscious. *UGH!* Kipper could hardly stand to think about it.

"Are you ready?" Jenny asked, poking her head into the little room where Kipper had ensconced herself with a com-console to record and receive videos.

"Yes," Kipper said, distractedly. "No, wait, I mean, I'd like to record one more message."

"Be quick!" Jenny said. "Oxo-agua stops for no cat. Or otter, for that matter. But, an otter wouldn't ask it to stop." She grinned, wide and whiskery.

Kipper shuddered, and the fur all up and down her body fluffed a bit. "How long..." She could hardly even talk about it. The mere *idea* of oxo-agua gelling in her throat choked her words to a halt. She tried again. "How long will we have after the ship is flooded before, you know, the *stasis* happens?"

"I'd say twenty minutes, give or take. Just enough time for Captain Cod to hand over control of the ship to Emily."

"To Emily?" Kipper asked in amazement.

"Who did you think was going to fly the ship while we're all in stasis?"

"How does *she* avoid the stasis?"

"She doesn't," Jenny said, "but she's an octopus. Her muscles are freakishly strong, and she's designed for living in a high pressure, high viscosity environment. At least, compared to what we're designed for."

"I see," Kipper said. She was still reeling from this new piece of knowledge, namely that the chef would be flying the ship. "Has she, um, flown the ship before?"

"Sure," Jenny said.

Kipper felt better hearing that. Then, Jenny continued.

"Why, Emily's the one who stopped us from rocketing straight into the cold, dark eternity of an interstellar voyage when the Ryderian engines were first installed."

Kipper's feline curiosity got the better of her, and she asked, "How do you mean?" before she could stop herself.

"You know the captain."

Kipper's ears flattened in impatience. "Yes."

"He hadn't really thought the stasis part through. He only meant to test the engines—see if they'd start right. He didn't exactly have a plan for how we were going to, well, stop the ship."

Kipper could picture it. A ship full of otters, gelled in stasis, unable to hit the *off* switch. Fortunately, they happened to employ an octopus chef, who must have made her slow, invertebrate way from the kitchen to the bridge when she finally realized something was wrong.

"How far out did the ship make it?" Kipper asked.

"Emily realized what had happened around dinner time," Jenny said, "And she taught herself the ship's controls surprisingly fast. So, we weren't much further out than the orbit of Neptune."

Speechless. Kipper felt utterly speechless. It truly amazed her sometimes that anyone followed Captain Cod's orders. Yet, here she was, doing the same.

"Emily's a good pilot," Jenny said. "You'll be in good tentacles."

"Right," Kipper said. "I think I'd better record that last vid now. If you don't mind."

Jenny bobbed her head to acknowledge Kipper's request for privacy then disappeared back into the corridor.

Kipper turned to the vid-cam monitor and took a deep breath. Feeling completely unready, she hit record. "Josh," she said as her brain switched gears from octopus pilots to cat colonies. "I've just found out about the attacks on *Europa*." Kipper paused a moment, weighing her options. She wanted to tell Josh off for misleading her, for being as secretive and superior as his entire society. She wanted to tell him off for even being *in* such a secretive and superior society.

But this conversation wasn't going to happen real time, fact to face. Her private video to a prospective paramour might not *stay* private. It was also going to be the only direct communique between New Persia's rescuers and New Persia's sister colony before those rescuers arrived.

Kipper stayed her spiteful tongue. Mostly.

"The *Jolly Barracuda* will be in Jupiter System by the end of the week. We're only one ship, but we have a big cargo-hold. It won't be comfortable, but if New Persia has supplies ready, we can rescue... a hundred colonists?"

Kipper lowered her head to her paws, dug the claws into the skin before her ears. *"That's not enough.* Doggarnit, Josh!" She glared at the mirrored image of herself on the vid-cam's RECORD-screen, "Why did you all have to be like this? If all the wealthy, elite, *purebred* cats like *you* had spent their power and money to help *all* cats, instead of building this exclusive castle in the sky..."

Kipper's whiskers quivered. *This would get her nowhere.* She flexed her claws and exerted the raw willpower necessary to still her whiskers.

"Well, you didn't, did you?" she said. "So, New Persia has one tabby cat and a borrowed otter ship coming to help them. I hope that will be enough."

Kipper slammed her paw down on the keyboard, shutting off the vid-cam. She sent the message, unedited: no flirtatious addendums, no wistful hoping to hear from him when she got out of stasis. None of that. In fact, Kipper hoped she wouldn't hear from Josh again. She didn't need all the frustrating emotions he inspired. If she wanted to fall in love, there were plenty of perfectly nice mixed-breed cats on Earth.

She hadn't wanted to fall in love, though. At least, not with another cat. Maybe with a *place.* A way of life.

Kipper shook herself, ears and whiskers thoroughly flapped, to get the very thought out of her head: she could *not* be in love with a way of life that involved breathing *gelatin.*

She was still sitting there, dazed and confused by her revelation, when Jenny poked her head back around the door. "It's time!" Jenny said. "Let's go to Jupiter!"

Kipper's tail fluffed, and she couldn't keep her claws from unsheathing. They squeaked on the flooring as she followed Jenny to the barracks. Other otters were already in the bunks, and Trugger shot her a huge grin when he saw her.

Sitting on her own bunk, Kipper felt her heart race as she heard the sound of the vents opening under the floor. Within moments, oxo-agua seeped up from the iron grates spaced around the floor of the room and everywhere else on the ship. The otters around her joked and chatted, but she couldn't hear any of it. All she heard was the sound of oxo-agua, sloshing and splashing.

When it reached the level of the bunk, she closed her eyes. It was bad enough to feel the liquid rising around her body. She couldn't stand to see it. She started to hyperventilate as the oxo-agua reached her shoulders. She knew she'd have to dunk her head soon and take that horrible lungful of oxygenated liquid into her lungs. The thought terrified her. As she took her final breath of air, Kipper thought, *Terror is a lot like exhilaration.*

When she opened her eyes in that *other* atmosphere, she looked up and saw the silvery layer of air above her. The first time she'd done this, Trugger had held her down. He'd forced her to stay under, rather than let her flop about like she was drowning. This time she'd done it herself. That felt better.

Jenny caught Kipper's eye and signed, "As soon as the atmosphere change is done, Captain Cod will send Boris to join us. Then he'll set off the EM-field."

Kipper nodded.

"The captain stays in a room right off the bridge. Closer to Emily."

Kipper nodded again and looked at the dwindling layer of silver air above them. The silver rose higher and higher, broke apart into separate bubbles as it hit the ceiling, and then was entirely gone. Sucked through vents, pushed into pressurized chambers. Where it would be stored until the *Jolly Barracuda* needed a gaseous atmosphere again.

Kipper wondered what the ship looked like now. She'd only seen it from the outside when the inflatable storage units for the oxo-agua were full. At those times, the *Jolly Barracuda* looked kind of like a missile being strangled by a pair of angry inner-tubes.

Since the *Jolly Barracuda's* gaseous atmosphere was so much more compressible while stored, those storage units were probably mostly deflated right now. The *Jolly Barracuda* might look a lot better that way. *More like a spaceship should.*

Kipper's reverie was interrupted by a swaying sensation in the oxo-agua around her. Boris swam past. He settled on his bunk, looked around the room at all the otters watching him, and signed, "T minus one!" Then he lay back on his bunk, as did all the other otters.

Kipper's heart pounded. She felt the blood rushing through her ears. She forced herself to lie back calmly, and she tried to breathe evenly. Each breath was liquid, and for the first time, she was grateful for that. Then she felt a prickling under her fur, which could have been her imagination, and she suddenly thought to clamp her eyes shut.

The gel congealed in an instant. It was like the oxo-agua hugged her all over—inside and out. Every part of her body froze, from her closed double-eyelids to her lungs. No more breathing. Not until Jupiter. *Wouldn't she die of oxygen deprivation?* Her mind started to panic inside an immobile body. *This was a nightmare.*

Then the temperature started to drop, and as Kipper felt her heart slow, she remembered: the cold would shut her body down. She would survive this nightmare and wake up in Jupiter

System. *She hated this.* Right before her mind slipped away into blessed unconsciousness, she thought, *"Thank goodness my eyes aren't open."*

CHAPTER 11
EARTH

Only two hours until Alistair planned to storm the senate assembly, and Trudith was completely lost. She didn't get lost easily. She'd been all over the back streets and alleys of New LA. In her old life, as a thug, she'd tailed many a cat through every unsavory part of the city.

She could only assume Petra was going somewhere incredibly top secret. Or she knew Trudith was following her.

At first, it was only an inkling in the back of Trudith's mind. Leading Trudith on a wild goose chase *was* the kind of thing Petra would do, but Trudith had never been spotted by a cat she was tailing before. Of course, most cats weren't Petra.

Petra led Trudith three times around the same block. "*Okay,*" Trudith harrumphed, stepping out of the shadowed leeward side of a building that Petra was studying the signs on *for the third time*. She was a smart cat; she couldn't be *that* lost.

"This is just insulting," Trudith barked.

"Yes, it is," Petra snarled, "But you're the one who started it." She took a cautious step toward Trudith. All the fur on her face and arms fluffed out. She must be scared of Trudith, no matter how hard she tried to hide it. "What're you doing following me around like the common thug who beat my sister up? *Or* are you not as reformed as you pretend to be?"

Trudith took a step back. How had this turned on her? A moment ago, she was the good guy, and Petra was sneaking around town.

"Are you on Morrison's payroll? Is that it?" Petra asked with a sneer and another step forward, though her fur was still fluffed.

"Wait, what?" Trudith was confused. How could she prove that she wasn't on Morrison's payroll? *She wasn't, right?* Trudith was so confused that, suddenly, she wasn't even sure. "I mean, I don't get any money from him, if that's what you mean..."

Petra skewed an ear.

Maybe this was exactly what Morrison would want—Alistair's two closest henchmen turning on each other. Maybe Morrison had schemed it all. "How would Morrison get me to do what he wanted without telling me he wanted it?"

Petra skewed the other ear and rolled her eyes. "Never mind," she said. "You're clearly not on Morrison's payroll." She looked thoughtful and added, under her whiskers, "Unless you're a much better actor than I think you are." After a moment's consideration, she dismissed the thought. An evil glint appeared in her eye, only to be replaced a moment later by an almost vapid look of innocence.

Cats are so complex, Trudith thought. She could hardly keep up when Petra actually talked to her. Understanding the multifarious thoughts and feelings that flitted across Petra's twitching ears and gleaming eyes? Trudith hadn't a hope. She knew better than to even try.

Shuffling her paws and grinning nervously, Trudith said, "As long as we're both out here, I suppose, well, we could head to the senate assembly together? I mean, we might as well. Right?"

"Yeeeees," Petra said, stretching the word out between her tiny, pointy feline fangs. "Why don't you lead the way?"

Trudith shuffled her paws again and lowered her eyes, avoiding Petra's piercing gaze.

"Oh, I see," Petra said, sarcasm dripping from her voice. "You're *lost*, aren't you?" She didn't wait for Trudith to respond. She clearly already knew the answer. "I guess I'll have to show you the way."

Trudith's jowls gaped in an even more nervous grin, and her tail started to wag reflexively. "Oh thank you, Petra!" she said. "Thank you!"

The silence between them grew tense and heavy as Trudith and Petra walked through the maze of alleyways and rundown neighborhoods full of dilapidated buildings. Trudith wanted to fix it. She wanted to say something that would ease the tension and make Petra like her again. Except Petra had never liked her.

Trudith didn't know why.

She had been following Petra around town, thinking about breaking into her desk drawer, and generally mistrusting this sister of her two closest friends. Maybe, Trudith thought, Petra had a point. Maybe all of this really was her own fault.

When Petra said, "You know, Trudith, I have an idea for something you could do to help Alistair out," gratefulness flooded through the big, loyal, black dog. *She would do anything to help Alistair.* She could hardly believe her luck that Petra would, of her own accord, offer a chance for Trudith to win redemption.

Only a flicker of uncertainty surged through Trudith when Petra said, "I think you should kidnap Senator Morrison."

Trudith didn't say anything, and the two of them walked on in silence again for a while. The tension was different this time. Very different. *Was Petra serious?* Trudith was afraid to ask.

"If you can't do it," Petra said, "That's okay."

Trudith raised an eyebrow, stretching the brown spot above her eye into the shape of a jelly bean. Was Petra trying to egg her into this by challenging her ego? *That wasn't going to work.*

Unfortunately for Trudith, Petra sensed she was losing her and changed tactics.

Petra said, "I kind of hope Alistair doesn't win. If he did, it would mean living in this big publicity spotlight for even longer, and I am ready to be *done* with that." Petra cast Trudith a sidelong glance. "Soooo," she added to make her position completely clear, "It'll be better if you leave Senator Morrison be. If you kidnapped him, then Alistair would probably win. And I wouldn't want *that*."

Trudith, sweet but senseless soul that she was, bought it hook, line, and sinker. She wanted to please Petra, but her loyalty to Alistair outweighed anything else. "You really think that kidnapping Senator Morrison would help?" she asked.

"Of course," Petra said as matter-of-factly as she could.

Trudith was tired of looking stupid in Petra's eyes, but she was also reluctant to take such a drastic action. Kidnapping was the kind of action Alistair would look down on. "How?" Trudith asked. "How would it help?"

"Weeeell," Petra said, "Are you familiar with the rebellion of Mai Mai, the great Siamese king of South Texas?"

The jelly-bean shapes of both of Trudith's eyebrow spots answered that question. Which wasn't surprising, as Petra had made King Mai Mai up.

Petra quickly spun a complex tale of her invented king's last minute capture by the Texan pug dog mafia. "And that's why there isn't a monarchy in South Texas anymore," Petra concluded as soon as Trudith's head looked like it was spinning enough. "I'm quite sure the same tactic would work here."

For good measure, Petra threw in a quick, but verbally ornate, analysis of the parallels between Senator Morrison and King Mai Mai. It boiled down to: they're both evil and need kidnapping.

Trudith didn't say anything, but she didn't have to. Petra could read her body language just fine. Trudith's jaw line had taken on a determined edge, and she was holding her head stiffly forward. Completely unaware that she'd been played, Trudith spent the rest of their walk in silent contemplation.

When they arrived at a familiar bus stop, Petra parted ways, claiming that she had a few things to pick up at her apartment. Mostly, she wanted to separate herself from the impending excitement. Guileless, Trudith nodded absently and continued walking on to the capitol building alone.

She was trying to hatch a plan, but planning had never been Trudith's strong point. When she'd been a thug, she'd just followed her targets—who were usually low-life cats, living on the fringe—until they were alone. Her greater size and strength, combined with the cats' lack of social agency to affect reparations after the fact, did the trick.

Senator Morrison wasn't *that* much smaller than her; he was rarely alone; and, he had a *lot* of social agency to affect reparations after the fact. Probably jail-time style reparations. Trudith didn't think she'd like those, and, worse, they'd probably reflect badly on Alistair.

So, no jail.

This meant she needed a plan. A *sneaky* plan. The kind of plan Petra could come up with and may have already had in mind but had somehow failed to mention.

Trudith had been doing her brain exercises. She would have to put them to the test. As senators began to arrive at the capitol building, Trudith paced the grounds. She stared hard at her paws and tried to force her brain to think, but, all she could think was that her claws were getting awfully long, and she'd need to get them ground down again soon.

She tried staring up at the sky and soon found herself daydreaming about Kipper instead of planning.

Finally, Trudith settled on watching the senators arrive, wearing their expensive-looking suits. They were all dogs, of course, except for Senator Adinew. He was one of those fancy breeds, according to Alistair and Petra. He mostly looked thin and orangey-brown to Trudith. When he arrived, he was wearing a nicely cut, sleek powder-blue suit. It complimented his fur strikingly, but it seemed a little flashy to Trudith. For a senator, anyway.

Arg! Trudith thought. *What was she doing?* She was supposed to be coming up with a plan, and instead she was watching the senators like they were a fashion show. No plan at all.

Yet, her brain still felt like a pulled muscle from all her concentrated *attempts* at planning. With a jowly sigh, Trudith decided to give her brain a rest.

When Senator Morrison arrived, surrounded by his Greyhound guards, Trudith defaulted to her standard operating procedure. She fell in step, following the senator, hoping to spot a moment of opportunity.

Senator Morrison went straight up the wide marble stairs and into the foyer of the capitol building. His three Greyhound guards flanked him right through the lobby and into a senate room antechamber. There was no point in following him there. It would be impossible to kidnap a senator from the middle of the senate hall.

Trudith hung around the lobby, keeping an eye on the door to the antechamber, feeling awkward, and trying to look nonchalant. She felt both confused and relieved when Alistair arrived. She was glad to see him, of course, but she wasn't sure how to reconcile his presence with her plans.

"Has the assembly started yet?" Alistair asked. He had a laptop computer under his arm, and he looked harried. "Is Petra here? Have you seen her?"

Trudith started to answer, but Alistair was already asking new questions.

"Do you know how to hook up one of these things," he waggled the laptop, "to a projector? Do you know what kind of projector they have in there?"

Under the pressure of all those questions and the embarrassment of knowing the answers to so few of them, Trudith could feel the inside of her ears turn bright red. Fortunately, with the way they flopped, no one would be able to see it.

"Quit pestering Trudith," Petra said, walking up from behind. "She has *other* things to do." Petra glanced up at Trudith meaningfully. "And I've already got everything worked out." She took the laptop from Alistair, grabbed him by the arm, and dragged her littermate toward the senate antechamber where she'd apparently been the whole time. Over her shoulder she called, "Trudith, you'll get a good view of the action from the lower level pressroom." She pointed toward a corridor with the laptop.

Trudith followed the gesture and found herself in a balcony-like room. It was like a balcony in that there was a chest-height wall enclosing it, but Trudith was still on the ground floor. Instead of looking down, this room looked up and across the senate hall. Petra was right. It was a good view.

The senate hall was a large, tiered oval room. Most of the senators were at their desks which were arranged in several concentric semi-circles on the lowest tiers. Each desk had a lamp, and most of them had open laptop computers.

Trudith took it all in, but she kept her focus on Senator Morrison. He stood in the doorway to the antechamber, which was under an actual balcony for the general public to watch from. He was arguing with Alistair. Petra had already made it to the center of the semi-circles, where she was attaching various cords to her laptop.

As Trudith watched, the argument between Alistair and Morrison grew more and more heated. Morrison was practically barking at him. Several other senators noticed Petra, and, after a quick consultation, the dachshund and Scottish terrier senators shoved Senator Adinew her way. He looked annoyed. His ears were flat, and his tail swished behind his powder blue suit.

When he got to Petra, Trudith couldn't make out the words, but she could hear that they came out in a hiss.

Then the video started. Everyone went quiet. Petra looked pleased with herself, tail swishing wildly as she beamed up at the image of her sister projected on the wide, empty wall that served as a video screen.

"Senators, citizens, members of the press," the recording of Kipper said.

Trudith didn't see any citizens in the upper balconies, though she noticed there was a Chihuahua sleeping in the corner of the pressroom she was in. He wouldn't be too happy when he woke up, to find out that he'd missed all the exciting news by sleeping through what he clearly expected to be a boring assignment.

Trudith felt bad for him. She would have woken him up, but out of the corner of her eye, she saw her target move. Senator Morrison left the hall.

One breath and Trudith was back outside the pressroom. A handful of heartbeats, and she had the door to the senate antechamber in sight. Senator Morrison couldn't have emerged yet.

With her eyes locked on that doorway, Trudith strained to hear the echoes of Kipper's video-speech in the senate hall.

No use. The sound was too muddled from travelling through walls and by turning around corners. But Trudith knew the gist of the speech anyway—Kipper and a band of heroic otters, at Alistair's behest and relying on the senate's generous support, were on their way to rescue New Persia. If the senators played along, they could claim the credit.

It was the senators' reactions that would be interesting, and Trudith might not be staying long enough to hear those. Every muscle tensed in her strong, black-furred body when she saw Morrison's long, orange muzzle emerge from the antechamber. He looked about furtively, and then he darted out of the building like the quick orange fox jumping over the lazy brown dog.

Trudith was no lazy brown dog, and she kept pace. Outside the capital building, Senator Morrison took a few quick turns until he was in a deserted grassy side yard. Trudith could hardly believe her luck. He couldn't have picked a better spot for her to kidnap him if he'd tried.

"All right," Morrison said, pulling out a cell phone and holding it up to his ear. "I'm alone."

Intrigued, Trudith hesitated. She wondered what she might learn by listening in on Morrison's side of this phone call, but she didn't get to find out. A giant fawn-colored, black-muzzled bull mastiff dressed in street clothes stepped out of the bushes and wrapped his paws around Morrison's bulkily-fluffy orange neck. Morrison's voice strangled to a halt, and the phone fell out of his paw.

"Joey?" Trudith said.

"Trudith!" the bull mastiff exclaimed. "I, uh, wasn't expecting to see you here!" He looked around nervously, Morrison still hanging by the neck from his massive paws.

"It looks like you weren't expecting to see much of anyone here," Trudith said. The two dogs then exchanged a knowing look reserved for those in the thug trade, meant to accompany verbal innuendoes about the unpleasant nature of their work.

Suddenly, the entirety of the situation registered in Joey's mind. He looked at the senator in his paws and startled, as if he hadn't remembered there was anything there, let alone an important senator. Joey dropped Morrison's neck immediately, and, then, in an odd gesture, dusted off Morrison's shoulders and straightened his rumpled jacket.

Morrison, a fluffy little thing compared to the other dogs, stepped back quickly. "You're Alistair Brighton's bodyguard," he said to Trudith, looking back and forth between her and Joey. Trudith was larger than Morrison, but Joey was almost twice his height and bulk, and, unlike Morrison, little of that bulk was fur.

"*And you—*" Morrison addressed Joey, but his words sputtered to a halt. He clearly didn't know how to say *are a big thug who was throttling me.*

So Trudith said it for him: "Are a big thug who was throttling you."

"Er, right," Morrison said.

"This is Joey," Trudith said. "We used to work together, back in the day."

Joey looked uncomfortable.

"You're a hired goon," Morrison said to Joey. In his sharp navy suit with orange fur overflowing the collar, Morrison looked in control again. "Someone hired you to bump me off, then. Who was it?"

"No, jus' kidnap you! I mean... No, I mean, I wasn't working for anyone."

"Oh really," Morrison sneered. "You were just strangling me for fun then?"

"I... slipped?" Joey tried. If he'd been a smaller dog, his awkward discomfiture would have made him seem to shrink away. As it was, Joey looked more like a sofa with nowhere to hide.

Morrison looked down his long nose disapprovingly. "I'll be filing a formal complaint against you with the police, of course. Last name, please?"

Joey gaped. *"Why would I tell you that?"*

"Blevins," Trudith said. When Joey glared at her, she shrugged. She was legitimate now. If Joey wasn't, that was *his* moral quandary to wrestle. Never mind the fact that Trudith had been planning a similar course of action. That was different. It was for Alistair.

Senator Morrison interrupted Trudith's thoughts, saying, "You *might* have told me your last name, because then I would have told the police you were cooperative. After the fact." Morrison glared at the befuddled bull mastiff. *"You can leave now,"* he said pointedly.

Not knowing what else to do, Joey lumbered away. Trudith felt bad for him. In the past, she'd have had his back. Why, they even used to be on the same scramball team! *Come to think of it...* "Hey Joey," she called. "Does the scramball league still meet on Tuesdays? Is there room on the team?"

Joey's serious snub-face brightened. "Oh yeah!" he said. "We could use a player like you! Interested in coming back to the team?" His tongue lolled as he grinned.

"Maybe!"

The goon and reformed former-goon grinned at each other. Senator Morrison rolled his eyes impatiently and huffed his long cheeks. When Joey was around the corner of the capitol building and out of sight, Trudith said, "You know, Joey's not a bad guy. He didn't mean any harm."

"To *you*, perhaps. To my neck, he meant *plenty*."

Trudith looked the angry senator over. He would prosecute Joey to the full extent of the law. That was clear. Fortunately for her buddy Joey, she was the only witness, and she'd interrupted him before any real harm was done. A little roughhousing among dogs was all in good fun, and Morrison would have trouble proving otherwise. It should only count as a minor infraction. A slap on the wrist, legally speaking. Goons had to get used to those; it was a hazard of the job.

Gosh, it was going to be fun to start playing scramball again! If she had time.

The senator was looking at Trudith strangely. "Ye-es?" she said.

"Thank you for saving me," Morrison said stiffly. He hurried on before Trudith could get too comfortable with the 'thank you.' He said, "I'd like you to set up a private meeting between myself and your employer, Mr. Brighton."

Trudith gave Senator Morrison a steady, serious stare. Her jowls were set tightly, but the thoughts in her head were bouncing like super balls between her floppy ears.

Was she hearing what she thought she was hearing? Was it all that easy? Did it count if it was that easy? Petra would discount anything Trudith did on any technicality, but Trudith wasn't doing this to impress Petra. She was trying to help Alistair.

"Senator," she said, "I'm sure that can be arranged." She laid a heavy black paw on the senator's expensively-suited shoulder. "In fact," she said, "if you'll come with me now, I'll take you to the Brighton headquarters."

"Shouldn't we wait for the end of the senate meeting?"

"No," Trudith said, a slight tone of menace, a growly tone, entering her voice. "It would be best if you came with me *now*. *Quietly*." The grip of her paw on his expensive suit tightened ever so slightly.

"Oh, very well," Morrison said with an airy tone. "I hate senate meetings anyway. Lead the way."

Trudith escorted the senator back to Alistair's headquarters. She had no idea whether she'd kidnapped him or merely provided the secretarial convenience of arranging a meeting time for him. She was extremely confused.

CHAPTER 12
JUPITER SYSTEM

Gel encrusted eyes flittered open to the wavery sight and watery feel of oxo-agua. Kipper felt cold and icky. *Are we there yet?* she thought, but she knew better than to try using her lungs. There's not much point in signing if no one's looking at you. Given the state of her own gooey eyes, she'd be surprised if anyone was.

A few more groggy minutes and Kipper felt she could risk sitting up. She was alone in the barracks, but that wasn't surprising. She was the only crewmember who'd never been cryo-gelatinated before.

She felt the fur along her arms and was surprised to find the gelatin entirely gone. Of course, she shouldn't have been. The gel was caused by an EM-field, and the phase shift between liquid and colloid oxo-agua was as instantaneous as the cessation of that field.

She remembered the colloidal oxo-agua hugging her. She shuddered, and hugged herself. Space was a crazy place.

Kipper worked her way through empty corridors of the *Jolly Barracuda* toward the bridge. As she went, the gravity lurched in different directions at varying strengths, making swimming even harder than usual.

Kipper had no post on the bridge, but that's where the action would be and, possibly, answers about the weird gravity. Besides, if the *Jolly Barracuda* received any more broadcasts from the Persians, she would be the best suited to understand any subtle details. Cats are all about subtle details. Otters not so much. And that made her the cultural liaison.

Before she reached the bridge, floating and ricocheting along the ship's hallways, Kipper happened upon the squiggly sight of a tangle of tentacles. She floated gently toward them, and lightly touched the quivering bundle. Emily's skin, normally a mottled grey, flushed flat white. Buried between two sucker-covered arm-bases, one of her yellow eyes opened.

"Emily?" Kipper signed. "Are you okay?"

The tentacular huddle shuddered. Then, a few wispy tentacle tips signed, *"Tired."* The miniaturized quality of the sign—being done with the tentacle version of fingertips instead of entire arms—gave the visual effect of a whisper.

Kipper's heart melted. Moving through a gelatin atmosphere must be *exhausting*. Poor Emily. Kipper reached out her paws and scooped up Emily's tentacly mass. A few tentacles curled around Kipper's arms, hugging onto her. With Emily clinging lightly to her chest, Kipper awkwardly swam her way down the corridor to the galley. The kitchen at the back of the galley was Emily's home and sanctuary.

Kipper laid Emily gently in the back of the room, between a cupboard and a countertop. Her sucker disks immediately latched onto countertop, anchoring her as the gravity shifted unpredictably. Kipper braced herself against the cupboard.

When Emily's tentacles started to stretch out, slowly expanding to fill the space in the room, Kipper felt relieved, though, she still didn't feel right leaving Emily in this state. Whatever was happening on the bridge could wait.

"I'll make some oolong graplets," Kipper signed, partly in hopes of reviving Emily further and partly to distract herself.

Kipper knew where the ingredients were, and got right to work. The graplets were a delicacy Emily had invented—a soft, flavor-infused gelatin coated in a thin skin. They satisfied some of the otters' desire for *drinks*. There wasn't a great deal of *thirst*, per se, in the liquid atmosphere of the *Jolly Barracuda*, but there was still a social, cultural desire for drinks to accompany meals.

Emily had developed a fondness bordering on addiction for oolong tea in this form. Kipper had to wonder if the mildly caffeinated quality of the oolong tea graplets played into Emily's addiction. Did caffeine affect an octopus' metabolism the same way it affected a cat's or an otter's?

Kipper wasn't sure, but Emily did perk up when her tentacles felt the oolong graplets. She passed them from sucker disk to sucker disk along her tentacles, moving inward toward the base of her arms. Emily's mouth was at the intersection of her arms, under her body. In Emily's current pose, Kipper couldn't see her mouth, but she knew Emily had a sharp beak—the only non-squishy part of her body—that she used to puncture each graplet before swallowing it.

When she finished the graplets, Emily waved her tentacles loosely for a moment. Then, she began signing.

"I wasn't ready," she signed, golden eyes staring blankly ahead of her.

"Ready for what?" Kipper signed, though she wasn't sure Emily could even see her in this state of shock.

"I knew what our mission was." Emily signed, halting with her arms in place at the end. The next signs were quick and decisive: *"I should have been ready."*

Kipper was getting seriously worried, and the lurching gravity wasn't helping. She wondered if she'd get straighter answers on the bridge, but she wasn't sure Emily should be alone. Before Kipper could make up her mind, Emily fixed that eerie yellow gaze sharply on her.

"The warships attacked before Captain Cod woke up," Emily

signed, her movements precise and hollow. "I had to dodge them." Her tentacles fumbled, tripping each other. "I think... They're working on repairing the hull."

Kipper felt the oxo-agua in her lungs turn to lead. "Repair?" she signed.

"*It'll be fine,*" Emily reassured herself. She sure as roaring lions wasn't reassuring Kipper. "We knew we were heading into a war zone. *I should have been ready.*"

Watching Emily sign, Kipper had already started backing away, treading water, dog-paddling away from the kitchen, backwards through the galley. She didn't think she'd be any help at all on the bridge, but maybe she could help with repairs.

Kipper left Emily in her shocked reverie, and turned tail to swim as fast as her cat body could carry her. She searched the corridors of the ship, looking for a repair crew, *hoping* she could help, and, all the while, those words—"*war zone*"—echoed in her mind.

Kipper worked her way forward from the aft of the ship. She tried to swim down the middle of the halls, but the gravity kept pulling her up against the floor or the ceiling or the walls. Mostly, she tried to avoid bumping her head. Window by window, Kipper learned not to look at the dizzily spinning stars outside. It was bad enough to feel the ship's movement in the pit of her stomach. Seeing it didn't help.

When she found the repair crew, it was simply two otters— Felix and Destry—hemming and hawing over a terribly disturbing bulge in the wall. The fake wood paneling had buckled and split from floor to ceiling. One of Captain Cod's beloved giant canvas paintings of a sailing ship, coasting along the rings of Saturn with dolphins dancing beside her, hung over the bulge. The acrylic glass protecting it from oxo-agua had broken into a spider web of cracked lines, and the gilt frame had snapped, tearing the canvas halfway down the middle.

"Oh my goodness, what did that?" Kipper signed.

"The enemy ships, of course," Destry signed.

"We need to reinforce it," Felix added. "I'm thinking: the tables from the galley."

"Good idea!" Destry signed. "We could use another pair of arms." He looked over at Kipper meaningfully. Shortly thereafter, she found herself in the galley, helping to unbolt one of the tables from the floor.

When they had the first one freed, Kipper and Felix hoisted it over their shoulders and set off to swim the table through the lurching, narrow hallways of the ship. Felix took the front end and did all the tricky work of navigating corners and angling the table properly. Kipper just provided exactly what had been asked for: another pair of arms.

Destry stationed himself in the galley with the ratchet. By the time, Kipper got back there, all the rest of the tables were unbolted. They floated eerily, swaying in formation together as the gravity shifted. A particularly strong pull caused several of the tables to slam into the ceiling, and Destry narrowly dodged out of the way.

Kipper didn't get really worried though, until she and Destry got the second table transported. They arrived in the hall with the bulge to find Felix drilling a series of holes in the wood-paneled wall. The painting had been removed and carelessly discarded farther down the hall.

"What... What are you doing?" Kipper signed.

"I need to have holes to bolt the tables into the wall with," Felix signed awkwardly, electric drill weighing down one paw.

"Why do you even have a drill on a spaceship?" Kipper signed, thinking furiously about how thick the wood paneling was, how thick the hull was beneath it, and how deep those drill holes went.

Felix looked at her strangely. It was a look Kipper got from the otters on the *Jolly Barracuda* a lot. "Help me hold this table up," he signed, completely failing to answer her question or address her rapidly multiplying concerns. She wanted to tell herself that a seasoned space otter like Felix wouldn't drill holes all the way through the hull into outer space, but she also wanted to tell herself that the captain wouldn't stick them all in stasis and then send the ship barreling uncontrolled toward deep space. One of those had already happened, so she wasn't sure what—other than luck—would stop the other.

Nonetheless, Kipper swallowed her concerns and helped Destry lift the table up to the wall. They held it in place while Felix bolted it, flat side against the buckling wood paneling. They repeated the process twice, which left three tables still floating dangerously about the galley.

"Will this really fix the hull?" Kipper signed as the three of them stood around admiring their work.

Felix and Destry wobbled—the liquid atmosphere version of shuffling their feet. Then Felix signed, "No. But, it buys us time."

"And maneuverability," Destry signed. "The tables will strengthen this patch of hull against all this, you know, stress being put on it." Destry got a distant look in his eyes as he finished those signs, and the gravity lurched sideways as if to punctuate his point.

Felix also looked worried and signed, "I think we'd better get back to the bridge."

Kipper gave a last uncertain look at the three tables, essentially stapled to the wrongly curving wall, before following Felix and Destry on their swim to the bridge. She had no experience with space battles, but neither did any of the rest of the crew from what she could tell. Besides, whether she'd be a helpful addition to the bridge or not, the lure of the knowledge she might find there was irresistible.

Peeking around the end of the corridor, peering into the bridge, Kipper saw a confusion of otters. Because of the echoey, ocean-depth silence, each otter had to face Captain Cod, waiting for eye contact before, in turn, signing any messages to him. The proceedings had a strangely regimented feel. All eyes turned to the center of the bridge and the captain, waited, and then snapped back to their consoles after his signed answers.

Watching the conversation, Kipper was able to gather that three unidentified ships were pursuing them. Captain Cod had the *Jolly Barracuda* doing barrel rolls, zipping around asteroids, and popping out from behind moons like a blackbird from a pie to avoid them. That explained the gravity.

"What did the ships hit us with?" Kipper asked Trugger when he drifted to the back of the bridge to join her.

"What do you mean?" he signed.

"Torpedoes? Missiles?" Kipper had to spell out those words, not knowing the signs for them. "Some kind of laser beams?"

Trugger looked amused briefly, but then his whiskered face went dead serious. "No," he signed, "They punched their ships right into us. Whole ships. Ship to ship. *Blam.*" He punched one fisted paw into the other in what was clearly a descriptive gesture rather than an official sign.

Kipper's eyes widened, black pupils crowding the green irises almost entirely out.

"Apparently," Trugger signed, "it was only a glancing blow. I'm not sure we could withstand a straight on hit. Fortunately, we can outrun them. Their hulls may be tough, but we're faster!"

Felix had been watching their conversation and added, "It won't do us much good though if we can't stop and give that bump they put in our hull a real repair. Those tables won't hold for long."

"Tables?" Trugger signed.

"Isn't there anywhere we can hide for a while?" Kipper asked.

Trugger shook his head. "They've spotted us every time we've tried ducking behind a big asteroid or moon."

Kipper looked at the view screens arrayed across the front of the bridge. The deadly ships following them were visible from several cameras showing rear views. Other screens showed the asteroids all around them. One screen showed a pockmarked moon—larger and rounder than the asteroids. Then there was Jupiter. Giant, covered in creamy ripples. The most giant object Kipper had ever seen with her own eyes.

"What about Jupiter?" she signed, her paws moving as if without her. "Could we hide in Jupiter?"

"Under its surface?" Felix asked, but Trugger was already swimming over to the captain. He tapped Captain Cod's arm lightly, and when Captain Cod turned, Trugger signed to Kipper, "Say that again."

CHAPTER 13
EARTH

Trudith was a big, black, bag of fur-coated turmoil. She expected Alistair and Petra back from the capital building any minute, but that had been true for half an hour's worth of minutes now, and it made her extremely nervous to have Alistair's arch-rival in their headquarters.

Everything Senator Morrison looked at, everywhere he laid a paw—Trudith felt the responsibility of guardianship. Worse, he kept trying to make small talk, but between his stentorian style and Trudith's terse responses, it felt more like an interrogation. As Senator Morrison's kidnapper, Trudith was pretty sure she wasn't supposed to be the one being interrogated.

"So, why are you working for... Mr. Brighton?" Senator Morrison barked in a shrill tone. He meant to ask, *"Why are you working for a cat?"* His words were close enough, though, and Trudith got the idea.

She started to answer but realized her escapades with Kipper weren't actually public knowledge. She wasn't sure how much to say. "Er, actually..." she hedged, maneuvering herself to where she could see out the window. *Why wasn't Alistair back yet?* She'd heard the clamor of Senators signaling the end of Kipper's video before she and Senator Morrison were fully away from the building. *How much more could there be to talk about?* "I guess I'm just comfortable working for cats. I mean, Alistair. *Mr. Brighton*," she fumbled.

Senator Morrison sneered. "Yes, you look comfortable."

Talk about sarcasm. If Trudith didn't know better, she'd have thought Senator Morrison was a cat. Her jowls set in a frown as she looked at this powerful yet strangely petty dog. She wasn't sure what to do with him. She'd like to throw him out on his ear, but that would either amount to insulting an important guest in Alistair's office or letting her prisoner escape.

How *had* a dog like him managed to get elected? Did anyone bother to meet politicians before voting for them?

The door rattled and burst open, portending Petra. Alistair never treated doors that way. Sometimes Petra did—mostly when she was angry. Trudith flinched, expecting wrath, but as Petra stepped through the door, her jaw fell wide. "You..." Petra's eyes flicked frantically back and forth between Trudith and the senator. "I didn't think you could actually do it," she said, her eyes settling on Trudith, wide with awe. "Or that you *would*." She suddenly looked terribly skeptical. "*What have you done?*"

"Excuse me." The senator seemed completely oblivious to— or, at least, uninterested in—the fact that Petra had been speaking at all. "When *will* Mr. Brighton get here?" His bushy canine form dwarfed Petra's feline body. But they had two things in common: they were both bright, flaming orange, and they both had short tempers. "I've *been* waiting."

Morrison glared. Petra bristled. It was enough to make Trudith wonder if the tempers ran with the fur color until Alistair slipped in, shutting the door quietly behind him and breaking the palpable tension before it had a chance to explode in barks and hisses. He was orange too, but he radiated easygoing calmness.

"Mr. Brighton," the senator said in a harsh, commanding voice that brooked no argument. "I have a proposition for you."

Alistair took in the scene, and Petra seethed quietly at the way the senator had dismissed her the moment her brother entered the room. Morrison, however, stood tall (as tall as a Sheltie could) and leveled Alistair a gaze suggesting, whatever this proposition might be, Morrison would not take "no" for an answer.

Now Trudith understood how Morrison got elected. When there was space at the top, Morrison stepped into it. If there was a power vacuum, he was there. Confident. *Controlling.*

Alistair, for all his mellowness, was not a cat to be controlled.

For that matter, few cats were controllable. Most cats, like Petra, dealt with controlling dogs like Senator Morrison by turning them a cold, cold shoulder. Maybe among cats, that worked. Among dogs, it was tantamount to ceding dominance. That's what made Alistair so special. He didn't take Senator Morrison's power play personally; he didn't get persnickety and cut himself out by trying to cut Morrison out. He just said, "All right. Lay it on me."

Morrison gave Alistair an appraising stare. Both politicians stood there, unbending. Neither one suggested they take their seats. Get comfortable. Relax. As it became clear that neither one would, Morrison contrived a cough, breaking eye contact first. He smoothed the ruff of white mane, overflowing his suit jacket. When he glanced back up, Trudith could have sworn Morrison looked impressed. And pleased.

"I will withdraw from the race for the senate," he said.

Petra's breath hitched. Alistair laid a paw, almost automatically, on her arm. It steadied her long enough to let Morrison continue uninterrupted.

"You will win the race," he said.

This time, Alistair's steadying paw was not enough, and Petra spat, "What's the catch? There's got to be a catch."

Morrison glared at Petra briefly, but he didn't deign to acknowledge her verbally when he continued. She wasn't important enough in the hierarchy within the room. "I will be devoting my energies, full time, to running for president. Mr. Brighton, I would like you to run as my vice president."

"President of the country?" Trudith asked.

"*What else?*" Morrison barked, sarcasm dripping from his teeth. Yet, with all the mockery in the world, he still had deigned to answer Trudith, meaning he rated her higher in the hierarchy than Petra; probably merely by right of her being a dog.

"Wait," Alistair said, finally looking ruffled. "I mean, what?"

"That catch doesn't make any sense," Petra said. Stepping closer to Trudith, she whispered for only Trudith's ear: "I can see how you managed to kidnap him. He's completely loony. You didn't rough him up did you? Knock his brain loose a bit maybe?"

Trudith thrilled at the secret confidences from Petra. Before she could whisper anything back, Morrison's commanding bark took the floor again.

"You will carry significantly more weight as my running mate if you're in the California senate."

"Wouldn't *you* carry more weight if *you* were in the senate?" Petra sneered.

Morrison didn't look at her but said, "I've been in the senate for two terms, and it's time for me to move on."

The two orange coated politicians stared at each other. Trudith couldn't help a slight whimper escaping her jowls.

Alistair said bluntly, "I won't be a pet cat. If you think you'll have me in your back pocket because you gave me something I may have rightly earned anyway—'cause that recount is looking *mighty* close—then you are sorely mistaken."

Alistair and Senator Morrison kept staring at each other, but the tension was different now. Alistair had laid claim to his position. He would not budge. Morrison looked angered by it but also grudgingly respectful. "Fair enough," he said. "I will expect you to use the powers of vice president as your own conscience dictates. In return, you will stand by me in this presidential race, lending your support base to my ticket."

Alistair dipped his ears in acknowledgement and acquiescence. "We have a deal," he said, offering his white-socked paw.

Morrison reached a paw forward. The fringe of his long fur fell drapingly from out of his short vest sleeve and along his arm. His paws were white too. Blazing-orange fur coated the rest of them, but the two enemies promised a queasy peace over a dove-white handshake.

Trudith wondered if being allies with Senator Morrison would feel all that different from being enemies with him.

"I'll have my secretary contact you with further information," Morrison said, pulling his paw back and stepping toward the door. "Right now, I have an election to withdraw from."

"And another to join," Alistair said, but the senator had already shut the door behind him. The meeting had been abrupt and unexpected; it left Alistair's head spinning. Trudith was even more befuddled. Her prisoner had simply walked out of the door right in front of her. Should she have stopped him?

Alistair's wide green eyes turned to each of his companions faces, searchingly.

"You know, Alistair," Petra said through clenched fangs. "I'm not sure *I'd* vote for you on that ticket."

"I'll vote for you," Trudith said. "On any ticket." She grinned winningly at Alistair, even though she could feel Petra's eyes burning into her from the side.

"Vice president," Alistair said. "That's a lot of power."

"So's president," Petra said. "Or have you forgotten that Senator Morrison has been weaseling laws through the senate to ban cats from space travel? To require that they carry special ID at all times? Pay *separate* taxes? And *you know* those taxes will be higher than dog taxes. Not lower."

"Even so, I'd get a one-in-three veto and the right to call sessions of the congressional senate. Not to mention the cultural effect of having a cat be vice president. It would energize every feline in this country!" Alistair looked dazzled. He was clearly visualizing kittens in lonely, hopeless, yet overcrowded catteries across the country holding their chins up and their tails straighter as they set themselves higher goals than they would have ever dreamed before seeing Alistair Brighton take the office of vice president.

Petra sighed. She knew that look in her brother's eye. "You're making a deal with the devil," she said, but she accepted his decision. At least, she was choosing to seem that way. Trudith didn't buy it for a second and resolved to watch Petra even closer from now on. Though, she wasn't sure how to manage that. Most of her attempts to clamp down on Petra so far had backfired in entirely unpredictable ways.

"It's a deal I can't turn down, Pet." Alistair's eyes looked genuinely soulful. He was contemplating committing his fate to the paws of a dog who wouldn't shake paws with him if given a choice. "Senator Morrison has the influence and machinery to run a national campaign. We had a few volunteers until the election, but now our office is the *three* of us!" He held his paws out, indicating the rented room with beat-up desks, ramshackle hand-me-down computers, and not much more. "He has an entire fleet of hired Greyhounds. You heard him! He has a secretary. He has money."

"Has it occurred to you," Petra said, "that he can't win without you?"

Alistair cast his eyes down. "He wouldn't offer me the deal if he could. I still can't turn it down."

"All those cats are going to turn out and vote for *you*, and you're going to stick them with an anti-feline bigot like Morrison as president!" Whether she could change Alistair's decision or not, she was angry, and when Petra felt something, she made sure everyone else in the room with her felt it too. Anger and wrath sparked from her as if her very fur was a live wire.

"Let's focus on the good we can do, okay?" Alistair said. Trudith nodded enthusiastically, but Petra stormed out of the office.

In the calm after the storm that was Petra, Trudith asked, "How did the senate meeting go?"

Alistair blinked, changing mental gears. "The California Senate voted sixty-five/thirty-five to officially support the actions of the otters attempting to rescue New Persia colonists."

"Oh," Trudith said. She was feeling much more comfortable with Petra out of sight. Though she was a little afraid that Petra might come storming back in again. You never knew with cats. "That sounds... helpful?"

"Does it?" Alistair asked, his voice rising in genuine surprise.

"Well," Trudith said. "I'm sure that, well..."

"I suppose it does make a statement about otters being our allies," Alistair said, looking pensive.

"It's certainly better than voting to declare war."

"You're right, Trudith. War and peace lie mainly in the public's perception of them, given that the Uplifted States doesn't have anything like a space military—if the senate supports the otters, then peace lasts a day longer. And every day of peace is worth fighting for. You know, Trudith, it's easy to get cynical and tired in this job. Thank you for putting me back on track."

Trudith felt her chest inflate with pride, but then Alistair burst the bubble.

"Of course, there's no sense in getting too dreamy-eyed," he said. "Realistically, Petra's right. I'm making a deal with a devil, and the least I can do to obviate that calamity is learn everything I can about him."

Trudith didn't like where this was heading.

"I'd like you to work on that," Alistair said.

"How do you mean?" Trudith woofed.

"Get to know Senator Morrison."

"Spy on him?"

"Not really spy. Just, *learn* about him."

Trudith thought that sounded an awful lot like spying, though she didn't like to say so. It was more something she'd expect from Petra than Alistair. Sometimes, Trudith almost forgot that her alpha cat was a *cat*. Nonetheless, he was still alpha.

"I'll get right on it," Trudith said.

CHAPTER 14
JUPITER

Flippant comments turned into full-fledged half-baked ideas so quickly on the *Jolly Barracuda*, it made Kipper's head spin. She wanted to scream, "Don't listen to me! I'm not qualified to make recommendations!" But the *Jolly Barracuda* was already flying full tilt toward Jupiter's Great Red Spot.

Next time, Kipper would know better than to let her paws wander around forming signs on their own. She'd keep them tight in her vest pockets, like they were now. Of course, that presupposed there would be a next time, and, watching that Great Red Spot swell, closer and closer, on the central viewscreen, Kipper wasn't at all sure about that.

"We're entering the thermosphere. Angle of descent seventy degrees," Boris the pilot signed towards Captain Cod before turning back to his post.

Kipper felt the steady weight of Jupiter's gravity replace the erratic lurching of the past hour. It pulled her down. She saw a few otters treading their flippered feet to keep floating, but all the others—herself included—began settling to the floor of the bridge.

The fore viewscreens showed only masses of ruddy gas

clouds. The stars were gone. The entire horizon was Jupiter. The entire horizon was one *Spot* on Jupiter.

"Entering the stratosphere. Expect turbulence."

Kipper could barely see the dangerous ships on the rear viewscreen. They'd dwindled to spiny, dark shapes, and they made Kipper think of pine cones.

Shortly, they'd be lost to view as Jupiter enclosed around them.

Boris signed, "Flattening angle to thirty degrees. Troposphere, here we come!" Rolling, roiling clouds of phosphorus and sulfur enveloped them. Boris punched his fist upward in triumph. "Find us in that!" he signed tauntingly for the benefit of enemy ships that could no longer see his ship, let alone him.

Captain Cod set a paw on Boris' shoulder, and the pilot turned to read the captain's paws as he signed, "Bring the ship up to speed for a stable, internal orbit so we can begin repair work. I want a crew out there, patching the hull as soon as possible."

Boris nodded his whiskered face, but when he turned back to his console, his posture grew increasingly tense and frustrated. Furthermore, the turbulence buffeting the ship seemed, at least to Kipper's sea-sick stomach, to be increasing.

"There's too much drag at this level of the atmosphere to set up a stable orbit," Boris signed. "We'll have to keep the thrusters running or our orbit will rapidly decline. Worse though,"—Boris looked really frustrated—"the controls aren't *working*."

"It's the winds," Jenny signed.

"We're caught in a storm?" Captain Cod asked.

"The entire Great Red Spot *is* a storm, Captain," Jenny answered. "It's a hurricane that's been going on for centuries. I thought you knew that."

Captain Cod looked at her blankly. He chewed on his

whiskers a bit. The entire bridge crew waited tensely for their captain's response.

Kipper signed subtly to Trugger, "That's got to be the biggest hurricane in the solar system."

"I wouldn't bet against you there," he signed back.

"All right then," the captain signed, pulling his dignity—what he ever had of it—together after this latest blunder. "If it's been going on for a century, I don't suppose there's any point trying to wait it out."

Jenny shook her head. Captain Cod chewed his whiskers some more. The ship lurched in the storm.

"What's the pressure differential on the hull?" Captain Cod asked.

"There's a difference of about point three atmospheres right now." Jenny signed, reading the numbers from her console. "Since we've only lost 500 liters of oxo-agua in the half hour since our hull sustained damage, we should be good for... ten hours."

While the captain deliberated and chewed on his whiskers, Kipper signed to Trugger and Felix, "We're losing atmosphere?"

Trugger shrugged. "How should I know? You were the one helping the repair team."

They both looked at Felix who signed, sheepishly, "That bulge was on a seam between two plates in the hull. As Jenny said, it's a really slow drip, but, yeah. Oxo-agua's been leaking out of the ship."

Kipper signed, suddenly terribly claustrophobic on this metal monster that was the merest of molecules inside the great expanses of toxic Jupiter, "Those poison gases... they're not... *leaking in?*"

"Oh no," Felix signed. "Not at this level of Jupiter's atmosphere. The oxo-agua's still leaking outward up here."

Kipper failed to feel comforted.

Meanwhile, the captain reached the end of his deliberations

and signed his verdict. "If it's a hurricane," he signed, "there'll be a calm in the center. Eye of the storm and all that. Right?"

Jenny nodded, looking only slightly stricken.

The captain concluded, "Then we'll let the winds push us there!"

"*Brilliant,*" Trugger signed. "Bravo."

"We have no idea how long that will take!" Jenny signed frantically. Boris also looked disgruntled; his webbed paws gripped his console and flexed like he wanted to punch something.

"We were aiming for the center," the captain pointed out.

"*Approximately,*" Jenny signed. "It's thousands of kilometers —*tens* of thousands of kilometers—wide!"

Before the tense atmosphere on the bridge could turn to mutiny, Felix shot forward and upward, against the pull of Jupiter's gravity, into the center of the bridge. Floating above everyone's heads, he pointed an arm toward the aft viewscreen. The sight there caught everyone's breath. Two of the spiny, black, vaguely coniferous spaceships had followed them into Jupiter's atmosphere. They hung in the yellow clouds on the viewscreen like angry hornets on a bed of golden sunflower petals.

"They're still chasing us?" Jenny signed.

"I'll drop us half a kilometer. Maybe the clouds are thicker down there," Boris signed.

The captain was back to chewing his whiskers, watching the viewscreen intently. "Hold steady," he signed with one paw, the other resting on Boris' shoulder. "I don't think they've seen us."

Boris began to object, but the captain grabbed his paws, quieting him. The captain signed, "The turbulence may be worse in the thicker clouds."

"That's true," Jenny signed.

Everyone on the bridge waited. The dark shapes moved closer

on the viewscreen, and Kipper could see various officers cast their captain uncertain glances. Kipper had never seen the crew doubt their captain before. Boris had his paws clamped tightly on the controls, ready to roll the ship out of the alien ships' way at a moment's notice. Even Trugger looked tense. But the alien vessels, black and ominous, passed overhead uneventfully. They hadn't seen the *Jolly Barracuda*, just like Captain Cod said.

"Where are they going?" Jenny signed.

"Are they looking for us?" Kipper asked.

The captain, however, had regained the blind confidence he was accustomed to and made use of it. "Now, as I was saying," he signed, "if we let the ship drift with the storm, we should find ourselves safely at the quiet center in plenty of time to effect repairs to the hull."

Jenny and Kipper shared a look. Neither of them was quite so sure. Boris signed furiously about deteriorating orbits and coefficients of friction, but the captain looked relaxed and ready to let the ship drift. As long as Boris, who had the helm, was busy arguing physics at an uninterested captain, the ship did exactly that. She drifted.

Fortunately, Boris was a tip-top pilot with fantastic aim. When he aimed for the exact center of a cyclone three times larger than the entire planet Earth, by golly his ship hit within mere kilometers of the calm in the center of that storm. Perhaps there had been an element of luck involved. Either way, no one on the *Jolly Barracuda* would ever challenge Boris to a game of darts again.

"The winds stopped," Jenny signed.

Captain Cod swirled a victory pirouette in the middle of the bridge. Everyone else stared past him at the ragged raft of wedged edges darkening the horizon in the view screen.

"What *is* that?" Boris signed.

No one answered. No one knew. The anonymous, hostile

ships flew up to it, slowed down, and *docked* inside a massive hangar that opened for them and then closed behind them.

"Oh my god," Jenny signed. "It's their mothership."

"No," Boris signed. "Look at how it's built. That's not a ship." The massive, alien object was wide, deep, and *thin*—except for a rudder-like tail that jutted out beneath it. "It's designed for coasting through these clouds. It's a *sail station*."

The *Jolly Barracuda* hadn't escaped its assailants. It had followed them home.

CHAPTER 15
EARTH

Two days ago, Trudith was a dog on the up and up. Her alpha was the only honest politician, and she was his right hand dog. Today, she was a dog back to her old tricks; trailing, eavesdropping, spying, and —kind of —kidnapping.

Trudith didn't want to be the old dog who couldn't learn new tricks, so she put her all into doing things differently this time. She didn't break into Senator Morrison's lavish estate; she didn't contrive for him to "lose" his phone; and she certainly didn't corner one of his lackeys in a back alley and offer to rough him up either more or less depending on the quality of his information.

She did the last thing she would have done before she met the Brighton family: she called her target up and explained the whole situation to him outright.

"I don't understand," Senator Morrison said over the phone.

"I'm supposed to spend some time with you. Get to know you."

"*Why?*" the senator asked. "Why do you even have my number?"

"It's listed," Trudith said.

"I should fix that," the Senator grumbled.

"Look," Trudith said, gruffly, "My employer is concerned about the kinds of compromises he might be expected to make in working with you. He's assigned me the task of... getting to know you. So, um, what kind of food do you like? Are you more of a Shamrocks fan or are you a Tusks dog?"

"I don't follow scramball. *This is ridiculous*," he woofed not quite softly enough for Trudith not to hear him. "If it'll get you off my back, I'll tell you what. I'm going to a luncheon this afternoon—part of a social convention. I won't have a lot of time for you at it, but I'm sure you'd be welcome to join everyone." There was something wolfish in the way Senator Morrison said she'd be welcome, but Trudith wrote down the address he gave her and thanked him anyway.

It all made sense when Trudith got there. The luncheon was being held at an upscale restaurant downtown, and every dog in the restaurant was either a waiter or almost indistinguishable from Senator Morrison. Trudith stood out like a tree in a lily pond.

It was a Sheltie convention, a giant meet-and-greet for all the pointy nosed, bushy-maned Shetland Sheepdogs in New LA. Aside from a few tricolor and blue merle dogs, they were almost entirely Senator Morrison lookalikes. Short, orange, intense— miniature collies with an ax to grind, because dogs that short always felt like they had something to make up for. It was kind of creepy.

Trudith had a sense of what Kipper must have felt like in Siamhalla. She was the only mutt here. Even the waiters were meticulously coiffed poodles. Oh, and one Greyhound, looking out of place, towered over the Shelties and stood by Senator Morrison's side. He must have been one of the senator's bodyguards, but, right then, he was functioning as a giant sign post, pointing out where in this homogenous crowd to find the senator. Perfect!

Trudith wended through the crowd, getting piercing, beady-eyed looks from all the Shelties who stood inches shorter than her as she passed them. They weren't dressed differently from any other crowd of dogs in New LA—vests and pants in recent styles, heavy on the pockets. However, the effect of the bushy manes trailing out of their collars and the white fur gloving all their paws made them look like a crowd in fancy tuxedos. Trudith felt underdressed in her uniformly short, black fur.

"Senator!" she said. "Hi!"

Senator Morrison glanced her way, but he was busy talking to a delicate, tri-colored Sheltie woman. He didn't look like he planned on breaking the tête-à-tête any time soon. His Greyhound guard, however, looked relieved to see another misfit in the crowd and lit up as soon as he saw her.

"There's a buffet over there," the guard said to Trudith eagerly. "Sir, if you don't mind, I'll show this friend of yours to the buffet?" Morrison grimaced at the guard who apparently understood the expression to mean approval. Morrison was probably grateful to have Trudith out of his way.

Trudith followed, and the guard, who said his name was Keith, led her to a well-laid table. They each took plates, and Trudith piled hers high with beef tarts and lamb brûlées. If the senator was going to brush her off, she might as well get a good meal out of it, and this meal looked fantastic.

"Wow," Trudith woofed after tasting one of the beef tarts. "Alistair should bring *his* guard along when he goes to things like this!"

Keith gave Trudith a tilted look from his long, gaunt face.

"'Cause I'm his guard," Trudith explained. "And I wouldn't mind going to a few more events like this." She wolfed down another tart or two. "So, what is this event anyway? The coalition for Shelties' special interests?"

Keith barked a laugh. "Hardly! There's nothing political going on here. Unless you count social politics."

Trudith laughed along to be congenial, but she didn't get it. "Social politics?"

"These breed mixers are one big marriage market," Keith said.

Trudith goggled, and Keith backpedaled.

"Not literally," he said. "But, every friend of mine who's let his mother talk him into going to a Greyhound Picnic has come back completely head over heels. They're usually engaged by the end of the month. That's why I haven't gone."

"Happy bachelor, eh?"

"That's right," he said, picking up a few more tartlets for his plate. "Besides, it's a little creepy, isn't it?" He popped a tartlet in his mouth. The morsel of meat and pastry was a single bite for him. "You know, like those cats up on Mars."

"I was thinking the same thing when I walked in here!" Trudith looked around again. Long noses, perky ears, and flowing manes everywhere. "It is creepy," she muttered.

"I guess there's something about meeting another dog who's so much like you. I mean, look at them! They have all these subtle mannerisms in common." Keith pointed to a dog who looked like a black and white photo-copy of the senator. "See that man, there? He's holding his paws in the same way the Senator does."

Trudith saw—he had his wrists high and his elbows low. Just like the senator. Looking around, Trudith realized that more than a few Shelties held themselves the same way, even the tri-colored woman with whom Senator Morrison was clearly flirting.

"I guess that's how breeds continue without the First Race here to arrange it anymore," Trudith said. She tried to shake the heebie-jeebie feeling out through her ears. The jog to her brain caused Trudith to realize something: the connection she'd just made with this guard might be exactly what she needed. Senator Morrison's guard was likely to be a lot more outgoing than the senator himself. By talking to him, she could do her job for Alistair without spending time directly with the senator at all!

"So," she asked, hoping it sounded casual and trying to quickly figure out what kind of information she should pursue. "Is that why the senator's here?" *That's it!* Trudith thought, *Stay on topic, but turn the conversation towards the target.* "He wants to get married?"

Keith shrugged. It was an impressive gesture on his long, narrow body. His expression stayed impassive, indifferent. Apparently, he wasn't that interested in talking about his boss.

"Hey," he said, suddenly brightening. "I heard the boss saying something about you and a buddy of yours discussing a scramball team the other day. Do you need a good thrower?" He pantomimed a high throw, and Trudith had to admit that height like that would be useful on any scramball team. Soon they were deeply embroiled in a debate of scramball tactics.

A few more twists of the conversation, and Trudith realized she wasn't learning anything about the senator. She was enjoying Keith's company, and that was what *he* seemed to have in mind.

"You've been put in charge of keeping me busy," Trudith said. "Haven't you?"

Keith rolled his eyes theatrically and grinned sheepishly. "*Maybe,*" he said. "But I'd be enjoying our conversation anyway. I mean, this is a lot better than most of the jobs Senator Morrison gives me. He's such a micro-manager! Most of the time, he writes little scripts for his guards if he expects us to talk to anyone."

"You're kidding," Trudith woofed.

"Nope. He puts them on flashcards." Keith pulled a pack of flashcards out of his narrow, pinstriped vest pocket. "These were for the senate meeting yesterday. They weren't very useful after your Mr. Brighton played that video though."

Trudith grinned, happily. "The cat in that video is my best friend," Trudith said. "She changed my life."

Keith tilted his head, triangular ears perked high. "There's something you don't hear very often."

"What?"

"A dog and a cat, best friends." Keith looked ponderous for a moment. "Here I am, complaining about how weird it is that all my Greyhound buddies keep marrying other Greyhounds, and there you are. Best friends with a cat. And working for one!"

"Your point?" Trudith said.

Keith looked around at the room filled with Shelties, a uniform monoculture of dogs. "I think," he said, "I've been keeping the wrong company. Want to get out of here?" He grabbed one of Trudith's paws, and his large oval paw pads felt smooth against hers. His brown eyes were serious. "C'mon," he said. "As long as I keep you busy, I'm doing my job. Let's skip this joint."

Trudith looked at Senator Morrison. He had a white paw on the tri-woman's arm, and several other Shelties stood and laughed with them. Trudith was not welcome there, and she knew it. Besides, she wouldn't learn anything that could help Alistair by listening to these Shelties joke and flirt. "Yeah," she said. "Let's go."

Trudith and Keith set their empty plates on a deserted table near the edge of the room and headed for the exit. Trudith wasn't sure what Keith had in mind, but he seemed to have a plan. As she followed him down the steps into the back parking lot, Trudith asked, "Where are we heading?"

Keith looked at her with brown eyes that had grown bright. His whip-like tail wagged. "Anywhere," he said. "I feel like I'm playing hooky."

"But you're not."

"Right."

Trudith thought about that and realized she didn't need to be playing hooky either. Even if hanging out with Keith made it feel that way. "I have an idea," she said, her tail starting to wag too. "Where does Senator Morrison go to church?" she asked. "Do you know?"

"It's the same church I go to, but that's not exactly what I'd pick for a first date," he said.

Even better!, Trudith thought, entirely missing Keith's comment about first dates. If Keith was a First-Racer—and he probably was—he'd feel completely comfortable in his home church, she reasoned. It was the perfect place to have a real heart-to-heart about their employers' intentions, what was right, and the future of the world. "Let's go there."

Keith looked at her quizzically, but he must have seen something in her eyes that he liked. "All right," he said. "I'll take you there."

CHAPTER 16
THE GREAT RED SPOT

The spiny wedge of an alien sail station loomed ahead on the *Jolly Barracuda's* viewscreen. Every otter on the bridge grew deathly still looking at it. Bewhiskered faces with oval noses and serious expressions stared straight at the behemoth in front of them. Then, one by one, they turned to look at their captain.

Shifting uncomfortably under the combined gaze and the weighty Jovian gravity, Captain Cod eventually signed, "It's big, isn't it?"

"Yes," Jenny agreed.

"Our weapons couldn't take it down," he signed.

"No," Boris answered.

Captain Cod rubbed his paws together meaninglessly. Trugger, his most loyal follower, tried to spare him the spotlight by signing, "This means the attackers on the anonymous ships are Jupiter... *ians?*"

Jenny shook her head. "Jovians, but I doubt they evolved here," she signed. "We have Deep Sky Anchor and Kelp Frond station, but it doesn't mean otters evolved in space."

"Right," Trugger signed. "But if they didn't evolve *here*, then where?"

As soon as she saw the look that crossed Captain Cod's face, Kipper's heart started pounding a mile a minute. She knew what he was thinking even before he signed: "We need more information."

Information was a spy's bread and butter. Kipper felt her fur fluff out, but she knew that floating in the oxo-agua the change wouldn't be visibly noticeable. Her fur floated about making her look like a scaredy-fluffball all the time in this atmosphere anyway. She didn't need to feel embarrassed, only terrified.

"Let's nose the *Barracuda* up closer to that behemoth," the captain signed. "Either under or above, wherever you think we'll get the least attention."

"Aye, Captain," Boris signed. He turned to the controls and began adjusting the *Jolly Barracuda's* position with carefully controlled thruster blasts. It looked like he was aiming for the topside of the space station.

"Now, Kipper," Captain Cod signed, turning to her. Just as she had expected. "While Felix and Destry get to work on repairing our hull from the *outside*, I want you to infiltrate that space station."

Kipper floated limply in the oxo-agua. If she'd been in a gaseous atmosphere, she'd have staggered and possibly fallen over. As it was, she simply drifted downward in the heavy gravity.

For a dread moment, Kipper felt her head pounding and her ears echoing in the thick atmosphere. She couldn't imagine putting on a spacesuit and climbing into that dangerous looking sail station to discover god knows what kind of lethal gas giant aliens who she'd have to hide from and possibly face down alone. *Alone.*

A flicker of a hope occurred to her, and Kipper signed before even finishing the thought for herself, "Captain, I don't have a spacesuit."

"That's not true!" Trugger signed. "I bought the smallest suit

I could find at Trailside when you decided to come with us and had it altered to fit you."

"*Thanks*," Kipper signed, trying to glare her sense of betrayal at Trugger since her paws couldn't convey sarcasm as well as her tongue. In spite of the dangerous mission it made possible, Kipper thrilled inside to think there was a special spacesuit for her. "But..." she stalled, thinking hard. "I'll need a team?"

Captain Cod blinked. "Of course," he signed. "Why didn't I think of that? This is a whole infiltration mission!" He looked thoughtful for a moment, chewing his whiskers again. "My goodness, should I have had a spy's assistant training with you all this time?"

"I volunteer!" Trugger signed, unable to wait any longer for the captain to actually ask for volunteers. If they'd been standing on land, he'd have been bouncing up and down to catch the captain's attention. As it was, he was just sort of vibrating mid oxo-agua. It was dizzying.

"Excellent," the captain signed. "Go prepare for your mission. I'll expect you to be ready in twenty minutes."

Trugger saluted heartily, bobbing his head to meet the thick paw at the end of his short arm. Kipper mirrored his salute, half-heartedly. She had a sick feeling in the base of her stomach and wondered if her fondness for the *Jolly Barracuda* and its crew was all an illusion caused by adrenaline addiction. If you spent enough time scared witless, perhaps you started to get a taste for it.

Trugger turned a tight curlicue in the oxo-agua ahead of her. Swishing his broad tail, he launched himself out of the bridge, grabbing Kipper's paw as he flew past. The momentum helped her keep up with him until she settled into swimming in his wake.

At the end of the corridor, Trugger twisted about, stopping to sign, "I think we should do our planning in the galley. There's nothing like a trip on the Ryderian engines to leave you hungry, and I don't think we should infiltrate an alien sail station on empty stomachs."

Paddling hard to keep up with Trugger as he took off down the next corridor, Kipper realized he was right. Her stomach felt cavernous and rumbly. Left to her own devices, she'd have spent the next twenty minutes obsessing over the ordeal to come. She'd have probably set one paw on that alien sail station only to collapse, faint with hunger.

Trugger summersaulted to a halt in the middle of the galley. The tables were still unbolted, but Jupiter's gravity had pulled them back down to the floor. The momentum of Trugger's wake pulled Kipper right into him. Untangling her water-awkward feline limbs, he helped her right herself. Once they were both floating freely, he signed, "What's wrong with Emily?"

The octopus chef was still much paler than usual. White flashes flushed her skin like a fever.

"She was captaining the ship when it was first attacked," Kipper signed. "It really shook her up."

"Right," Trugger signed. He turned tail and swam to Emily. With his furry paws, he stroked the octopus' long tentacles, two at a time. Her golden eyes stared at him, and the white flashes slowed down. Trugger kept his paws on her and stared his brown eyes into her gold ones until she settled out to her usual gray. "That's better," he signed.

"Thank you," Emily signed, twirling a few of her tentacle tips —as slender as sharpened claw tips—around his paws.

"It's okay to be scared," Trugger signed. "As long as you can whip us up some sashimi at the same time!"

Emily waggled her tentacles in her version of laughter and signed, "Already done," with two tentacles while pointing a third tentacle at a covered glass platter of colorful morsels on the counter. "Yellowfin tuna and mackerel," she signed. "I cook when I'm scared."

"A trait I love in every creature, great and small!" Trugger lifted the lid from the platter and tossed several of the morsels into his mouth in quick succession. Kipper joined him, and they finished off the platter in no time.

"Now," Trugger signed after putting the glass lid carefully back. "We need a plan."

"Yes," Kipper signed. "I've been thinking about that."

"And?" Trugger signed.

"I haven't got very far."

"Well, we need disguises, right?" Trugger signed, "We'll be infiltrating their space station. That means disguises."

Kipper blinked, and then her ears rotated about as if she'd misheard something and was looking for a sound that made more sense. Even in the dull quiet of oxo-agua, surrounded by otters who were practically blind when it came to understanding cat facial communication, her ears continued to reflect her every thought. "Are you serious?" she signed. "We have no idea what kind of alien life forms will be on that sail station. How could we possibly disguise ourselves to look like them?!"

"I guess that means we need a whole lot of different disguises. To be sure we're ready."

Kipper wondered if this was Trugger's way of dealing with stress.

Emily watched their conversation. The rectangular pupils in her golden eyes were widely dilated. "There's something you should know," Emily signed. Her flesh was pale again, although not flashing white like before. "You asked if these ships could be octopus space ships."

Kipper nodded, flattening her ears. Had Emily lied to her?

Emily's flesh grew paler by the second. "I know they're not," she signed, "because the octopus empire has had dealings with them before. Hundreds of years before otters and cats were even uplifted. The octopus empire is ancient." The white flashes returned, and Emily's tentacles began quivering so badly she could barely sign.

"Slow down," Trugger signed, "I can't make any of your signs out."

Emily managed to sign the words, "I wish I knew something that could help you. All I know is: *be careful*," before giving up and curling all her tentacles in close to her. In her fear, she became an eerily small, coiled ball of whiteness that hung in the kitchen's atmosphere, falling slowly through the Jovian gravity to the floor. It demonstrated how much of her size was an illusion caused by the motion of her eight long arms.

Trugger's whiskers drooped; his usually cheerful face frowned. "You shouldn't be left alone," he signed to Emily. "Destry has the most training in medicine, so I'm gonna swim back to the bridge and get him." Then, turning to Kipper, he signed, "I'll meet you at the secondary airlock. Your spacesuit is in the supply closet with the others. Get your space suit on, and we'll figure out the rest when I get there."

Kipper swam to the airlock, hoping to draw out the time she had left before this unsettling mission began. The aliens were most certainly hostile. She had every reason to expect the same from them in person as in a ship to ship confrontation. She should be ready for guns. Or blasters. Laser rifles? Sonic pistols? Kipper wasn't sure what kind of weapons to expect from hostile aliens living inside the upper atmosphere of Jupiter.

Once she reached the secondary airlock, Kipper found the supply closet filled with spacesuits. As Trugger suggested, there was one suit that stood out: it was smaller and looked like it had been altered to better fit feline proportions.

Kipper pulled the rubbery fabric of the suit up her legs, curling her tail into the left pant, and fastened the seals along the side of her torso. It was a stretchy material, fortunately, since despite the alterations, she could tell it had been built for an otter. The torso was long, and it bunched up around her middle. The limbs were barely long enough. The bulky space for a wide otter tail in back was simply unnecessary, even though it had clearly been narrowed for her. Whoever had altered the suit for Trugger must have done fast work, but it wasn't bad.

She slipped her arms into the sleeves and left the gloves dangling, attached at the wrists but without her paws in them, to maintain her dexterity a little longer.

Then, as she looked at the helmet and the complex breathing apparatus, not to mention the thruster pack, Kipper had an idea. Maybe Trugger's suggestion of disguises wasn't so far off.

CHAPTER 17
EARTH

As usual, Trudith's plans didn't work out quite the way she expected. Keith took her to his church, and he showed her where the senator usually sat. However, instead of settling into a long discussion of the senator's behavior at church, leading into a heart to heart about the senator's intentions, all Trudith learned about was Keith.

She heard about all the times he got in trouble as a puppy for playing hide and seek in the pews; the way he and his littermates used to each pick a word and whoever picked the word that the pastor said most during Sunday's sermon got to pick which kind of treat they'd stop for on the way home; and how he'd had a crush on an English Springer Spaniel girl who sat in the third pew and wore ribbons in her long, curly flopped ears, but he never got a chance to talk to her because her family moved away before he got up the courage.

"Do you know what I would've done if that Springer Spaniel girl had stayed in New LA for one more year?" Keith asked, leaning his long chin on the back of the pew in front of him. His whole body looked doubled-up and far too long in these pews. They were about the right size for Trudith, but Keith would've looked a lot more comfortable if they were just a little roomier.

"What would you have done?" Trudith asked, obligingly. None of this conversation was getting her anywhere with respect to the job she was doing for Alistair, but it was making Keith happy. She couldn't help her fundamental nature: she was a dog who lived to please.

"Same thing we're going to do right now," Keith said with a grin.

For a moment, Trudith thought he was leaning his muzzle toward her... for a kiss? but she realized he was just trying to straighten out his folded up body and stand up.

"Come on," he said. "Let's get out of this dusty church. It's time for an after church treat."

The treat Keith picked was ice cream, and the two dogs got cones from an old-fashioned feeling ice cream parlor. Keith selected the flavor of the week, bacon ripple, and Trudith went with her old standby, peanut butter. They sat together at one of the parlor tables with their cones. It was a warm day, so they had to eat fast to keep the cones from melting.

"I'm sorry," Trudith told Keith when he asked her if she wanted to follow the ice cream up with a walk in a park. "But this all feels like a distraction."

"It is," Keith said. "My boss assigned me to distract you, since your boss told you to, uh, what is it you're supposed to be doing?"

Trudith considered trying to explain her job in delicate terms, pussy-footing around the truth. Instead, she said, "Spying."

"Right. So, what's the big deal?" Keith said. "We already talked about that. We're having a good time and doing our jobs. What could be better?" His long-faced grin certainly was winsome, but Trudith refused to be distracted from her point.

"No, we're having a good time, and we're doing *your* job. Not mine."

Keith sighed, leaning back in the classy ice cream parlor chair, all metal curlicues and cherry-red vinyl. "All right," he said, "What do you want to know?"

Trudith blinked, her tail beginning to wag. "Really?" she said. "You'll just tell me stuff about your boss? I don't have to find a sneaky way to get it out of you?"

"Sure," Keith said. "He's not my favorite topic, but, if he's really what you want to talk about, why not?"

"Isn't it going against what your boss asked you to do?"

"My boss asked me to keep you out of his fur. As long as we're at an ice cream parlor, out of his sight, I don't think you're bothering him."

Trudith's tail wagged tentatively. She was getting tired of the senator treating her like she wasn't a threat. She supposed if he underestimated Alistair's cleverness in assigning her to learn about him, well, that was all the better for Alistair. "All right," she said, "Let's start with what you know about the senator's plans."

Keith told Trudith everything he knew about Senator Morrison. Either Keith wasn't kept in the loop or Senator Morrison didn't have any secrets because, according to Keith, he was exactly the slimy, bossy dog he seemed to be. He had no hidden agendas. His awful agendas—restrict cats' rights and start a war with the otters—were all out in the open. She wasn't learning anything she didn't already know.

Keith, on the other paw, was learning a lot from talking to Trudith and watching her reactions. He wasn't used to dogs who noticed cats as anything other than an inconvenience, let alone cared about them as people. Talking to Trudith opened his eyes.

"You really care about this stuff, don't you?" he asked.

"Well, yeah," Trudith woofed. "Don't you?"

Keith shrugged. He was such an easy-going guy. It was a trait Trudith liked. Sometimes. Alistair was easy-going. Even when

Alistair was losing the election, nothing really ruffled his fur. Nonetheless, it could also be infuriating.

"I just don't see what the big deal is," Keith said. "I don't care about space travel. One, it's expensive." He held out a claw, ticking off his first point. "Two, there's nothing up there but otters and an amusement park on the moon. So what? Big deal. We have better amusement parks right here in New LA." He held up another claw. "And, three, I dunno. We've got a whole planet down here." He held his arms out in an expansive gesture and grinned. "Are cats really feeling so crowded down here that they need to get into outer space to get away?"

"That's not the point," Trudith woofed.

"Explain the point to me, then," Keith said, and although the words sounded flippant, his expression made it clear he was serious. He truly wanted to understand.

Trudith told Keith everything. She told him how she used to work for Sahalie, until she met Kipper. She told him about the drive down to Ecuador with Kipper, and she told him about coming back up to New LA and springing Alistair from jail. She told him about the dreams Kipper and Alistair had shared with her. She told him about Kipper and Alistair themselves.

While they talked, the ice cream parlor began to close. A disgruntled young cat who scooped the ice cream drew the window shades and turned the "Open" sign hanging in the glass of the front door around. When he started picking up the chairs to put them on tables, Keith jumped up to help.

He might not get it—what it was really like for cats; the difference between a life of subtle privilege and a life of subtle friction, interference, and disappointment. At least he was a sweet and courteous guy. When he saw someone smaller wrestling with a heavy object, he offered to help. It just didn't occur to him how hard it must be to be smaller and need help, every day, every time.

Trudith and Keith left the cat sweeping up. They walked through the twilight streets of New LA, breathing the rapidly cooling desert air. Although Trudith didn't know it, while she had failed to gain any useful information in that ice cream parlor, she had gained a loyal ally.

CHAPTER 18
THE GREAT RED SPOT

When Trugger arrived at the airlock, he found Kipper in a box. It was a lightweight storage cubby, crammed full of spacesuits, with spacesuits draping over its sides. It rested on the floor of the corridor, rocking and rotating lightly in the currents of oxo-agua. When it turned so Trugger could see inside, Kipper was barely noticeable among the other spacesuits. If she turned her head so the faceplate of her helmet looked away from him, there'd have been no way to tell she was anything other than another empty suit.

"What do you think?" she signed, unfolding herself from the box. The gloves of the spacesuit dangled from straps at her wrists, tangling up her signs. "I bolted the suits to a box. It's a disguise!"

Trugger tilted his head to the side and his body followed in a little half circle swim. "You didn't harm the suits?" he signed.

Kipper hated it when the otters signed sideways. It was hard enough keeping up with Swimmer's Sign—a language she'd only known for a few months—without having to read it sideways. "No," she signed. "I put the bolts through the backpacks. We could pull the suits out pretty easily; getting the packs off would take more work." She looked at the drill she'd used to affix the bolts. It was the same drill Felix had used to affix the tables to the hull. She was pretty sure it could be used to take the bolts out if that was called for.

"It's a disguise," she signed again. "Like you suggested." Kipper felt like an idiot. She knew her spacesuit box made no sense, but she was scared and nervous. It had given her paws something to do while waiting for Trugger. While waiting to launch herself into the toxic atmosphere of Jupiter on her way to a terrifying, hostile alien sail station.

"I think it's brilliant," Trugger signed with a grin. "Will I fit inside too?"

Kipper shook her head. She pointed toward the supply closet and signed, "I made another one for you. It's in there."

"Genius!" Trugger signed, followed by a nose dive for the supply closet.

Kipper wasn't sure if Trugger's endorsement of the "disguises" she'd built made her feel better or not. She suspected nothing would really make the pit of terror, panic, and despair in her stomach go away until the residents of New Persia were safely stowed in the *Jolly Barracuda's* cargo bay, huddled together, flying away from those horrible, spiky, pinecone ships. She tried to hold that image in her mind—all those grateful flat-faced Persian kittens rescued by her.

Trugger emerged from the supply closet wearing a spacesuit and shoving his own disguise box. Kipper pulled on her spacesuit gloves and sealed them to the rest of her suit. Then the two of them shoved their disguise boxes into the airlock.

Trugger pushed a button in the airlock wall, and the door slid shut behind them. They were enclosed in a cramped compartment, barely large enough to hold both them and their disguise boxes. A window in the outer door showed the thick red smog of Jupiter outside. Kipper braced herself mentally as Trugger reached for the wall panel again. He pushed another button, but, instead of the outer door sliding open like Kipper expected, there was a kachunking in the floor and ceiling. She looked down and saw a tornado of bubbles thread its way upward, whirling outward and growing wide. The room filled with tiny, glittering silver bubbles. *Air?* she wondered. *No, it couldn't be.* Yet, clearly, it was. Precious, gaseous, breathable air.

Thinking it through, Kipper reasoned that the oxo-agua must be pumped out through the grates in the floor, and as the pressure in the airlock lowered, more and more of it evaporated. As much as she hated oxo-agua, it was the *Jolly Barracuda's* atmosphere, and it would be horribly wasteful to blast an airlock's worth of the stuff out into the upper atmosphere of Jupiter.

The airlock had a separate pump system from the rest of the ship, and *no otter had bothered telling her about it.* Could Kipper have come here and drained away the oxo-agua to give herself a break from breathing this nasty liquid any time during her months on the *Jolly Barracuda?* She wasn't sure, but, when she got back, she intended to find out. Kipper fumed. More than a few whiskery heads were going to roll when she got back from that scary alien space station. *If* she got back from that scary alien space station.

When the last of the oxo-agua—and, presumably the air, though that was harder to see—finished being sucked out through the grates in the floor, Kipper stood in the vacuum-filled room, ready to face the dangers outside. Her fury at her recent discovery made her strong. Cats and anger go well together.

Instead of reaching for another button on the wall panel, Trugger reached down and pulled one of his spacesuit's boots off. Kipper's ears would have twisted in confusion, but the limited space in her suit's helmet constricted them. The helmet's ears were much too small and rounded for her own, but cat ears are flexible. She'd simply mashed them in.

"What are you doing?" she signed clumsily with her gloved

paws. Trugger didn't answer her. He shoved his boot back on, and then he grabbed one of her ankles.

Reflexively, she tried to kick him off, but she felt just as clumsy standing in Jupiter's heavy gravity as she always felt floating in the oxo-agua. She couldn't see him well through her helmet's faceplate, but it seemed like Trugger was trying to work the latch that would undo her boot. She felt the click that meant he'd succeeded, and then he gave the boot a pull. Kipper would've fallen over or found herself hopping on one foot if her disguise box hadn't been right beside her. As it was, she toppled sideways, catching herself by grabbing the box's edge.

She stared at Trugger numbly as she felt the oxo-agua in her suit vaporize around her. It chilled her fur, and she felt a fizzing followed by a cold hollowness in her throat. Her whiskers shivered, but before the vacuum could do her any actual harm, Trugger shoved her boot back on. He flipped the valve to her oxygen pack, and her suit filled with blessed air.

A voice came through the radio in her helmet. It was Trugger saying, "It's a crazy sensation having the oxo-agua boil right out of your lungs, isn't it?"

Kipper coughed lightly. The transition from breathing liquid to breathing gas was much easier this way though kind of terrifying. "Let's just go," she said, her voice hoarse with the after effects of oxo-agua or maybe fear.

"Right." Trugger's voice echoed in the small space inside Kipper's helmet. "We'll want to try to bring these disguises back. I mean, we do have some extra suits onboard. But, well, in terms of general policy, it's good to have spacesuits around when you're on a spaceship. That's why I bought you one."

Kipper nodded and whispered, "Thank you. I like my space suit."

"No problem."

Kipper stared at the airlock's outer door, waiting for it to slide open. Instead, she felt a knocking against one of her gloved hands. She looked down and saw that Trugger was handing her a white plastic pistol.

"Nav-gun," he said. "It's basically a water pistol, actually. You shoot it behind you in space, and conservation of momentum causes you to shoot forward."

Kipper's ears flattened, despite the impediment of the close-fitting helmet. "We're not in space," she said. "We're inside the atmosphere of Jupiter."

"Right," Trugger said. "We'll use the spacesuit jetpacks to get around, but you still might want that nav-gun." Trugger guided Kipper's gloved paw to clip the nav-gun onto her space-suit near the waist. "You never know," he said.

Kipper swallowed painfully, imagining herself shooting a plastic water pistol at a hostile space alien. "*Okay*," she whis-pered. "You don't, you know, have any other weapons?"

Trugger laughed and bumped her shoulder congenially with a gloved hand. "We're not those kinds of pirates," Trugger said. "Don't worry, though. This is purely a reconnaissance mission, right? Get in, get the information, and get out."

Kipper nodded, still terrified and now wondering whether she should have hung on to Felix's drill. Though, it was easier to imagine accidently puncturing her spacesuit with it than successfully fighting off a hostile alien. "Right," she said, mustering a tone of certainty and command. "Let's get to it."

"Yes, ma'am!" Trugger answered. He punched a final button in the wall panel, and the outer airlock door slid. Dense, red smog blasted through the widening crack in the door, throwing otter, cat, and both disguise boxes back against the closed inner door to the airlock. Once the airlock finished re-pressurizing to match Jupiter's atmosphere, the wind in the airlock dropped down, leaving only the roar of red smog blowing by outside as the *Jolly Barracuda* flew along keeping pace above the black sail ship..

Kipper stepped toward the open door and found herself

standing at the edge of a precipitous drop into the heart of a gas giant. She peered into the smoggy red and orange gloom, and she was able to make out the expanse of the black, alien sail ship stretched out about a kilometer beneath them. "We need to fly down there," she said, pointing into the roaring, windy void.

"Do you remember the instructions on how to use the spacesuit's jetpack?" Trugger asked.

They'd given Kipper a crash course on most of the *Jolly Barracuda's* systems and functioning when she joined the crew—spacesuits had been included, despite the fact that none of them would have fit her back then. It had been a thorough tour.

"Yeah, I think so," Kipper said. She turned to look at Trugger; he was shoving his disguise box toward the open door. Once it perched at the edge, he climbed into it and took a safety cord coiled at his spacesuit's waist, pulled out an arm's length, and tied it to one of the spacesuit packs bolted onto the box.

"That's a good idea." Kipper pulled her box to the edge and attached herself to it, just like Trugger. Then, she climbed inside, among the crumpled up, empty spacesuits.

"What's our plan, fearless leader?" Trugger's voice came over the radio in Kipper's helmet.

Kipper set her jaw and said through her teeth, "We fly ourselves straight into the sail ship, ramming it just like they rammed us. When they come to check out what hit them..."

"They'll find boxes of empty spacesuits!" Trugger said.

"Right." Although Kipper's heart felt cold, she powered up her jetpack. In a numb daze, she said, "I'll go first." She whispered herself a count of three, and then the blast of her jetpack rocketed her and her disguise box into the freefall of Jupiter's heavy gravity and ruddy atmosphere.

CHAPTER 19
THE GREAT RED SPOT

The thick red smog whipped past Kipper as she flew haphazardly downward in her strange box-ship powered by the jetpack on her back. She felt the cold through the rubbery fabric of her spacesuit, and dancing wisps of red clouded her field of vision. Kipper's paws gripped tight to the front edge of the box, and her feet braced against the back.

She leaned her shoulders to steer the jetpack strapped to her back, but she wasn't good at it. She kept over-steering, wobbling, and constantly altering her grip on the throttle, jolting and lurching her way toward the sail ship.

Trugger, on the other paw, zipped past Kipper, shouting "Yee-ha!" over the radio.

The bizarre amalgam of spacesuits that constituted his tiny craft all stared at her with their empty faceplates as he disappeared ahead of her. She couldn't make out his face in any of them, but she could imagine him grinning. Crazy otter.

The idea of his manic grin, hiding behind the dark gleam of one of those faceplates, eased the tension Kipper felt in her chest. Her heart kept racing, and her paw squeezed tighter, bearing down on the throttle. As the smog closed behind that crazy otter, the crazy tabby-cat following him, raced to keep up.

A red glow diffused everything around Kipper except for the looming, black sail ship beneath her. It was a much, much larger vessel than the *Jolly Barracuda* or the pinecone ships. It grew larger, filling her field of vision until she squeezed her eyes shut, anticipating the collision. Her paw squeezed even tighter on the throttle as she braced herself for the impending impact.

A second ticked by in the self-imposed darkness of her tiny shut-eyed world. She felt the press of the blasting jetpack behind her, but other than that she felt suddenly, dizzyingly aware of the fact that she was hanging in the sky of a gas giant millions of miles from Earth.

WHAM! The disguise box slammed onto the top of the giant sail ship, and, after a few seconds, Kipper found sense enough to let go of the throttle.

All was eerie quiet. Kipper relaxed the muscles in her arms and legs now that she didn't need to brace herself inside the box. She opened her eyes and looked over the surface of the sail ship. She couldn't tell what it was made from—a dark metal, possibly something more synthetic. The light wasn't especially good, diffused as it was through the swirling red smog.

Kipper shifted her position among the empty spacesuits in the box. The strong gravity made her feel heavy and awkward. Her own body was an uncomfortable weight. For a brief, flicker of a moment, she almost missed the oxo-agua. *Almost.*

Kipper looked up and could see the light from the *Jolly Barracuda's* still-open airlock in the distance. It warmed the red smog to a dull glow, but the power of its illumination tapered off quickly. The bulk of the *Jolly Barracuda* was a mere shadow behind that light. It hung eerily in the Jovian sky, disturbingly small and far away, but, still, a safe, familiar presence.

The sun would never rise here. Every day would be an overcast sunset: glowing red smog turning to deep auburn and rusty black, then, after the pitch black night, without even stars, the daylong cycle would begin again. Sunrise and sunset combined in an everlasting melt of red, gold, and orange hues. Swirling eddies of gas mesmerized Kipper.

"Dum-de-dum-dum," came Trugger's voice over the radio. "We're on Jupiter!"

Trust an otter to make light of a weighty situation, and the situation got even weightier as Kipper watched the *Jolly Barracuda* hanging above them. The red expanse of clouds around the otters' spaceship lit up with bursts of fire, and the ship began rising higher, flying away. "The ship's leaving us!" Kipper cried.

"Oh, yeah, didn't I mention?" Trugger said over the radio. "They're flying to a stable orbit. It'll be easier to repair the hull in zero-gee vacuum than down here in all this crud and gravity."

"That makes sense," Kipper mewed, feeling small and kittenish. Her last anchor to home had just pulled out.

"They'll be back in about three hours. That's how long it takes to orbit this big ol' ball o' sky. Sky as far as the eye can see! Sky all the way down! Ha ha!"

Kipper couldn't tell, but she wondered if the stress of their situation was getting to Trugger. He was acting even giddier than usual. Somehow that made her feel better. If he was terrified out of his senses too, then she wasn't completely alone out here. Kipper peeked above the edge of her disguise-box and looked over the expanse of sail ship. She found Trugger's box to her right. She couldn't see him in it—it looked like a discarded box of junk, but, then, that was the idea.

"It'll be okay," she said, peering through the red wisps of cloud at his box. There was so much buoyant otter personality hidden inside that box and not the least sign of it to the naked eye. She meant to continue, saying reassuring words for the both of them, but she felt a vibration in the sail ship beneath her. It started gentle and grew to a ragged quaking.

Kipper whispered, "I think they're coming. Let's keep radio silence until we're inside, okay?"

Trugger whispered back, "Okay." Kipper had never heard his voice so serious.

Kipper closed her eyes and ducked her head back down. She turned herself so her faceplate faced the side of the box, and she worked at relaxing her body, but it didn't come naturally. Her muscles wanted to tense, ready to spring into action. Instead, she tried to loosen them and let herself sag into the box like any of the other, empty spacesuits.

When she felt the box lift and move, all her fur fluffed out. Her tail grew thick and brush-like inside the pant of the spacesuit where she'd tucked it, but she didn't let herself move. Not a muscle.

Every instinct inside Kipper screamed at her to jump up, bare her claws, spit between her fangs, and run, run, *run* away! Her breathing sounded loud, echoing in her own ears. She worried that Trugger could hear her breathless, puppy-like panting over the radio in his helmet. He'd pick up on her fear and get more scared himself. She'd have a useless, puddle of fear-ridden otter to deal with whenever they got out.

Kipper began to count silently in her head to stave off her panic. Before she got to ten, though, she felt a change in the atmosphere. The fabric of her suit pressed more heavily against her, and she heard clanking from the world outside her helmet. They must be inside the alien sail ship now. Cycling through an airlock, perhaps?

Oh my, Kipper thought, *oh my, oh my, oh my.* The aliens who'd built this vessel and attacked New Persia must be within paw's reach. Were several of them carrying her disguise-box together? Were they large and strong enough that it took only one? Or had they sent an evil alien robot minion to fetch these strange boxes that had crashed into their ship?

The desire to open her eyes and peek over the edge, to catch a glimpse of the mysterious aliens of the pinecone ships—true space aliens!—was immense, but Kipper kept her eyes squeezed shut and counted again to distract herself. Right now, she and Trugger were space debris. If she started moving and showed her face? Then she was a hostile alien who'd infiltrated their sail ship. She would wait. She would wait. She would wait. *Keep counting.*

The box jostled and dropped, knocking the breath out of Kipper's lungs. Kipper felt something poking her spacesuit and the others around her. Were those alien hands she felt on her suited back? Her heart raced. When the sensations stopped, Kipper had counted well into the high hundreds.

Kipper promised herself that if the box didn't move and nothing else poked her, she would try peaking out when she reached a thousand. No, two thousand. To be sure.

Time dragged so slowly; by the time she reached a thousand, she was relieved to be interrupted by Trugger saying over the radio, "Woo-oo-ooo! I am the ghost of empty spacesuits!" Then after a slightly manic sounding fit of giggles, he added in a more serious tone, "Shall we get out of these boxes and check out this alien space ship?"

"I said to keep radio silence," Kipper grumbled, but she opened her eyes and peeked over the edge of the box. The room she saw wasn't what she expected at all. She expected dark metal walls at severe angles and bizarre contraptions that looked like a cross between spaceship consoles and alien torture devices. Instead...

"Ferns?" Trugger said. "And horsetails? What is this? Some kind of flying arboretum inside of Jupiter?" They were surrounded by layers of green, lacy, bladed leaves.

"You are terrible at keeping radio silence," Kipper said. Though she was too perplexed by what she was seeing to properly rebuke him. There were plants everywhere, and they didn't look all that alien. They really did look like ferns, all different kinds and sizes of fern. Some were tall like trees, others were low underbrush. Altogether, they gave the area a tropical, almost prehistoric air. Kipper didn't feel like she was in a space-ship; she felt like she was in a natural history museum. It was an eerie, out of place feeling.

Something about all those cycadophytic plants inside a dimly lit, drably colored room (for the walls, or what she could see of them between the ferns growing right on them, were a dull dun color) reminded Kipper of fieldtrips to the museum as a kitten. "Are those Earth plants?" she began to ask, but she stopped herself before reaching the word *Earth*. Certainly, Trugger wasn't a First-Racer nut like most of the dogs back home, but she didn't want to tread too closely to the ideas that these strangely familiar plants were putting in her head. At least all this under-brush would give her and Trugger some sort of cover when they got moving. She wished their spacesuits were camo-patterned instead of flat gray.

"Do you think we can breathe in here?" Kipper asked.

"Uh," Trugger said, "Let me check the readings inside my suit. Your suit should have them too."

Kipper tilted her head to look at the row of digital readouts under her chin at the seam between her spacesuit's helmet and body. There were a bunch of numbers and abbreviations, but she didn't know what any of them meant.

"Right," Trugger said. "It looks like the oxygen content in this atmosphere is a little higher than we're used to, so it might make us a little giddy, but it's otherwise fine."

The idea of Trugger getting even giddier troubled Kipper, so she said, "Maybe we should leave our helmets on. You know, in case we need to make a quick escape."

"Right ho," Trugger said. "You're in charge of the spy mission, so I'll do what you say."

Unless it involves radio silence, Kipper thought. What she said was, "Come on, we need to learn something that will give us an edge over these aliens, and we've only got three hours to do it." With that, Kipper crawled over the side of her box, toppling the contraption in the process. She climbed into the ferny under-brush, feeling almost stealthy and catlike under its obscuring cover. The clunky spacesuit, however, interfered with the illusion, especially the empty flap flopping about in back for an otter's rudder-like tail.

"Keep low," she said to Trugger, keeping her voice down in case it carried. She didn't know what kind of hearing these aliens had or how far away they might be.

"I see an archway over there, to the left." Trugger pointed to a flat part of the wall, without any ferns growing from it.

"Do you think that's the airlock we came in through?"

"Could be," Trugger said.

Kipper turned herself around to get a complete view of the room. Behind them was a whole stack of other boxes, variously sized crates, and random equipment. Their disguise-boxes were down in front. "This looks like some sort of storage bay. Except for all the plants." Who was Kipper to judge? She hung out with a bunch of otters who filled their spaceships with liquid; filling a spaceship with plants was a lot less weird.

The arch Trugger had pointed out did look like some kind of hatchway, and there were a pair of open corridors to the right. "Trugger, why don't you go check out the archway," Kipper said. "I'm going to prowl around and check out those corridors. Try to keep low down, under these plants, and if any weird aliens come in here, well..." Kipper's voice broke off with a small, scared sound. She didn't have any advice for dealing with unknown aliens. That was why Captain Cod had sent them here —to make the unknown aliens *known*. "I'm... I'm g-going to see if I can get a look at whoever lives on this ship," she said, more for her own benefit, to bolster her courage by committing to the idea, than Trugger's.

The ferny greens came to the middle of Kipper's chest when standing up, so she crouched low and let her helmeted head disappear beneath their cover. She tried to duck under their blade-like leaves to keep them from swaying too much with her passing.

When Kipper reached the open corridors, she chose the one closer to the arch Trugger was examining. The corridor had lower ceilings than the cargo room, and the ferns were thinner on the floor but thicker on the walls. There weren't so many of the tall, tree-like ones that were scattered among the underbrush in the cargo bay. However, there was still enough underbrush that Kipper could crouch down, paws to the floor and crawl forward under its visual protection. Unless, of course, these aliens saw infrared? Kipper shuddered. At least she'd learned one thing about them: based on the height of the ceiling in the corridor, she guessed they were taller than most cats. Possibly the height of a tall Greyhound, or taller. Maybe *the height of humans*.

For a moment, Kipper felt ashamed to be crawling on four paws like a primitive cat. If she was on a human ship, then she should meet that ancient race standing tall and proud. Except, if the aliens on this sail ship were humans, then *humans* were murdering otters and cats on Europa. That couldn't be the humans of the history she knew. Could it? She hadn't read much First Race doctrine, but she didn't think that murdering non-believers was supposed to be the First Race's style. More like rewarding the believers and leaving the rest of the world to rot on Earth.

Kipper heard the radio silence in her helmet change—the subtle change that always happened right before Trugger started speaking. Just then, she saw movement in the ferns ahead of her. Her heart pounded, and her paws froze. She hoped the ferns would shield her. She hoped the radio wouldn't give her away.

"These controls are really weird," Trugger said. His voice sounded painfully loud in Kipper's helmet, but she couldn't do a thing about it. She couldn't remember how to work the controls.

"They look like, well, like they were designed to be used by tentacles," Trugger said. "Like the little entertainment station Emily keeps in the corner of the kitchen, you know?"

Kipper wished he would stop talking. The movement in the ferns was getting closer. Despite wanting to stay frozen like a statue, a subconscious instinct caused Kipper to shrink away from the center of the hall, closer to the dirt floor and closer to the wall of the corridor.

"You don't think this could be an octopus ship?" Trugger asked.

Kipper lay flat on the dirt floor now, holding her breath and terrified. She couldn't have answered Trugger's question if she wanted to, because her throat constricted with fear.

A heavy, taloned footfall in front of her answered Trugger's question: not octopi.

Sharp claws. Large claws. One larger than the others.

"Kipper?" Trugger asked. His voice stopped. Maybe he'd remembered her earlier order for radio silence. Kipper hoped it wasn't too late.

The clawed foot passed in front of Kipper—passed her by—and Kipper felt the tightness in her throat release, just in time to realize that while the taloned alien didn't seem to have heard Trugger, it might see him if he wasn't under cover when it got to the cargo room. "Trugger, *get down!*" she rasped into the radio. "Get down *now!*" She had no way to know if he'd obeyed, but, great and holy First Race, she sure hoped he had.

Kipper had seen statues, paintings, and alleged, ancient photographs of humans, and that was not a human. That was not a primate's foot. That was a creature with murder in its heart and vicious, curved talons that made her own claws feel like kittens' toys.

Curiosity got the better of Kipper and, as the ferns in her corridor settled back to stillness, she dared against her fear to creep toward the cargo bay, following the alien. She moved slowly and cautiously, keeping close to the wall, but she could hardly account for how her need to see that alien pulled her onward. It would be much safer to stay still.

At the entrance to the cargo bay, Kipper's sense of the reality of her situation slipped away. It was too surreal. With a cat's insane curiosity outweighing fear, she raised herself slowly upward and poked her helmeted head, ever so slowly, above the cover of the ferns.

The alien's long, narrow head tilted to the side, and its tail, wide at the base and slender at the tip, swayed menacingly. It examined their disguise-boxes. The alien was easily three times her height. It wore simple, brief clothing over its shoulders, chest, and down to its thighs. Where the rough, green cloth of its uniform didn't cover it, the alien's body—arms, legs, tail, and head—was covered in gleaming black feathers. At its elbows, the tip of its tail, and the crest of its head, the feathers exploded in plumes of brilliant fresh-blood red.

"Oh my god," Kipper whispered, falling silently to her knees, safely beneath the ferns. As safe, at least, as she could be as long as she stayed on this most dangerous vessel. "This is heresy!" The image of the alien was burned into her eyes.

Kipper had never thought herself a believer of First Race doctrine until the moment she saw it disproved: humans were not the first species off of Earth. They'd been preceded. "This is wrong," Kipper whispered. "This is so wrong." She continued mumbling unintelligibly about dogmatic dogs and their damned First Race doctrine until Trugger's voice in a hoarse, frightened whisper broke through the radio of her helmet.

"I don't understand, Kipper," he said. "Can you see the alien?"

"Yeah," she said, pulling herself out of her reverie. She looked around at the Earthly ferns surrounding her and said, "It's a dinosaur."

It was an impossible, unbelievable, heretical demon from the murky, apocryphal times that came before the distant, barely remembered beginnings of human pre-history. Yet there it was, proving billions of deeply faithful First-Racer dogs wrong. Dinosaurs existed, and they had spaceships.

"Humans *were not* the *first race* off our native rock," Kipper whispered to herself in awe.

"A dinosaur?" Trugger said, sounding suddenly interested. "You mean those giant reptile-bird-skeleton thingies from ancient human religions?"

"Yeah," Kipper said. "I'm looking right at one." Even though she'd crouched down, low to the dirt ground again, she could still make out the shape of the dinosaur, obscured by fern leaves, ahead of her. "It has red feathers."

"Neat!" Trugger exclaimed and, with a sudden rustling in the ferns ahead, his helmeted head popped up. Kipper could see the light gleam off of his faceplate, and she could just make out his wide-eyed look of wonder that turned to horror when the dinosaur's head tilted toward him. "I think it's some kind of raptor," Trugger said, his voice gone wobbly. "And, uh, well, I think it sees me."

Kipper had no weapons at her disposal save the nav-gun clipped at her waist and the jetpack strapped to her back. Kipper decided to bet on the jetpack instead of the equivalent of a squirt gun. She gripped the jetpack throttle and launched herself bodily straight for the feathered raptor.

Before she could even think through what she was doing, Kipper had slammed against the surprised alien, knocking the two of them over. With the element of surprise on their side, Trugger thought quickly. Both Kipper and the alien were still recovering from their rocket-powered collision, but Trugger was already busy binding the raptor's talons with safety cords from the Trojan spacesuits and shoving it bodily into the disguise-box. By the time he was done, the angry bird-like alien was trussed like a turkey ready for baking. Which, as a coincidence, was exactly the metaphor Trugger used as he crowed about his success to Kipper.

"Shall I interrogate our turkey?" Trugger asked of the dizzied tabby. She was having trouble keeping up.

"Um, you don't know *dinosaur* language? Do you?" Kipper asked, getting to her feet and looking at the quick work Trugger had made of the much larger alien. Its powerful hind legs, smaller arms, and tail didn't entirely fit inside the box, but the spacesuit tethers tied tightly around them, digging into the dark plumage.

Kipper found it hard to believe that Trugger had simply tied up those sharp talons at the end of such strong, curved legs without shying away. On the other paw, *she'd* rushed the raptor while it was still standing, clearly a moment of complete insanity.

"I don't know its language," Trugger said. "That's true. But, I'm sure I can learn something from it."

Kipper wasn't as sure, and she was concerned about leaving Trugger alone with the raptor, no matter how securely it seemed to be tied up. "What if it calls for help?" Kipper asked.

Trugger took a step, carefully, toward the raptor and reached gingerly with a space-suited arm towards an electronic gadget clipped to the alien's clothing. He gave the device a tug and then stumbled quickly away with the gadget in his paws.

The raptor let out a warbling screech, but Kipper surprised herself by pouncing close enough to pull a free spacesuit tether out of the box, loop it around the raptor's feathery yet lizard-like snout and pull it tight. The screech ended, but the raptor glared at Kipper with eerily round, orange eyes. Its pupils narrowed to pinpricks of black in an expression that made Kipper shudder.

"There, see?" Trugger said, holding out the electronic gadget he'd freed from the raptor's clothing. "This looks like a communication device. Without this or, well, the use of its mouth, I don't think it can call for help."

"Or answer questions," Kipper added shakily. She still held the end of the tether taught against the raptor's snout.

Trugger came over and helped her tie it in a secure knot. "I think I can figure something out. Besides, we're looking for clues about how to beat these aliens. I can't think of a better place to start than with one of the aliens itself."

"Maybe," Kipper said. She still felt they should explore more of the sail ship. They did need to beat these aliens, but that mostly involved beating their ships. Splitting up seemed dangerous, but they were working with a limited amount of time. "All right," she said to Trugger. "Use the external speakers on your helmet though, so you don't have to take it off. And keep your radio open so I can hear you."

"Will do," Trugger said. His next words echoed strangely between Kipper's helmet speakers and the external speakers on Trugger's suit broadcasting outside. "Now! As for you..." He spoke to the raptor and brandished the confiscated electronic gadget. Kipper didn't listen to the rest of his words. She could hear him, but her mind was focused on the task at paw. Trugger's voice became a dull blur in the background as she crouched back down, sinking below the level of the ferns. She put her front paws to the floor and began moving, stealthily towards the open corridor.

She stayed low and close to the wall, weaving among the plants so as not to disturb their stalks lest the motion in their leaves give away her presence. Trugger's voice anchored her comfortingly to the reality of the *Jolly Barracuda* and the friends coming back for her. Everything else around her made her blood pulse with fear and uncertainty.

As she neared the end of the corridor, Kipper could see that it opened into a much larger room beyond. At first, she thought the floor fell away because she couldn't see any more ferns ahead of her, though they clearly continued to cover the walls. When she reached the seeming-ledge at the end of the corridor, however, she found the reality much stranger.

The ferns stopped, because the floor turned to glass or some other clear, hard substance. The floor looked smooth and empty —a window looking down on the swirling red gases of Jupiter below. It didn't feel smooth or slippery like she expected when she tested it with a paw. The surface gave a bit under her suited paw like the feel of a tumbling mat. It made her feel like she was perched on the surface of a bubble, ready to pop.

Kipper looked up and found the ceiling, approximately as high as the ceiling in a First Race ruin, matched the floor: another clear window, this one showing the ruddy Jovian atmosphere above.

Although Kipper tested the clear floor with her paws, she didn't want to step into the open. She didn't see any raptors in this large room, but there were archways leading to other corridors all around. A raptor could appear from any one of them at a moment's notice.

Kipper kept close to the wall, letting the ferns that grew out of it continue to cover her, and followed the edge of the giant room.

CHAPTER 20
THE GREAT RED SPOT

As Kipper made her way around the edges of the cavernous room, the clear floors and ceiling began to make more sense to her. Raptors came and went through various archways, flocking over the bubble-like floor with a spring in their strong legs and a swing to their feathered arms. Based on their build, Kipper would have been surprised if they could actually fly; their wings didn't seem large or broad enough relative to their overall mass, but, in this setting, they looked like dark birds, winging through the Jovian sky.

The raptors didn't seem to notice the spacesuited tabby cat, hiding in their ferns along the outer wall, and, according to the prattle from Trugger that Kipper heard through her helmet, they hadn't missed their captured crewman yet.

Kipper didn't dare open any closed doors she encountered, instead limiting her explorations to open archways. Most of the corridors and open rooms she could get to through the open archways were much the same—lined in ferns, occasionally featuring outgrowths of larger, tree-like plants from the floor, or filled with objects that looked like a cross between furniture and abstract art installations. Kipper assumed it was furniture.

After half a dozen such rooms, Kipper grew frustrated with

her discoveries. She felt increasingly nervous about the distance between her and Trugger, not to mention the sheer number of raptors between them. Yet, she needed to learn something that could help Captain Cod defend New Persia. She resolved to try at least one more room.

Kipper almost skipped right past the open arch, ducking from the ferns on the one side on to the next. The room on the other side of the arch wasn't safely blanketed in greenery; however, it was the first open room she'd encountered that didn't emanate with either the rosy glow of Jupiter's sky or the harsh yellow lights that filled the rooms without transparent floors and ceilings. The difference intrigued Kipper, and she decided to take a risk.

Kipper waited until the nearest corridors cleared of raptors as far as she could see through her leafy screen of fern shielding. Then she ducked into the dark, bare room.

The floor and ceiling were opaque and gray. The red glow of Jupiter leaked in through the open archway, but it was only a dim illumination. Kipper's cat eyes were good at seeing in the dark, and they adjusted.

In the center of the room stood a dais, a risen surface that came to her chin height and spanned most of the length of the room. Kipper approached the dais, intrigued by the way it filled the room. Was it a stage? Why would there be a stage in such a small room?

When Kipper reached the edge of the dais, she tipped herself up on her toes and peered over the top, trying to decide if she should climb on top of it. However, the top wasn't flat. She was surprised to find the inside of the dais hollow and filled with liquid. Perhaps it was less of a dais and more of a restraining wall around a pool or aquarium? As her eyes continued to adjust, Kipper realized she could see pale figures moving inside. They were hard to make out, but their white shadows reminded Kipper of Emily.

Then a tentacle splashed over the edge and reached toward her.

Kipper leapt back, heart racing. Caution told her to run, leave the room and get back to Trugger. Curiosity told her to stay. She followed her curiosity. Kipper edged around the dais that she now recognized for an aquarium, looking for a window in or a control panel to examine. She crouched low as she moved, hoping to avoid the reach of any more grasping tentacles.

When she reached the back side of the aquarium, Kipper heard footsteps enter the room. The walls of the aquarium protected her from immediate discovery, but she was trapped inside the room. Once again balancing caution against curiosity, Kipper flattened herself, completely, against the floor and, slowly as she could, she poked the top of her head around the edge of the aquarium. Her ears were flat against her head in terror at her own ridiculous audacity. However, she was rewarded with a surprising sight.

Several raptors stood in the room, dressed in uniforms made of the same rough green cloth as she'd seen on all the others, but these uniforms were subtly more ornate. Better tailored, perhaps. Certainly, sporting more decoration. Two of the raptors had orange plumes of feathers at their elbows, tail-tips, and on the crests of their heads in addition to the black feathers that blanketed the rest of their bodies. A third raptor sported bursts of yellow plumage.

The raptor that stood in the center, however, had plumes of brilliant royal purple feathers where the others had orange and yellow. The way the others stood beside and behind the purple-plumed raptor, their heads tilted toward him, indicated that he was their leader.

Kipper had grown nearly used to the idea of dinosaurs hiding out in the skies of Jupiter. Creeping around their ship, dodging them, how could she not grow used to the reality of them?

Everything she'd known before leaving the *Jolly Barracuda* behind to come to this sail ship had been wrong: humans were not the first species to leave Earth; the solar system was not a safe place —owned, run, and operated by jolly otters.

Dark demons from the pre-history of her world lurked under the surfaces, ready to attack, and those demons were stranger than she imagined. At first, Kipper could hardly believe what her eyes saw. The purple-plumed raptor breached her understanding of the entire situation in one mind-bending, world-altering way: out from his black-feathered shoulders eight pale tentacles rose, stretching away from his body like a hideous set of extra, twisting, writhing arms.

The purple-plumed raptor with his pale tentacle arms was a strange hybrid creature, the sort that was supposed to stay relegated to nightmares on only the darkest, loneliest, rain-pounded nights.

The purple-plumed raptor creature gestured to the other raptors, directing their motions with both his feathered, taloned arms and squirming tentacles. His ten fore-limbs worked in clear concert, all a piece of the same unutterable being.

Kipper's eyes dilated, and she wanted to pull back behind the tank. Yet, she watched, frozen in horror, as the other three raptors—first the yellow-plumed one and then the two orange— reached into the tank and pulled out struggling tentacle clusters of their own.

Only, they weren't mere tentacles. As the struggling, writhing balls of flesh were pulled from the aquarium, Kipper saw their mantle-bodies and yellow eyes, eerily similar to Emily's. The octopi lashed their pale tentacles, reaching for the aquarium, fighting and scrabbling to return to the liquid. With taloned hands, each raptor pulled a single octopus out, gripping it firmly at the base of its mantle, where all eight arms met in a small, beaked mouth.

Each raptor lifted an octopus over its feathered head and

lowered the struggling cephalopod into an electronic-looking harness at its shoulders. As each octopus came to rest in its harness, its tentacles suddenly, startlingly relaxed. The eight limbs stopped struggling and became raptor limbs, moving in concert with feathered arms—just as the tentacles on the purple-plumed raptor had moved.

Night-black feathers and dagger sharp talons contrasted hideously with soft, pale, waving tentacles that grew from the raptors' shoulders. They were horror incarnate.

The yellow eyes of one of the octopi fixed on Kipper. Its mantle-body was a limp lump of flesh, fixed to the raptor it rode. Wires from the electronic harness disappeared into the base of the raptor's skull, probably connecting its brain to the brain of the octopus. Would the raptor turn its head toward Kipper, following the piercing gaze of those yellow eyes? *Had she been discovered?*

The tentacles continued to move as they had before, none of them reached to point at her. That watchful yellow eye continued to stare at Kipper, but the raptor carrying it turned with the others, and all the raptors left the room.

Kipper closed her eyes and tried to breathe a sigh of relief, but her panting breath would not slow down. The sight of that yellow eye was burned into her mind. The octopus had seen her. She knew it. Yet, the raptor had not.

When her breathing finally slowed, Kipper opened her eyes and raised herself to look in the aquarium again. Pale tentacled figures moved inside. The raptors hadn't taken them all. Were they normal octopi like Emily? Did Emily know about them? Was this why she'd been scared?

Without thinking it through, Kipper pulled off the gloves of her spacesuit and left them dangling from the straps that attached to her wrists. Her paws formed the Standard Swimmer's Sign for the question, "Who are you?" She held her paws high enough to be seen from inside the aquarium and, despite shaking, signed the question again.

The movement inside the aquarium changed. Yellow eyes stared through the wavey surface at her.

"Who are you?" she signed, again and again.

Then, she added, "Help me." Suddenly, her feelings rushed out through the language of her paws, "I'm terrified," she signed. "I don't know what's going on, and I need to find a way to stop these dinosaurs from hurting my friends. They're hurting cats and *kittens*. I need to stop them, and I don't know how." Her paws took on a life of their own, speaking all her fear and uncertainty. She didn't expect an answer, but she couldn't stop her paws from rushing on, signing about Emily and New Persia and the leak in the hull of the *Jolly Barracuda*.

The pale figures moved beneath the surface of the aquarium. More and more yellow eyes watched her, and they began rising toward the surface. Finally, a bumpy pair of eyes emerged and stared levelly at her paws.

Kipper's paws slowed to a halt, mid-sentence. The octopus watching her raised a pair of tentacles and reached out. Kipper held still as the tentacles explored the fur of her paws. She was used to the soft feel of Emily's tentacles under oxo-agua, but, now that she was dry, most of what she felt from the octopus' touch was wetness.

The pair of tentacles pulled back. The octopus' eyes continued to float barely above the surface, watching Kipper, but more of the octopus' tentacles rose up, breaking the surface. Slowly, the octopus formed signs of its own.

At first, Kipper was too surprised to translate the word shapes she saw in its tentacles. They weren't Standard Swimmer's Signs, however, some of the figures were familiar. She couldn't make all of it out, but she thought... she thought she could make out some. Perhaps it was a related language.

The octopus signed the word *slavery*, or maybe Kipper only

thought it did, because she was looking for that word, expecting it. She thought the octopus signed the word *help*, too. Was it asking for help, offering to help her, or refusing to help her? She couldn't tell, but she was pretty sure the sign for *help*—or, at least, a sign similar to it—was in there. Many times.

Kipper repeated the sign, *"Help. Yes."* She didn't know if she was asking or offering or simply trying to connect on the word that was most recognizable.

"Trugger," she said, into her helmet. "I found the tentacles that must be meant to work those controls you found."

The speakers in Kipper's helmet stayed silent. Trugger didn't answer. How long had he been quiet for? She hadn't been paying attention to him. "Trugger?" she said. *"Trugger?"* Worry for her friend overpowered the pressing, strangeness and urgency of her communication with the octopus. "Trugger, are you okay?"

Finally, the speakers in Kipper's helmet crackled to life. "I think we need to leave soon," Trugger's voice said, low and scared. "Very, very soon."

"What happened?" Kipper asked, stepping away from the aquarium. The octopus she'd been signing with reached two of its tentacles out and wrapped them, tightly, around her wrists. Two more of its tentacles grabbed the gloves dangling from her spacesuit.

"The electronic gadget," Trugger said, "it's broadcasting raptor voices. I think they've started looking for our captive. How quickly can you get back here?"

"I don't know," Kipper said. Her paws signed, as best they could trapped in the vise-like grip of those freakishly strong tentacles, *"I need to leave. My friend needs help."* She took a step away, pulling her arms against the tentacles, but the grip didn't give. Instead, the octopus let itself be pulled forward by her, onto the edge of the aquarium. Kipper startled at the sight of the octopus emerging from the water, skin all wrinkled and horny.

During her moment of discomfiture, the octopus leapt with its other tentacles and wrapped itself around her spacesuited body. It squeezed against her, climbing up her shoulders. It settled behind her helmet, placing itself much as the other octopi had been placed on the shoulders of the raptors.

There was no electronic connection between Kipper and the fleshy sea-creature riding on her back. The tentacles that filled her peripheral vision, clinging to the side of her helmet's faceplate and waving in the air, were not hers. She could not control them. Neither did they restrain her anymore.

Kipper couldn't stay here while Trugger needed help. In spite of the octopus on her back, Kipper raced for the archway she'd entered through. The tentacles slowed her down, grasping with powerful sucker-discs at the nearest wall and sticking solidly to it. "Let go!" Kipper signed, holding her paws above her head. She couldn't tell if the octopus behind her bothered to read her paws; she didn't know if it would even understand her signs. It ought to understand her thrashing movements and pulling, though.

Suddenly, the pull against Kipper's body let up, and she crashed to the floor. As she pulled herself onto her knees, she saw something in her peripheral vision—an object gripped in one of the tentacles that rose out of her shoulders. She turned around to see it better, but the tentacles turned with her. She couldn't directly see what the octopus held.

Kipper saw an open cabinet in the wall that she hadn't noticed before. Inside it were metallic objects, shaped to be held by a paw or talon. Shaped like guns. The octopus had armed itself.

Kipper's heart lurched to think that a hostile cephalopod was perched on her back, pointing who-knew-how-many guns at her head. She thought about grabbing one of those weapons for herself and shooting it blindly over her head, down her back, trying to knock the octopus off.

But she wouldn't know how to work it. She'd be as likely to shoot herself or be disarmed before figuring the gun out as to succeed. She could use her nav-gun, but squirting an octopus with a water pistol seemed more ludicrous than helpful.

Kipper remembered the calm way those yellow eyes had looked at her, tentacles signing smoothly in a foreign sign language, trying to communicate with her.

Kipper found a glimmer of hope inside herself that the octopus on her back was her ally instead of her enemy, despite the guns it held. She clung to that hope. The octopus was a slave of these raptors, hoping for escape, as much as she was. She had to believe that. The octopus held her firmly—it could restrain or, likely, kill her if it wanted to. She had to trust it.

Kipper pulled her spacesuit gloves back on and sealed them in place. She rose to her feet, struggling to keep her balance with the new weight on her shoulders and crawled her way toward the open archway. This time, the octopus let her leave through the archway. It didn't interfere as she crept through the ferns of the corridors, making her way carefully, steadily back through the sail ship towards the cargo room housing Trugger.

As Kipper retraced her steps, the cephalopod on her back settled into being nothing more than a slight extra weight and a niggling uncertainty in the corner of her mind. By the time she made it back to the first large chamber she'd encountered in her explorations, Kipper thought she was home free. There was only this last chamber to edge her way around. Then, a short corridor. That was all that was left between her and Trugger.

A screeching, rising sound—instantly recognizable as an alarm—began wailing.

"I thought that was about to happen," Trugger said over the radio in her helmet. "The voices over that gadget have sounded increasingly frantic. On the upside, I know exactly what these raptor voices sound like when they hit their breaking point."

"This means they're actively looking for us now."

"Possibly," Trugger hedged. "If I were them, I'd send someone to check out the airlock where they lost contact with the raptor we captured."

The cyclical rising and falling tones of the alarm made Kipper's fur fluff out all over. The pressure of her spacesuit against her fluffed fur felt itchy and uncomfortable. Her heart pounded. She didn't think she could stand creeping, an inch at a time, around the wide perimeter of the giant chamber ahead of her. If she wanted to get to Trugger before more raptors got to him, she didn't have time. The alarm drilled that knowledge into her.

Kipper made a choice: she broke from the cover of the ferns and ran for it, straight through the middle of the chamber. Speed over safety. Maybe it wasn't the best choice, but Kipper was terrified out of her mind.

"Trugger?" Kipper hissed through her teeth as her paws pounded, four-legged, full-speed, against the strangely cushy, transparent floor. "Can you get that airlock open? We need a way out of here!" Kipper thought she heard raptor voices shouting at her, but she ignored them.

"I dunno, Kipster," Trugger said doubtfully.

Kipper tried not to think that she and Trugger might be trapped on this ship with these hostile raptors. *Try to figure it out,* she hissed then lapsed into labored panting as she continued to run.

Kipper crossed onto the ferny floor of the final corridor. She could hear the raptor voices close behind. More frightening even, she could hear punctuated blasting sounds. She felt wobbles of pressure whenever she heard them. Were the raptors shooting at her? If so, they weren't missing by much.

Kipper couldn't risk looking back, but her question was

answered when she came to the end of the corridor and Trugger stared at her wide-eyed. He exclaimed, "What in the name of the holy nightingale is *that*?! You grew tentacles and found guns?"

"Uh," Kipper said. "Apparently?"

"I could use some tentacles and guns." Trugger looked at his raptor captive, clearly wondering why it didn't have tentacles for him to appropriate.

Kipper risked whirling around to see behind her. As Kipper turned, the octopus on her back twisted around too, bringing its tentacles into her peripheral vision. As Trugger described, the octopus kept firing the guns it'd grabbed, keeping the raptors—also tentacled and wielding firearms—at bay. Nearly half a dozen of the raptor-octopus hybrids advanced through the corridor

"First Race!" she swore, but her paws were already saying something different. Held out and up so the octopus on her back could read them, Kipper's paws signed, "Can you work the airlock? We need to get out of here!" She didn't know if the octopus could understand her signs, let alone her clumsily suited paws. She backed up the Swimmer's Signs with frantic pointing at the airlock.

Two of the octopus' tentacles waved in her periphery, unencumbered with weaponry, and signed something Kipper didn't understand.

Kipper ran to the airlock and pounded on it with her paws. She pointed to the cryptic control panel.

The tentacles kept signing cryptically and shooting at the raptors crouched in the mouth of the corridor.

Kipper seethed in frustration.

"I have an idea," Trugger said. He pulled one of the empty spacesuits out of the discarded disguise boxes and waved it around. He opened the suit at the neck, flipping the helmet back. The empty hole into the body gaped open.

Suddenly, the octopus leapt from Kipper's back. She had no

idea an octopus could jump like that! It slithered, pulling itself tentacle by tentacle, over the ferny floor. When it got to Trugger, it grabbed the spacesuit he was holding with its large sucker discs at the base of its tentacles. The octopus dragged the suit and itself into the archway, and climbed up the curved wall. Tentacles moved quickly over the controls, and the door in the archway slid open. As the octopus focused on the airlock controls, though, it neglected firing at the advancing raptors.

Kipper and Trugger found themselves ducking gunfire. The raptors advanced from the mouth of the corridor, heading for their captured compatriot. Kipper and Trugger fled for shelter in the newly opened airlock as the gun-wielding raptors stopped to free the captive raptor from the disguise box. It would only be a matter of moments before the others had him free, and, sure enough, shots soon rang off the airlock walls.

Instead of returning fire, however, the octopus crawled into the airlock after Kipper and Trugger. It handed its guns—all three of them, more than Kipper could hold effectively in her paws—to Kipper. Then, the octopus squeezed itself through the small neck-hole of the empty otter-shaped spacesuit. It pulled the helmet after it, closing itself inside.

The spacesuit lay crumpled on the floor, looking nearly as empty as it had before the octopus crawled inside. Then, tiny, delicate tentacle tips emerged from the neck, visible through the helmet's faceplate. They signed in miniature parody of the usual signing done with an entire tentacle: *"Help. Help."*

Kipper felt frustrated that the octopus was wasting time when it could be closing the airlock door to protect them all. Trugger, however, helped the octopus seal itself in the otter-shaped spacesuit, adjusted the suit controls to air-tight, and pressurized the otter-shaped metallic cloth bag.

Meanwhile, Kipper struggled with one of the guns. There was a catch and a trigger, not too alien after all. Once she figured out the trick of clicking the catch only a moment before pulling the trigger, she was able to fire the gun easily enough. She squeezed off several successive shots in the general direction of the raptors.

The gun was projectile based. Kipper hoped it wouldn't run out of ammunition. Picking up a second gun for her other paw, Kipper fired them both haphazardly at any raptor that dared approach. She expected Trugger and the octopus to seal the airlock in front of them, closing a shield between them and the raptors. She grew more and more impatient, ducking and dodging gunshots from the raptors, as she waited for the doors to slide closed.

A sudden blast knocked Kipper backward. She lost her footing and her stomach clenched. The airlock receded from her. Thick red gasses swirled past her into it. Panic hit, but a cool, rational center inside her refused to give in. She tucked her guns under arms, so as not to lose them. Then her paws grasped frantically, seeking the throttle for her jetpack, and she felt a surge of relief as she closed her suited fist, squeezing the blasters on her back into glorious life.

She shot upward. The red and yellow gases streamed past her faceplate, and she saw the open airlock fall away beneath her. The raptors fell away too, blasted unprepared into Jupiter's atmosphere; they diminished into tiny specks, plummeting beneath the sail ship. *First Race!* Kipper hoped the octopus wasn't among those tiny specks.

Kipper leaned her shoulders forward, changing the angle of her flight and prepared to dive after the falling raptors if necessary. She couldn't let the octopus, who'd helped to save her, fall to its death in the crushing atmosphere of Jupiter.

Fortunately, she spotted Trugger clutching the crumply spacesuit to his chest with one suited arm; an alien gun—the third one, Kipper didn't have enough paws for—held in the paw of the other. His jetpack flared. He was aimed toward the rear of the sail ship. Kipper followed his lead and watched as he landed on the sail ship's roof, protected from the howling Jovian wind by a fin-shaped protuberance on the ship's hull. Kipper tried to copy his landing, but it didn't go quite as planned.

Trugger landed on his feet, suggesting he had a lot more practice with jetpack maneuvers than Kipper who landed in an awkward barrel roll that ended when she slammed into the looming fin-protuberance. Cats don't *always* land on their feet.

"You all right?" Trugger asked.

"Yes," Kipper hissed. She tried to right herself and regain dignity, but instead she stumbled, tripping over the useless, otter-shaped tail of her spacesuit. "We should hide here until the *Jolly Barracuda* comes back for us." She sank against the surface of the sail ship. All the extra weight from the triple-Earth gravity exhausted Kipper.

The surface of the sail ship stretched out around them, larger than a dozen scramball fields. In the thick atmosphere and howling winds, three spacesuited figures crouched in the shadows would be almost impossible to see.

As she looked at the surface of the sail ship, though, the dull gleam of her reflection in the seemingly metallic surface reminded Kipper of how the ceilings had looked on the inside: *transparent*. From underneath, she wasn't hidden at all.

CHAPTER 21
EARTH

Many light minutes away, deep in the middle of night on her side of the planet, Trudith slaved away, scribbling mathematical figures and variables in a notebook. She was working on solving physics equations that—by a bizarre coincidence—described the way light bent through transparent surfaces and bounced off of reflective ones, much like the surface Kipper had collapsed on, exhausted. Like a one-way mirror it was transparent on one side and reflective on the other. The equations defining it's properties were fascinating.

Trudith took her new mental workouts seriously, and she had been learning a great deal of math, physics, chemistry, and anything else that she could get workbooks for in the popular *"Puppy Guide!"* brand.

Unfortunately, even if Trudith had been able to share her remarkable progress at understanding optical physics with her tabby cat friend, flying rapidly through the upper atmosphere of Jupiter, it wouldn't have helped Kipper find a place to hide on the top of the raptor's sail ship.

CHAPTER 22
THE GREAT RED SPOT

The entire ship wasn't transparent, Kipper realized. The room with the airlock where Trugger and Kipper had emerged from their disguise boxes had opaque ceilings. The room with the octopus tank did too, as well as several of the hallways. For all Kipper knew, she was slumped against one of the opaque parts of the ship right now. Her tired body wanted to believe, but her paranoid cat's mind couldn't stop thinking about how much the surface of the sail ship reminded her of the one-way mirrors she'd seen in cop shows.

Except, there weren't police dogs on the other side of this mirror. There were crazed, blaster wielding dinosaur birds with enslaved octopus tentacles. *Octo* tentacles meant *eight* blasters per raptor, with all those horribly be-clawed raptor talons still free. Kipper didn't like that.

"Kipper?" Trugger asked, his voice coming through the radio in her helmet. "Do we have to keep radio silence out here again?"

Kipper was busy staring along the surface of the sail ship, looking for changes in texture or seams that would provide clues as to which parts were opaque. She spared just enough brain power to answer Trugger's question with a tired, "What?"

"Well," he said, "I thought it would be nice to sing a sea shanty together while we wait for the *Barracuda*."

"Sure," Kipper said. She hadn't heard Trugger. She was imagining a fleet of police dogs showing up to rescue them. On Earth, Kipper hadn't been much of a fan of police dogs. They were as likely to laugh at a cat in trouble as help one. Out here, however, she would take any allies she could get.

Kipper would be relieved to see flashing red and blue lights cut through the orange Jupiter fog. Black and white cab cars would drive right up on top of the sail ship, and big, strong dogs in blue uniforms would jump out, holding guns, and set up a protective perimeter around her, Trugger, and their rescued octopus companion.

Perhaps *relieved* wasn't the right word. *Confused* might be more like it. Kipper wondered whether the air in her spacesuit was quite high enough on oxygen. The singing in her ears didn't help her believe in her own sanity.

"*...on a spinning iceberg!* Come on, Kipster," Trugger said, breaking off his song. "Don't you know this one?"

Before he could launch into another verse of *"What do you do with a drunken penguin?"*, Kipper decided it was time to stop hallucinating an action adventure film where police dogs save the day and start being proactive about her own safety.

"Trugger," she said, "the surface we're hiding on is transparent from underneath. The raptors aren't going to have any trouble finding us. We can't hide out here singing about penguins until the *Jolly Barracuda* gets back. We'll have company long before then."

The radio in Kipper's helmet went silent after she finished speaking. Then Trugger's voice crackled through, "I wonder if this octopus we rescued knows a good hiding place." Trugger lifted one of the floppy legs of the crumply otter-shaped space suit. In response, the spacesuit's torso contorted in a spasm, and then more tentacles shoved their way into the helmet, squishing against the faceplate. A single eye popped incongruously up from the neck and blinked mysteriously at them. The octopus' other eye must have been stuck in the neck seam. Octopi were weird.

"Well, we could try asking it," Kipper said, raising her paws. She stared dumbly at her spacesuit gloves.

Even if she could form recognizable signs with her gloves on, there was no guarantee the octopus would understand them. It would have to squeeze its eye back down out of the faceplate to make enough room in the helmet to sign back to her, and then it wouldn't be able to see any response she gave it, unless it squeezed its eye back up again.

"This is no good," Kipper said. "We should just start moving. See what we can find."

"That way we'll be a moving target, at least," Trugger said.

Or, Kipper thought, *we'll make ourselves even more obvious up here by tramping around until we're sure they've seen us.* Regardless, Kipper couldn't ignore the feeling gnawing in her gut that she was out in the open, and she *needed to hide.*

Kipper clipped the two alien projectile guns onto extra carabineers on her spacesuit's belt next to the unused nav-gun. She and Trugger each grabbed one of the octopus' spacesuit arms. The body sagged between them, leaning forward at the head, where most of the octopus' bulk seemed to be situated. The legs and rudder-like otter tail dragged on the ground.

Kipper wondered how the octopus was doing inside. The spacesuit provided fresh oxygen, but it couldn't provide an atmosphere friendly to the octopus' gills. Unfortunately, there was nothing to be done about that. The octopus would simply have to hold out until the *Jolly Barracuda* came back for them.

As soon as Trugger and Kipper stepped away from the protective shadow of the fin-like protuberance on the sail ship's surface, the gale force of Jupiter's wind knocked the breath right out of them. Kipper was amazed that she kept her footing, but she soon realized there must be some kind of special gripping technology in her spacesuit's boots. She vaguely remembered Trugger telling her once about space boot technology being based on gecko toes, though she wasn't sure if he'd been serious or if the comparison had been more akin to one of the bird metaphors so popular among the Barracuders.

"Rollicking raptors!" Trugger exclaimed over the helmet radio. He pointed with his free paw toward the horizon of the sail ship.

Kipper was dismayed to find Trugger's exclamation had been dead serious. Several twelve-limbed spacesuits climbed over the edge of the sail ship. Kipper counted three suits total, gleaming with the yellowed light of search beams. Fog swirled in the swaths of light cut by the piercing rays.

"Do you think they've seen us?" Kipper whispered. Her voice sounded small and kittenish. She didn't want to get caught up in another firefight. *Never mind,* she hissed. "Let's not wait to find out. *Run.*"

Kipper tugged on the arm of the spacesuit that she and Trugger dragged between them. Trugger stepped quickly to follow her. In a mad dash, Kipper led them directly away from the group of raptors. She hadn't thought any farther ahead than that when she saw another one of the pinecone shaped space-ships flying toward the sail ship from above. She wondered if it was going to dock like the ships she'd watched from onboard the *Jolly Barracuda. How many pinecone ships were docked inside this sail ship?*

More ships than Kipper wanted in the talons of murderous raptors. The raptors had more than enough ships to rain down terror on all the cats and otters in Jupiter System.

Everything would be better if the raptors had fewer ships. Everything would also be better if Kipper were inside of ship right now instead of fleeing for her life with nothing to protect her fur but a spacesuit and a jetpack.

That gave Kipper an idea.

Grand theft spaceship.

"Forget waiting for the *Jolly Barracuda*," Kipper said, trying to keep her breath steady as she ran. "Let's steal ourselves a spaceship."

Trugger and Kipper kept running across the surface of the sail ship. Kipper's own breathing echoed in her ears, but her suggestion wasn't greeted with any of the excitable exclamations she had expected. As they neared another protuberance in the mostly flat surface, Kipper veered for it, pulling Trugger and the octopus with her. They ducked, panting, out of sight of the piercing searchlights. Kipper was painfully aware that they might still be perfectly visible to any raptors standing inside the sail ship directly beneath them.

"*You're not saying anything,*" Kipper said.

"I don't know what to say," Trugger answered. "You're suggesting that we go back inside—where we were being shot at —and make these scary dinosaurs *angrier* at us?"

"Yes," Kipper said, trying her best to sound like a full grown cat in charge of the situation, instead of a lost kitten.

"That's crazy."

Kipper felt ashamed for making such a stupid suggestion but the more she thought about it, the less she could think of any valid alternatives. "When you've eliminated the impossible, whatever remains, no matter how stupid, is what you have to do," she muttered. "Look, we can't hang out here, dodging those raptors for another two hours."

"True," Trugger conceded, peering around to look at the raptors. Kipper didn't need to look. She knew they were getting closer.

"I don't like our odds on a firefight with them," she said. "And our jetpacks won't keep us aloft for two hours if we fly away from here."

"Most definitely true."

"So, we go back inside. We have nowhere else to go. And if we go back inside, we might as well try to steal a spaceship."

Trugger was silent for a long time. It scared Kipper that, right now, *she* was the crazy one.

"Okay," he said. "But I get to name the spaceship."

"Deal," Kipper said with relief, wondering whether she'd end up with a spaceship named for a bird or another fish like the *Jolly Barracuda*.

"So, how do we get back inside?" Trugger asked, but, before Kipper could answer, the descending pinecone spacecraft lowered to the edge of the sail ship. It cast a bright light across the surface of the ship, blinding them momentarily and silhouetting all the irregularities across the sail ship's surface.

As Kipper's eyes recovered, she said, "We follow that. Jet packs on three: One. Two. *Three.*"

Jet packs blared. Kipper and Trugger careened across the surface of the sail ship tethered to each other by means of the octopus' spacesuit that they each continued to clutch by an empty arm. They tugged each other erratically as each of them adjusted the thrust, alternately over and under compensating.

They flew low over the sail ship taking the most direct course to its edge. Their boots bumped and dragged as they skimmed over its surface. Finally, the surface gave way beneath them, and they flew over the yawning chasm of Jupiter. A tight turn, with Kipper in the lead, pointed the three-suit conglomeration down and back, following the path of the pinecone spaceship.

It was a massive, looming object; smaller than the sail ship, by far, of course. However, the sail ship was so large as to become a piece of land, an island, floating in the ruddy sea of Jovian gases.

The pinecone ship was closer in size to the *Jolly Barracuda*, and that size could be felt viscerally in a way that the sail ship's size could not. It was too large to comprehend as a single object.

The pinecone ship, on the other paw, was on a scale with the giant mansions of Wooftown movie stars, and giant mansions are not meant to hang, floating above you, in the swirling sky—even if that sky is orange and red without a trace of anything resembling land to be seen below.

Doubt glimmered in Kipper's heart. Despite the tall tales Captain Cod told about her wresting control of the *Jolly Barracuda* from him single handed, a spaceship this large was not something that a single cat—or even a cat, an otter, and a captured octopus—could fly. It took an entire bridge crew and engineers and, well, familiarity with the ship's layout and design.

Nonetheless, Kipper tilted her body, aiming herself for a loop that would curl around the pinecone ship and back to a neat landing on the topside. A sheet of light had opened in the sail ship ahead of them—hangar doors, if Kipper wasn't mistaken. Her landing didn't turn out as neat as Kipper hoped. Trugger slammed into her, squishing the octopus' suit between them. They tussled awkwardly to rearrange themselves among the jutting angles of the pinecone ship's upper hull. It was uncomfortable, but they were safely out of sight, hidden between dark metal turrets, as the pinecone ship pulled into the hangar bay.

Kipper helped Trugger lay out the octopus' suit then got herself situated in a pounce-ready crouch. So far, the octopus had been much more burden than help ever since crawling into that spacesuit. She couldn't blame the octopus for being useless inside an otter-shaped spacesuit. Her own altered spacesuit felt uncomfortable enough, and she was essentially otter-shaped compared to the octopus.

Kipper hoped the octopus would revert to its former incredibly useful state once they managed to break into this spaceship, take it over, and were faced with an alien helm to control.

The adrenaline in Kipper's veins started to slow down as she thought about that. What were the chances that this octopus would really know how to control one of these ships? This octopus was a *slave*, not a legitimate member of raptor society. Besides, even if the octopus were a trained pilot, it took a lot more than one pilot to run a ship as large as the *Jolly Barracuda*. Sure, the crew could rig up the *Barracuda* so that Emily could pilot her on a short, pre-planned flight, but that didn't mean Emily would be able to break into a ship the size of the *Barracuda*, start her engines from cold, and take off without a flight plan.

That all assumed the crew either didn't put up much of a fight or happened to all disembark at once, leaving the ship nice and empty.

"This plan is crazy," Kipper said.

"Oh ho, no you don't," Trugger replied. He stood up peering over the turret. "I see my ship over there, and you are not depriving me of the chance to name such a beauty. We have a deal."

Kipper rose out of her crouch, placed her paws on the edge of the turret and slowly lifted her head high enough to see over. Instinct flattened her ears, even though it made no difference in hiding her. The rounded ears of her space helmet didn't flatten with them.

Kipper's tip-toe position afforded her a better view of the hangar. It was wide—housing at least two other pinecone ships. She wasn't sure if there were more on the other side. The ceiling was low, at least, from her vantage point on top of the pinecone ship. The raptor who piloted it must be good at precision parking.

Then, Kipper saw what Trugger had been looking at: a much smaller vessel perched on the floor of the hangar between this pinecone ship and the next one.

The small vessel had two wings, angled backward from the body of the craft. Its shape reminded her of a whirligig seed from a maple tree. Kipper used to find whirligig seeds as a kitten and drop them to watch them spin downward like tiny helicopters. If the tiny vessel was designed to spin like that, Kipper wasn't at all sure she liked the idea of being *inside* it while it dropped down towards the heart of Jupiter.

Yet, Trugger was right about one thing. That smaller vessel looked like it would be much easier to capture and probably easier to pilot than a pinecone ship. Based on its size, Kipper estimated the whirligig was designed for a crew of two or three. Kipper was leading a crew of two or three. Perfect.

"Do you want to know what I'm going to name it?" Trugger asked.

"Tell me when we're flying it free through the skies of Jupiter," Kipper answered. "It'll give me something to look forward to." *Something more believable than successfully stealing a ship straight out of the raptors' docking bay.* Besides, even if they did get the whirligig out of the docking bay, there'd be raptor ships following, guns blaring, behind them. It would probably be a good time for a bird or fish-based pun.

Kipper unclipped the stolen projectile guns from her spacesuit's belt. With a gun in each paw, she clambered onto the top of the turret and looked around. She could see raptors at the back of the bay. A stream of them came from the rear of the pinecone she was perched on, and none of them looked up to see her. They were dressed in cloth uniforms like the raptors she'd seen inside. As she watched, they disappeared one by one through an airlock-like door. Presumably, they were returning to the leafy arboretum innards of the sail ship.

The last raptor even turned off the lights. The docking bay plunged into darkness.

"You bring the octopus," Kipper said to Trugger. She switched on her spacesuit's headlamp, cutting a path of light straight from her to the whirligig. "I'll keep us covered." Kipper didn't think there were any raptors left in the docking bay, but she felt safer with guns. Holding them at the ready made her climb over the bumpy hull of the pinecone ship more awkwardly, but her otter-shaped spacesuit and the Jovian gravity had already robbed her of her cat's grace. She didn't consider the extra inconvenience of the guns a huge loss.

The rounded hull of the pinecone made it possible to clamber nearly half of the way down before letting go and leaping. She hit the floor with a thud, but she stayed on her feet. Trugger was less lucky.

Kipper offered an arm to Trugger, never letting go of her guns, and he pulled himself up. He dragged the floppy octopus-filled spacesuit with him. Kipper worried about their noise, but the cavernous room stayed dark. Realistically, the swaths of light from the headlamps were probably a greater risk.

Kipper turned back to the whirligig. She followed the bouncing light from her headlamp directly to the winged ship. Once she reached it, Kipper held her paw out. She touched the reassuring solidness of the whirligig's hull.

Kipper decided to risk getting a better look at the docking bay from her new vantage point. She turned her head and watched the disk of light from her headlamp jump around the bay. It fell flat on the back wall, a small circle at such a distance. It caught on the angled hull of another pinecone ship and became an irregular, oblong ellipse. Scanning quickly to learn as much as she could, Kipper made out several small ships parked further on. Their shapes were different: one was pointed like a dart; another was blocky with a dish shape on top.

"Why this ship?" Kipper asked over her radio. "Those ships look fine too."

"This one looks fast," Trugger said without the least hesitation. It was enough for Kipper, even if she wasn't sure his reasoning made sense. "How do you think it opens?" he asked.

"I don't know," Kipper said. "But maybe our friend does." She tucked the gun in her left paw under her other arm, leaving one hand free. She touched the faceplate of the octopus' spacesuit. When she had the attention of the single yellow eye staring out from the helmet, Kipper pointed at the whirligig spaceship.

The tentacles in the octopus' spacesuit receded down the neck, disappearing inside the spacesuit's body. Kipper didn't know what that meant, but she knew the octopus couldn't help them from inside the spacesuit.

Trugger held up the spacesuit with a paw under each armpit. The helmet sagged forward, empty now, and Kipper reached over to unclamp it. After a tense moment, the tentacle tips began to emerge, and the octopus climbed out.

The octopus' fleshy tentacles looked different in the dry docking bay atmosphere than Emily's looked under oxo-agua. There was a soft, almost fluffy quality to Emily's skin. This flesh looked slimy, like the pink skin of an open wound. Where Emily floated gracefully, nearly flying through her liquid atmosphere, these tentacles were pressed down by the unrelenting Jovian gravity, without any cushioning from the gaseous atmosphere.

Like a ropy mass of animated intestines, the octopus crawled down the outside of the spacesuit, over the floor and straight up the outer hull of the whirligig. It stretched its tentacles across a rectangular hatch on the hull, splaying its body into a wavy star of flesh that bled from pink to ashen gray. Then the octopus' skin darkened to a coal black that blended in with the hull.

Kipper questioned her eyes. She blinked, but she could no longer make out the octopus against the metal of the hull. *Had the octopus fled?* she wondered, but, then, the hatch swung open, and she saw a bulging blur in the path of her headlamp that looked to be the octopus climbing inside the whirligig. Stepping closer, Kipper saw a panel on the exterior of the open hatch. It had the same controls designed to be worked by tentacles that had been on the airlock.

She didn't waste long examining it. Instead, she gave Trugger a gentle push on his arm, gesturing for him to go inside. She followed close on his heels and grabbed a handle on the inside of the hatch, allowing her to swing it shut behind them.

The interior of the whirligig was tight, probably designed for only one or two inhabitants. Perhaps a pilot and gunner? Kipper hoped the whirligig had weapons. She feared they'd need them.

The octopus busied itself at the front of the whirligig's cabin, tentacles stretching and waving, working controls. The control panel lit up with a multitude of lights and indecipherable computer displays.

Amazingly, one of the displays made sense to Kipper. It looked like a graphical representation of the sail ship, marking all the other ships in the docking bay with a pulsing light in their own position. She recognized the configuration of pinecone ships and smaller ships surrounding them.

"I can read that one," Kipper said pointing.

"Yeah, it's a map," Trugger agreed. "It'll help us figure out if they're pursuing us."

Trugger and Kipper watched in silence as their octopus helper continued to clamber around the control panel, stretching its body into changing shapes like a loop of string, wound around a kitten's paws, for a game of Cat's Cradle.

"I wonder what's taking so long?" Trugger asked.

Then Kipper realized: the octopus was contorting into such bizarre shapes because he was having trouble reaching all the controls. "Oh!" she said. "This ship isn't designed to be piloted by an octopus." She stepped closer, and the octopus locked an eye on her. She thought she saw gratitude. Then, the octopus reached for her with three tentacles, grabbed on, and shifted its weight onto her shoulders again. "It's designed to be piloted by an octopus *joined to a raptor.*"

From its new vantage, the octopus was able to move its tentacles much more freely, reaching higher and farther than when its body had been pressed against the control panel, clinging to it like a spattered stain of jelly on a wall. Things started happening much faster.

A hum began in the floor, resonating through their space boots. More lights came on—clearly external as Kipper could see their effect through the suddenly visible side windows and fore-screen. They lit up the space around the whirligig in the docking bay. Finally, a screeching voice boomed throughout the ship. Kipper couldn't understand the language, but the voice sounded like a raptor. And it sounded angry.

"We need to get out of here," she hissed, as if the octopus on her shoulders could hear. As she finished the words, she lurched forward. The whirligig was moving! The octopus' tentacles wrapped around her shoulders kept Kipper from falling. Trugger, however, slammed into the front control panel. The whirligig listed eerily to the side and then began zooming forward.

Kipper couldn't tell if the octopus was driving the ship or if Trugger had inadvertently hit the thrusters. Either way, her heart caught in her throat: the closed docking bay doors were rushing toward them!

The tenor of the screaming raptor voice over the whirligig's sound system raised several notches, matching the panicked screaming in Kipper's own head. Kipper wondered if this was how the raptors sounded to Trugger right before starting that alarm.

The docking bay doors began to open. Either the octopus had mad skills, or the raptors didn't want their docking bay door smashed to pieces even more than they didn't want a whirligig stolen. Kipper felt sick realizing the octopus had been playing a game of chicken.

Kipper, Trugger, and their octopus pilot slipped out of the docking bay and into the thick currents of Jupiter's atmosphere like a maple seed falling onto the surface of a fast flowing stream.

CHAPTER 23
EARTH

Trudith heard barking as she approached the Campaign Headquarters early in the morning. The blinds were closed against the harsh slant of morning light. Trudith couldn't see inside, but she recognized Lucky's voice shouting.

The door burst open, rattling on its hinges. Lucky stalked out past her, barely bothering to throw a grumbled greeting her way. That wasn't like him. He was a genial, pleasant dog most of the time. One of the easiest people to get along with that Trudith had ever met. He probably had to be, she figured, to survive being married to Petra.

Trudith watched Lucky walk away, radiating anger as if he had his own personal storm cloud floating over him. She wondered if she should follow after him—see what was wrong and try to make him feel better. But she didn't know Lucky that well. If it had been any other acquaintance, Trudith wouldn't have let that stop her, but Lucky was Petra's. Trudith didn't like to cross Petra, and if Lucky was storming out of the Brighton offices, it was probably over a fight with Petra. Trudith didn't want to take sides.

Besides, Petra was already glaring at Trudith with narrowed eyes through the wide open door. "Don't let me stop you," she hissed. "I can see you want to go commiserate with him. *You poor dogs,*" she mocked, *"always having to put up with the crazy, spiteful cat."*

"No," Trudith woofed. She came into the office and gingerly closed the door behind her.

"Too afraid?" Petra tried to sound mocking, but her voice broke, belying the illusion.

"I was wondering what Lucky did to make you angry." Trudith's sympathetic tone knocked the wind out of Petra's sails.

Angry orange ears flattened. It was hard to be cruel to someone who was being insightful and kind to her, but Petra didn't know how to cheer herself up without treating Trudith like a verbal scratching post.

"It's about that torbie woman who came with us to the demonstration," Petra said dully. She didn't elaborate. She merely sat at her desk, hunched before the computer, looking glum.

The lines of morning sun from the half-open blinds cut across Petra's fur making it glow in stripes. She wore a green sundress with strappy shoulders instead of the usual vest and pants. It looked light and summery, utterly at odds with the demeanor of the cat wearing it.

"I like your sundress," Trudith said.

Petra's ears perked up, and then one of them skewed to the side as if she was questioning the motives of any dog who would dare compliment her right now. Her skewed ear circled back when Petra decided that Trudith wasn't clever enough to be insincere.

"Thanks," Petra said.

Trying to maintain the rapport that had suddenly sprung up between them, Trudith blurted out, "I went on a date last night."

One of Petra's ears skewed again. Her eyes narrowed. She

was trying to figure out what Trudith was up to, but Trudith wasn't up to anything other than trying to cheer Petra up and connect with her. Eventually, curiosity got the better of Petra and she said, "Oh?" in a very leading way.

Once Trudith got talking about her trip to the ice cream parlor with Keith, it rapidly became clear that she really did want to talk. Trudith would have preferred pouring out her confused feelings to Kipper, but, in the absence of her best friend, her best friend's sister was a decent substitute, especially since Petra was so baffled by being the sudden recipient of such open camaraderie that not a single barbed word sprang to her tongue.

Sure enough, Petra *wanted* to abuse Trudith, take her anger out on the nearest available target, but she found herself too fascinated.

Trudith picked apart every moment of the previous evening, every detail of Keith's behavior, even her own actions and reactions. She analyzed and extrapolated just like a cat.

Was Keith sincere in his regard for her, Trudith wondered, or was he merely trying to play her for some scheme of Senator Morrison's? If he was trying to play her, then should Trudith double-scheme him by playing along? If he really liked her, could she make use of that to benefit Alistair? And, if she did, would that, in turn, destroy Keith's regard for her? Was that a trade worth making?

Trudith felt caught between the beginning tendrils of a fluttery feeling inspired by Keith's clearly romantic overture and her firmly rooted loyalty to Alistair.

Spending so much time around cats had rubbed off on Trudith. Her brain spun in crazy circles, but that meant the wheels were turning. When Trudith's brain was working, it became clear that she was a sharp dog.

For once, Petra's ears stayed straight toward Trudith as she spoke, instead of twisting about as if she'd rather listen to anyone—any*thing*—else. Her eyes held a plain, straightforward expression instead of the usual glare she reserved for her brother's bodyguard.

Before Petra could completely shatter her image as the scary, mean cat in Trudith's mind by reciprocating her friendly confidences, though, a window popped up on her computer screen to interrupt their conversation. An incoming message from the *Jolly Barracuda*.

Trudith's heart leapt when she saw those words. It was like she had summoned a message from Kipper by confiding in Petra. It made little rational sense, but Trudith felt like she'd earned Petra's good will and was being rewarded.

Petra started the vid file playing, and a window popped up onscreen with an image of blurry gray stripes. The image readjusted itself, and Kipper's face became visible. She must have been hunched up close to the camera, because her face was about all they could see.

"Hi guys," Kipper's voice said through the tinny computer speakers. Petra paused the video.

"What are you—" Trudith began, but Petra was already setting up the software to send a return video.

"Hey Kipper," Petra said, looking at the computer screen where a pinhole camera recorded her. "I don't know how far away you are. I don't know what the lag time is. But, in case you're still waiting for a reply out there, you should know that I'm going to watch your video right away."

"Me too!" Trudith chimed in, pressing her head up against Petra's, hoping to squeeze her face into the video frame. "Hi Kipper! I miss you!"

Petra glared at Trudith with flattened ears, but she didn't let the dog's interruption stop her. "A few quick things you should know: Morrison backed out of his senate seat in a bizarre deal-with-the-devil that Ali's fallen for. They're going to run for president *together*."

"Morrison will be president and Alistair vice president!" Trudith exclaimed. "Doesn't that seem backward?"

Petra kept talking, but she'd set a precedent when she tried to cut Trudith off; the dog talked right over her. Kipper would simply have to sort out the mess when she heard it.

"You know," Trudith continued, musing, "People really ought to just flip the names when they vote for Morrison/Brighton. Draw a little arrow or something?"

Petra finished her own tirade about Alistair's questionable choice and turned to look at Trudith with skewed ears.

"You know, a little curvy arrow," Trudith pantomimed the imagined arrow with a blunt claw. "Pointing at both names to show that they should be reversed because they're *really* voting for Alistair. That way Alistair could be the president and Morrison would just be vice president!" Trudith concluded triumphantly.

Petra rolled her eyes and snapped the video recorder off. "That is the dumbest idea," she said. "Have you no sense of how politics work?" Acid dripped from Petra's words, but it was less concentrated acid than Trudith was used to. Petra's argument with Lucky must have really gotten to her.

Petra unpaused Kipper's video and dialed up the speed to two-hundred percent. There was no more time to argue as Kipper began explaining in an eerily fast, high-pitched voice how she and the otters of the *Jolly Barracuda* had been attacked, fled into the atmosphere of Jupiter, and unwittingly discovered a giant sail ship.

The playback caught up with the live stream around the the part of the story where Kipper, Trugger, and the freed octopus began plummeting into the heart of Jupiter on their stolen vessel. The video slowed down to real time, and the pitch of Kipper's voice returned to normal.

"Trugger named the ship..." her voice caught for a moment

before she continued. "He named it *Brighton's Destiny*. For Alistair. For all three of us."

Trudith looked over at Petra, and it seemed like her ears stood a little taller, her whiskers a little straighter. There was a new sparkle of hope in her eye that matched the look in Kipper's eye on the screen.

"After some fancy flying, we rendezvoused with the *Jolly Barracuda*, and parked *Brighton's Destiny* in one of the cargo bays. Boris and Destry have been looking it over, trying to learn what they can. Jenny and Emily have been talking to the octopus we rescued. Captain Cod and Trugger are trying to work out a plan of attack. I convinced the captain that I should come in here—" Kipper's ears flicked and her eyes turned away from the camera, looking around the room she was in, which the camera barely showed, "—and send the news of what we've learned home."

Kipper drew a deep breath through her teeth. "Did you know that the airlocks can be drained of oxo-agua independently of the rest of the ship?" she asked rhetorically. *"And none of the otters told me about it."* Her green eyes sparked with anger. *"Anyway,"* she said through gritted teeth, "I figured it'd be easier to send a message home from here. That way, you can edit it up and have a video for the press instead of just a written statement. People need to know about these raptors."

Kipper paused a while, seeming to collect her thoughts. "The octopi already knew about the raptors. When Emily met the octopus we rescued, she began signing right away in a language I don't know. It wasn't Standard Swimmer's Sign. It was kind of creepy. Maybe just because Emily looked so scared." Kipper looked scared.

"Apparently, there are octopi on Earth with religious beliefs similar to the Doctrine of the First Race. Except, instead of believing humans uplifted dogs and cats, they believe raptors uplifted octopi. And instead of believing that humans will return one day, bringing love and happiness to everyone..." Kipper's voice hushed a level: "They believe raptors will return and destroy them."

The word *destroy* hung in the air in between Trudith, Petra, and the video recording of Kipper.

"We're orbiting Jupiter," Kipper said, "but, as soon as we've regrouped a bit and Captain Cod has come up with a war plan, we're going to fly to Europa." There was heaviness in Kipper's voice. "I'll wait in the airlock as long as I can for a return message, but, whenever the captain's ready, I... Just in case, you know... I love you guys."

The picture of Kipper disappeared. The video stream ended.

A hush hung over the office. Petra's ears were flat, and Trudith's jowls taut. They both looked stricken. They both wondered what they'd do if they lost Kipper. They both wondered if they'd ever hear from Kipper again.

"Do you think she got our message?" Trudith asked.

"If she did," Petra said in a bleak voice, "she'll send another one." Petra didn't say that the video they'd just watched had been nearly thirty minutes long, and they hadn't received a reply yet. "How far away is Jupiter?" Petra asked, meaning the question for herself. She had no expectation at all that Trudith would know, but that fact was in *Our Solar System! Puppy Guide!*

"It's about five hundred million miles from the sun," Trudith said.

Petra blinked. "What?"

"Earth is about a hundred million miles from the sun," Trudith continued, remembering a word problem she'd done recently. "So, Jupiter is anywhere between four hundred million miles and six hundred million miles away."

Petra hadn't expected an answer, and Trudith got a huge rush from her look of surprise. Trudith wondered if she could push that look over into actual *respect* by carrying on with the math until she actually got a useful number.

Straining her memory now, Trudith said, "Since there's about eleven million miles in a light minute..." Her eyes rolled up in concentrated thought. "Let's make that ten. It'll be, uh, forty to sixty minutes for a message to get here from Jupiter!" A huge grin broke across Trudith's muzzle. She felt immensely triumphant.

The look on Petra's face hadn't turned into respect, however; it had turned into irritation. Most likely, Petra was irritated by what the math proved—namely, how far away her only sister was right now—but, it was much easier and more satisfying to be mad at Trudith than at cold, unalterable facts.

"*Stupid dog wasting time doing math,*" Petra muttered under her whiskers as she reconfigured the video camera to send Kipper another message. She didn't turn it on. The truth was: she didn't know what to say to Kipper. Neither of them did. Neither of them wanted to say final, parting words. The pressure was too high.

"What if she doesn't come back from Europa?" Petra breathed. It was the softest whisper, but Trudith heard. And Trudith took a risk: she wrapped her big, black-furred arms around the tiny orange cat. If Kipper was her sister—and Trudith liked to think of Kipper that way—then Petra was her sister too.

The hug didn't last long. It's not safe to hug a cat for long. Their claws come out, and they get all sharp. Nonetheless, Trudith's show of support had made its point and something inside Petra melted. She looked to Trudith and said, "Lucky and I were going to adopt a kitten." She halted, her ears still flat. "Do I tell Kipper? We were going to wait to tell anyone until it was done, but now I don't know if it'll happen. What if I never get another chance to tell her *anything?*"

"Is that what the fight is about?" Trudith asked. After her impressive feats of mathematical memory and simple arithmetic, the question seemed dull and plodding to Trudith as soon as she'd asked it. She ought, she felt, to be able to work out the nature of the fight between Petra and Lucky through cleverness alone!

Petra shoved a copy of the morning paper at Trudith. The paper was folded open to an article about Topher Brooke—a popular pug dog comedian, known for his anti-feline shtick. Trudith skimmed the text, but it was hard to read with Petra staring at her. She couldn't concentrate under all this pressure. Time was ticking away, and every extra second meant it was less likely a message could make it back to Kipper, crouched in that airlock, circling Jupiter in time.

"I don't understand what this has to do with you and Lucky," Trudith admitted. "It seems to be about Topher Brooke... having kittens?"

Petra snatched the newspaper back clawfully. Trudith heard the paper shredding.

"Not kittens," Petra said. Her ears splayed on her head in a befuddled expression. "Hybrids? They're..." she looked at the paper in her paws again. "They're half-dog, half-cats. He and his wife have been trying... Artificial insemination? Gene therapy? I don't know. I don't get it."

Trudith looked at the paper again. The picture of Topher Brooke showed him standing in front of a black cat, shielding her from the camera. "Topher Brooke is married to a cat?" Trudith asked. "That doesn't make sense. He *hates* cats."

"That's an *act*," Petra said. "Irony? Satire? Fictional persona? Do any of those words mean anything to you?" Petra shook her head. "Sheesh. Yes, he's married to a cat. He's a cats' rights activist, and his wife is a cat." Petra paused, looking at the paper with that befuddled expression again. "And they've managed to have a litter of—puppies? kittens?—*something* together."

"Wow," Trudith woofed. She hadn't realized that was possible. According to the *Puppy Guide!* on biology she'd been working through, dogs and cats didn't even have the same number of chromosomes. That alone should mean they couldn't reproduce. Apparently, the *Puppy Guide!* book on biology was a little behind the bleeding edge of technology.

"Look," Trudith said, "I don't want to rush this conversation, since it's the first time you've ever really been nice to me and all —" As she said it, Trudith wondered whether those words were such a good idea. She hurried on past them. "But I don't understand what this has to do with you and Lucky, and, well, Kipper might be up there waiting to hear from us."

Petra's ears flattened and her whiskers drooped in an expression that Trudith could have sworn was chagrin. It didn't last long. Without even discussing it, Petra turned back to the computer and switched on the video recording software. Instantly, her demeanor was bright and cheerful. "Hi Kipper. We watched your message. It's so good to hear from you."

"It *is!*" Trudith agreed fervently.

Petra spared a glare for Trudith but didn't miss a beat saying, "We'll pass the important parts along to the media—" It looked like she had more to say, but Petra was relieved to see the words *incoming message* appear on her screen. "Oh, another message from you!" she exclaimed, interrupted herself. "We'll be right back—I mean—you know, we're going to watch the new message."

As Petra reached for the computer to switch from recording their own message to playing Kipper's, Trudith barked quickly to squeeze in a last few words: "Good luck saving Europa!"

Then Kipper was onscreen: "Oh, Trudith," she said, smiling through her whiskers. "I love that idea! Everyone should vote for Brighton/Morrison with a little arrow to show that they mean for Alistair to be president. He's exactly the cat to lead us through this war."

Petra looked at Trudith sourly. She was clearly jealous that the few words they'd received from her sister so far were for Trudith instead of her, but Kipper continued, saying, "Keep him honest, Petra? Okay? I know that Trudith will keep him safe, but he's going to need you if that conniving, controlling Sheltie has his ear now." Kipper shook her head. "God, I wish you were here now, Petra. I'm always so much braver when you're around." She drew a deep breath and looked down pensively.

Moments passed as Trudith and Petra waited with bated breath for their distant sister to speak again. Trudith wished she could be there with Kipper, but it was Petra that Kipper wanted.

"I'm going to volunteer to fly the *Brighton's Destiny*," Kipper said, turning her eyes back toward the camera. "An extra ship defending New Persia—even a small one—might help. And I have to do everything I can to help." Her eyes burned through the camera, her gaze steady and piercing. A look of such determination withered any doubt in its presence.

"I miss you, Kipper," Petra whispered. Nearly at the same time, Kipper's visage on the computer screen said, "I miss you guys. I have to go." And the video was over.

CHAPTER 24
EARTH

With Kipper gone, Trudith and Petra found themselves alone with each other again. Although it had only been a time-delayed ghost of her, Kipper's presence had filled the space between Trudith and Petra, bridging the gap between them. The emptiness she left behind was like a giant chasm. The tenuous bridge she had provided, crumbled away, leaving them with a gulf of silence.

Trudith cleared her throat, preparing for a leap into that gulf: "So, uh, adopting a kitten. That's a big decision, right?" Talking about anything was better than thinking about Kipper piloting a small alien spacecraft into a firefight over Europa, and Petra's topic du jour seemed to be kittens.

Petra didn't bite. Her shoulders slumped and her whiskers drooped. Trudith would have to bait the hook better. She tried for a more compelling question, "What are you going to do with the kitten?"

Petra glared and shot back the answer, "What does anyone do with a kitten?"

Trudith might not have succeeded at asking a more compelling question, but, by asking a more stupid one, she at least got a response.

"I dunno," Trudith said. "I thought you might be meeting with that social worker woman to set up some kind of stunt—something to make Alistair look good for the election. You know, like a video of him rescuing kittens from a burning building."

Petra stifled a snicker, then, too tired to maintain her coldness toward Trudith, she said, "No, Lucky and I just wanted a family." She extended a claw and began scratching idle patterns on the edge of her desk. "Growing up in a cattery, I never knew any parents. I wanted to see what it was like. By giving that gift to a kitten, well, it would be like going back in time and giving that gift to me. I thought I'd be able to see myself in the kitten's eyes."

Petra trailed off, her eyes staring into the middle distance. Suddenly, she shifted uncomfortably. Wrapping her paws around herself, she said, "Look, I know it's dumb, but I would have given anything to have parents looking out for me as as kitten, and, I figured, if Lucky and I had a kitten, then that kitten would have *me* looking out for her. And she'd have Lucky as a dad. Imagine that? A dog for a dad."

Petra looked up, and her eyes caught Trudith's. Her ears flattened as she realized the ridiculousness of what she'd just said. Trudith didn't have to imagine having a dog for a dad, or imagine any dad, or parents at all. She'd grown up with her own, real parents looking out for her, like most dogs did.

"You wouldn't understand," Petra said, her orange fur bristling.

Trudith was quiet for a while, but then she woofed, "I guess not, but that sounds like a nice reason for wanting a kitten."

Petra looked surprised, though still grouchy. "Thanks," she meowed.

"So," Trudith said, "what does this Topher Brooke thing have to do with it?"

"Isn't it obvious?" Petra meowed, eyes wide at the idea that even Trudith could be so dense. "I guess I have to spell it out for you?"

"Yes, thanks," Trudith woofed. "That would help."

Petra's eyes narrowed, looking for any way Trudith could be trying to trick her into looking a fool. No matter how she worked it in her head, Trudith was the one who looked a fool and was *admitting* it. Petra would *never* admit to being a fool. Even if she had clearly been one. Dogs were so weird.

"Whatever," Petra meowed. "Look, this article means that if Lucky and I really wanted to, we could have a litter of our own—children that are really ours. Both his and mine."

Petra stared at Trudith with an intensity that made the big black dog nervous. Especially since Trudith still didn't feel like she understood what Petra was saying.

"So?" Trudith woofed.

Petra threw her head back in an exasperated yowl. "Don't you understand anything?"

Now Trudith bristled. Petra had been being so nice to her—explaining things and sharing things—there was no call for her to fall back to her old patterns of blanket insults to Trudith's intelligence. "I understand lots of things," Trudith woofed, huffily. "I just don't understand what the big deal is about the difference between adopting a kitten and having a litter of your own."

Petra looked taken aback. Trudith didn't usually stand up for herself this way. "What do you mean?" she meowed.

"Well," Trudith woofed, "if the whole point is to give the gift of a family with parents to a kitten... That's what every cattery kitten dreams of, right?"

Petra hated to sound selfish, but, in this regard she felt selfish. "Yeah," she whispered under her whiskers, "but, the point is for the kitten to be *like me.*"

Trudith lowered her voice too. "A cattery kitten is like you—

in the most important way when it comes to wanting a family. You used to be one."

Petra had nothing to say to that, but it looked to Trudith like her point had hit home.

If Trudith had been a cat, she would have been thinking about how Petra's plans might affect her. Specifically, if Petra were to become busy with a new kitten, would she have as much time to interfere in Alistair's political campaigning? If she didn't have as much free time, might Trudith's life not become a whole lot easier?

Instead, Trudith found herself thinking about what life would be like for Petra and the newly adopted kitten. She'd never thought much about raising a litter herself. Trudith came from a litter of five, and she remembered how much trouble she and her four brothers had got into as pups. She wasn't close to any of her brothers now, but two of them already had litters of their own, and Trudith had heard enough stories about her nieces and nephews to guess that if she ever had a litter of puppies, they'd be more than a pawful.

Political goons, Trudith could handle. A half dozen rambunctious Labrador puppies? No, thanks.

While Trudith was lost in her reverie, imagining Petra's future, Petra found her mind focused on one very specific moment in Trudith's recent past.

A moment that had been captured in video.

A moment that could be important.

The more Petra examined that moment from every angle, playing and replaying it in her mind, the more she became convinced that it had exactly the right amount of goofy, guileless charm to captivate a nation of gullible dogs and cats who were less clever than her.

Petra called up the recent video exchanges with Kipper on her computer in separate windows. With a bit of scanning, she cued them up to two synergistic moments: Trudith describing how everyone should vote for Alistair with her pantomimed arrow gesture, and Kipper agreeing that Alistair was *"exactly the cat to lead us through this war."*

Petra played one clip and then the other. One and then the other. Again and again.

"What are you doing?" Trudith asked.

Petra's eyes were wide and wild when she looked at Trudith. "I have a plan," she said. "Well, part of a plan."

Trudith looked at the frozen images of herself and Kipper on the computer screen. "Does it involve putting these clips of video together into an ad campaign to win Alistair the presidency?"

"It's completely infeasible," Petra said. Her ears splayed as she considered the logistics. "But, yes."

Trudith shrugged. "Making a video can't hurt. We don't have anything better to do for Alistair right now."

"That's true," Petra said. "Senator Morrison had some of his lackeys bring over a schedule for Alistair and go over it with him the other day. They have everything mapped out—all the public appearances, every news outlet that will want to interview him. He doesn't need to do anything but show up when and where that Sheltie says for the next year, and be a puppet-cat for him. We're out of the loop."

Trudith felt a thrill raise the fur between her shoulders as she realized that—while Petra may be "out of the loop"—Trudith was finally *in the loop.* In Petra's loop.

"Do you know anything about video editing?" Trudith asked.

"No," Petra said. "But we don't want to do this ourselves. We want it to look professional."

Then Trudith got really excited. Her contacts on her scramball team were about to pay off. One of the other players—a salt-and-pepper furred poodle-mix—worked for an ad agency. After the stories Joey had told their scramball team about his run-in with Senator Morrison, anyone on that team would be happy to help out in a campaign against him.

Technically, Trudith supposed, this was a campaign *for* Senator Morrison to win Vice President, but it was still against the senator's interests, and that should be good enough. Right? The more she thought about it, the less Trudith realized she knew about how her scramball team would feel about voting for a cat.

Trudith started telling Petra her idea about involving the scramball team, hoping that Petra would offer to help her pitch the video plan to them. Petra was good at persuading people to do things.

Unfortunately, the more serious Trudith sounded about the plan, the less serious it sounded to Petra. Her orange ears wandered to the side—not in splayed annoyance but in simple inattention. Her eyes glazed over, and Trudith realized their brief partnership was already over. Trudith would have to persuade her scramball team herself.

"What do you think?" Trudith asked, grinning ingratiatingly, hoping to re-engage Petra. "Should we get to work on it?"

After a pause long enough for Trudith to wonder whether Petra had stopped listening entirely, Petra answered, "Yes, you should get to work on it." She rose from her desk and gathered up a jacket that had been draped over the back of her chair. Standing, Petra's orange fur caught in the striated light coming through the half-open window blinds. She glowed with fiery stripes, shaming the usual glow of her orange-on-orange stripes. "I need to find Lucky," she said, not even looking at Trudith.

Trudith understood. Petra had a lot on her mind, and her row with Lucky did need to be patched up.

"Sure," Trudith woofed. "I'll get the ball rolling, but, I'll keep you informed, okay?"

Petra made a sound that could have been a meow of confirmation, but it was hard to tell. She'd already turned away, and the creaking hinge of the front door as she left interfered with Trudith properly hearing her.

Never mind, Trudith thought. She would figure out how to rally her scramball team to the cause of Alistair for President on her own. Let Petra worry about adopting kittens—Trudith had a presidency to win!

CHAPTER 25
JUPITER

While Trudith phoned her scramball mates, rallying them to her cause, Kipper floated inside the *Jolly Barracuda*, treading water and watching Captain Cod sign a description of his battle plans for defending New Persia. Most of the crew assembled on the bridge to watch him, even Emily and the rescued octopus.

Captain Cod's paws moved with a deliberation and certainty that they rarely held. "We are about to embark on a dangerous mission. The *Jolly Barracuda* is not a warship, but she will not shirk from battle if honor calls for it. Nor will her crew."

In the oxo-agua atmosphere, the otters of the *Jolly Barracuda* couldn't raise a rousing cheer, but many of them did quick loop-de-loops or back flips before settling down to watch the captain's signed speech again.

"What we've learned from Ordol here—" Captain Cod spelled out Ordol's name, combined with a gesture to indicate the rescued octopus. "—suggests we're hopelessly outmatched. The raptors have an entire civilization floating inside this gas giant's atmosphere, and every sail ship hosts dozens of warships.

"Whereas, we are only one small cargo vessel, and the police force of our own civilization is centered between Earth and the asteroids. It would take weeks for any reinforcements to reach us, and we can't expect New Persia to hold out that long."

Kipper examined the faces of the otters around her. Even Trugger looked grim; Jenny clutched the end of her tail, fidgeting; and, both octopi were blanched white.

Captain Cod continued, "Thus, our mission is two-fold: first, we must confront the warships attacking New Persia head-on. An all-out assault will use our greater speed and maneuverability to their best advantage. We'll draw the raptors' attacks away from New Persia."

Captain Cod turned his eyes to Kipper before proceeding. His brown eyes stared at her with an intensity that made her very, very nervous.

"While we distract and divert the attacking vessels, destroying as many as we can in the process, Kipper and Ordol will fly the *Brighton's Destiny* to the surface, make contact with the New Persians, and begin organizing evacuation plans."

The intensity in Captain Cod's eyes turned to sadness as he signed, "The *Jolly Barracuda* can't carry very many refugees. If we fill our cargo bay, we can probably take a hundred and fifty, maybe two hundred refugees."

Kipper thought of the cargo load of fine art—whimsical, baroque and rococo paintings in gilt frames—that would have to be dumped. Nearly half the cargo bay was currently set up as the captain's personal art museum. She couldn't help but wonder whether some of Captain Cod's sadness was over that.

She couldn't doubt his feelings long. Captain Cod looked away from Kipper, turned his gaze to each of the other members of his crew in turn, and signed, "We can't do enough, merely rescuing a tiny fraction of the New Persians. So, I have decided to stay behind and form a group of freedom fighters to protect the New Persians who we can't rescue. I will be taking volunteers to join me."

The otters of the crew, floating in a crowded ring around the captain, shifted their flippered paws in a restless motion of surprise. Their whiskered faces looked long, but their eyes were lit with sparks of determination.

"For each one of us that stays behind," Captain Cod signed, "there will be room for another refugee on the *Jolly Barracuda*."

Jenny signed excitedly, "And there will be another warrior fighting alongside the New Persians!" Her foot-paws paddled, causing her to float forward. "I volunteer."

"Me too," signed Destry.

Trugger looked at Kipper before volunteering himself. Kipper's heart jumped each time another otter volunteered, until every last one of them had followed suit.

"But," she signed, "who will fly the refugees away?"

Captain Cod looked at her again and signed with steady paws, "I already thought of that." He looked proudly around at his crew. "I expected you would all be willing to stay and fight. You're a brave crew. But, the *Jolly Barracuda* will need someone to fly her."

Boris, the sea otter pilot with golden earrings bejangling his small round ears, bobbed his head dutifully and signed, "I can fly her home, Captain."

"Yes," Captain Cod agreed. "A ship needs her pilot." He pointed in rapid succession to Felix, Emily, and Kipper. "You'll also need our head engineer; our expert on maintaining mobility during use of the Ryderian engines; and Kipper to keep order among the refugees."

"What?" Kipper signed, feeling a burning at the tips of her ears. The white noise of the ship creaking, like distant whale song, was joined in her ears by an internal roar of outrage. "I should stay to defend New Persia!" she signed. If she could have spoken, her voice would have seethed. As it was, her paws trembled. She didn't want to be sent away like a kitten while all her friends stayed to fight.

She couldn't take the idea of abandoning her friends. She'd seen how terrifying these raptors were, first hand, and she didn't want to leave these otters who had become her second family behind to fight them without her. If they had to face such a terrible foe, she wanted to be right there, fighting at their side.

Instead of addressing her objection, however, Captain Cod merely signed, "That settles it then. The rest of us will be staying on New Persia to fight the raptors. With Ordol's inside knowledge, I'm sure we can keep them on their toes and hold them back. Let them do their worst, and we'll best them! In paw-to-paw combat if it comes to it!"

A number of Barracuders signed brave, eager, bloodthirsty words of assent. Captain Cod continued to sign, but Kipper's view of him was suddenly obscured by a cloud of murky grayness. The smoky cloud blasted into the atmosphere of the bridge, muddying the oxo-agua, and blotting out Kipper's vision. She felt the oxo-agua around her bump turbulently in a sudden storm of motion. All the otters around her were moving —had they taken off for their posts? or escape pods? Was the ship under attack?

Before Kipper could do anything, a sour, salty taste from the darkened oxo-agua hit her nostrils. She coughed violently as it burned in her lungs.

Doubled over, floating and coughing, Kipper was a wreck by the time she felt a paw on her shoulder. She hadn't realized she'd clamped her eyes shut against the salty sting until she opened them to see Jenny beside her. Jenny didn't look nearly as discomposed. Her eyes—like all the otters'—were much better protected in this liquid atmosphere by their third inner eyelids.

Squinting her less protected eyes, Kipper saw the murk in the oxo-agua clearing. She noticed a deep, thrumming, hum vibrating around her and a strong current blowing past. The pumps for filtering and scrubbing the oxo-agua must have been turned up high.

"What happened?" Kipper signed. "What was that?"

Jenny signed, "I think it was Ordol. He blasted us with ink."

Through the clearing murk, Kipper saw that most of the crew had swum directly to their stations. Captain Cod still floated at the center of the bridge. He signed, "Did anyone see which way Ordol went? We need him. Everyone fan out and look. Except you—" He pointed at Kipper. "I need to talk with you."

Otters summersaulted and dove away, streaming out of the bridge, until only Captain Cod, Kipper, and Emily, lurking at the arch of the door into the bridge, were left. Emily's tentacles writhed nervously, and her skin pigmentation had taken on rose-colored rings, scattered like leopard spots over her taupe body.

As Captain Cod began signing, Kipper signed simultaneously. Her paws spelled out, "Captain, I want to stay and fight."

His paws signed, moving much faster than hers, "Kipper, we've stumbled our way into a war. When back-up arrives from the asteroid belt, I think we otters can make a good showing, but an early victory is not a decisive end. If we want to win this war, we'll need back-up from more than the other otters in space. We'll need the support of Earth."

Kipper's paws trailed to a stop, and her ears slowly lowered. With small, slow motions, she signed, "I can't give you the support of Earth. I... have no power there."

Captain Cod signed, "You need to be a hero, Kipper. You need to return to Earth victorious—the only cat that was up here to make a difference when New Persia was in need. You need to shepherd home two-hundred refugees who would have died without you. You need to be an example for all the cats and dogs on Earth."

Kipper shook her head, but she knew the captain wouldn't back down. He might even be right. It made her mind spin that the foolish buffoon she was used to had turned into a clear-thinking military leader when the situation called for it. She hadn't known Captain Cod had this in him. This was why he inspired so much loyalty in his crew.

"How shall I select the refugees?" Kipper signed, resigning herself to submission.

"Find a leader you can work with—not the top cat. The top cat should stay behind to run New Persia until this battle is resolved." Captain Cod chewed his whiskers, showing some of his old buffoonish side, but it was belied by the cool-headed wisdom he imparted. "You'll want to take as many kittens as you can, but you'll need to have enough adults to keep them in line." More whisker chewing. "Give preference to nursing mothers, adults that have experience with kitten-care, and adults who won't be strong enough to defend themselves and survive the raptor onslaught if left behind."

Watching Captain Cod sign these instructions, the reality of what Kipper was about to face began to feel terribly *real* to her. With sinking ears, she signed, "Right. Kittens and elderly." The shape of those words on her paws made her think about all the cats who wouldn't fit that description. All the cats who would be left behind.

The captain saw her flagging spirits and gave her a friendly cuff to the chin, followed by signing, "Buck up, crewman. Jumpin' jaybirds will tap dance to paw-paw music before we let those raptors tear us down."

Visions of blue-crested birds with top hats and tap shoes pirouetted through Kipper's head, making her wonder whether this expression might be more believable than the *swimming ostriches* that so often colored the captain's language. She wished, like an ostrich, she could bury her head in the sand. Instead, she signed, "I guess we need to find Ordol, so that I can be ready for the flight down to New Persia."

At that, the captain gave a whiskery frown. "That blasted

coward! We're going to need him as a tactical expert, and, right now, he's holding the whole mission up!"

Given Ordol's current behavior, Kipper wasn't sure she wanted to trust him with the controls of *Brighton's Destiny*—or any mechanical device, let alone a spaceship that the future of New Persia and all her friends hinged upon.

Emily waved her tentacles to draw the captain's and Kipper's attention.

"Ordol's system is still in shock from spending so much time out of water. He needs more time to recover," Emily signed. "I have experience piloting space ships." A quiver of whiteness flushed over Emily's body, starting at her mantle and ending at her tentacle tips. It was brief, and then she returned to a healthy tan with rose-colored rings. Emily was scared, but who wasn't right now?

"Not raptor ships," Captain Cod pointed out.

Kipper signed at the same time, "I'll take a pilot who's volunteering—and who speaks in Standard Swimmer's Sign— over a wildcard who squirted me with ink like Ordol any day."

After a steady stare, the captain nodded his head gravely. "Your call," he signed. "That gives the rest of us more time to find what nook or cranny Ordol's insinuated himself into. Now get going, and start familiarizing yourself with that ship! I'll expect you to disembark as soon as we reach the orbit of Europa —that way you can finish the approach behind us, shielded by our diversion."

Captain Cod looked brave, but the tremble in his whiskers gave him away. Kipper put a paw up as if to shake his hand, but he threw both of his short arms around her shoulders, encircling her in a bushy-furred embrace.

Next he turned to Emily, who approached him with tentacles writhing in an ornate, eight-armed goodbye hug. Captain Cod broke away and signed, "Good luck, officers. You're the best chef and ship's spy we've ever had." At that he pirouetted away to face the front of the bridge where he floated, framed in the star-studded blackness of the main viewscreen.

Kipper thought, perhaps, the presence of the oxo-agua had hidden the trails of a tear down the captain's cheek fur. The stinging in her eyes suggested that it might also be masking a few of her own. She turned away too, willing herself to stay strong. Life was surreal, and she felt buffeted about.

Mere months ago, she'd been a simple secretary, moving from office to office, wherever her temp job took her. Yet, then, her life had been stable, predictable, and profoundly safe. She hadn't felt that way back then, but, looking back, she could see it now. Her fears back then were so small, nearly petty, compared to the fears that tightened her throat, already lodged with oxo-agua, and threatened to drown her now.

"Come on," Kipper signed to Emily. "Let's go see what we can figure out about my spaceship." Kipper stretched her paws out, spreading her toes into an ineffective doggy-paddle.

Emily wrapped three of her tentacles around Kipper's wrists and jetted herself forward by expelling a blast of oxo-agua from her siphon. Held firmly in Emily's grasp, Kipper was pulled along for the ride. Emily propelled them through the corridors of the ship, heading for the cargo bay where *Brighton's Destiny* had been parked.

Emily used her free tentacles to sign to Kipper. "*Your* ship?"

Emily adjusted her grip on Kipper, replacing the three tentacles around Kipper's wrists with a single one, snaked under Kipper's arm and around her back. This freed Kipper up to answer, signing with her paws, "Captain Cod says, I found it, it's mine. Law of the space pirates or something. Does that make me a captain?"

Kipper saw the tips of Emily's free tentacles wriggle in laughter, but then she signed, "At your command, Captain Kipper."

Shortly thereafter, Emily unhanded Kipper, removing her

suckered grasp from the cat's back. They had arrived in the cargo bay, and the strange double-winged ship sat enigmatically before them. Correction: *Kipper's* funny little double-winged ship. She shook her head, trying to wrap her mind around that idea. A couple months ago, Kipper couldn't even afford the ticket to ride the space elevator, and now she owned her own spaceship.

If only she weren't about to fly the same spaceship into the opening battle of what might well become a worldwide—if not solar system-wide—war.

CHAPTER 26
EARTH

While Kipper contemplated the opening moves of the interplanetary war facing them all, Trudith was hard at work trying to affect the war's mid-game by laying the groundwork for putting another Brighton at the forefront of the action.

So far, she had called a meeting of her scramball team and spent the morning scurrying around, gathering supplies for hosting the team properly at her apartment. Pork rind curls, Munchy-Crunchy peanut butter balls, and beef sticks sufficed for snacks. A good spread of snacks could put any group of dogs into an agreeable mood. Well, almost any group of dogs—all those Shelties at their big Sheltie meeting hadn't seemed too agreeable, and their food had been super fancy.

Scramball stadium fare would have to do here. It was all Trudith could scrounge up in her price range on short notice.

Trudith arranged all the furniture in her apartment— a couple dining chairs and a futon—to face her computer, and she loaded the video files so they'd be ready when her teammates got there. She had a whole pitch planned in her head, and she rehearsed it over and over again, while going about nervously fluffing and rearranging her various throw pillows until her teammates arrived.

Joey got there first. He liked to take credit for bringing Trudith back into the team, so she knew she could count on him to show early. Besides, his work as a goon kept him busy at night more than the afternoons. A number of the others wouldn't be able to make it until after work.

They started to filter in after Trudith and Joey had had time to get deeply into an argument about whether local, live scramball games or the big, televised games featuring world class players were more exciting. Trudith liked the visceral feel of watching a game unfold right in front of her. She liked the air in her nose, smelling the currents of the very wind that played across the field. She liked to feel like she could just jump up and join right in, even though she knew better than to actually do that.

Joey, on the other paw, liked knowing that the players he was watching, even if they were only images on a sterile screen, were the most agile, adept, clever scramball players on the entire planet. He felt like he learned new things about scramball, new ways of seeing it and new ways of playing it, just by watching them.

Trudith could understand that, but it still wasn't the same as watching a match in person.

Somewhere in the middle of their argument, the rest of the team had arrived. Although he wasn't on the team, Trudith had invited Keith, too. She told herself that she invited him because his connection to Senator Morrison could be useful, and, besides, he had expressed interest in joining her scramball team. However, the way her heart sped up when she saw him, and she felt suddenly both calmer and more nervous at the same time, made Trudith realize those reasons were just excuses.

She wanted to see him again, and she was taking a huge risk

including him in this campaign. What if he went straight to Morrison? What if he... well, actually, going straight to Morrison was probably about the worst he could do.

Trudith didn't think he would do that.

The whole scramball team was here now: Joey paced around the room gesticulating; the salt-and-pepper furred poodle in advertising sat on the futon, squeezed tight with a couple other dogs, mostly the smaller members; and the dining chairs had been claimed by some of the biggest dogs on the team. Keith, possibly the tallest dog in the room, draped himself over one of the dining chairs, which he'd turned backwards so he could lean forward with his arms resting on its back.

Trudith woofed a booming bark. "Hey guys!" Her voice came out louder than she meant it to, cutting right through a raucous argument over which pro-scramball team was best.

After a brief pause and glances in Trudith's direction, most of the scramball players went back to barking about their favorite teams. If Trudith had been talking to Petra and Alistair, she'd have their complete, annoyed, ears-flat-back attention after that booming bark. Cats don't like noise the way that dogs do.

Trudith woofed again, shouting even louder this time. "Guys! We've got to talk about this thing! This thing I called you here for!" She kept woofing, "Hey guys!" and "C'mon guys!" until the rest of the barking actually quieted down.

"That's better," she said. It was so much easier to get cats' attention! Walking over to her computer, Trudith started up the video of herself and Kipper. She hadn't done any editing yet—just spliced the two pieces together.

As it played, the scramball team watched. One of the small-breed dogs on the futon barked out, "That's the cat on the otter spaceship out around Jupiter, right?" Several dogs answered in the affirmative. One added the comment, "That's one brave cat. I wouldn't want to be on a spaceship near Jupiter right now."

When it was over, Trudith looked over her teammates, and said, "I know we don't talk about politics much as a team—"

A salt-and-pepper furred poodle named Dahlia interjected, "Politics are bad for scramball. We don't need to agree on government regulations to play sport."

Trudith's heart sank. Dahlia was the dog whose support—and advertising expertise—she needed most in this room, other than Keith's. She guessed from Dahlia's steely gaze that they weren't likely to share a lot of political views. Why else would Dahlia feel the need to interrupt and waylay her presentation?

Trudith soldiered on, saying "—but things are different now. This isn't a time for worrying about political parties and affiliations." She drew a deep breath. "I don't know how much attention you've all been paying, but there's a war happening in our solar system."

Joey barked, "That's just the otters."

Keith said, in a steady, commanding woof, "For now."

Other dogs looked at him. Some of them, including Joey, looked worried. Dahlia looked annoyed.

"It's not just otters," Trudith barked. "It's a whole colony of cats, too."

Dahlia barked, "It's a bunch of *spacers*. If they'd stayed down here on Earth, in the home the First Race left for us—"

Angry, Trudith barked, "Then what? They'd be safe from being attacked by vicious raptor aliens from Jupiter?"

The room fell silent, except for some awkward shuffling of feet and shifting of weight. In the heat of all the barking, Trudith had forgotten that she and Petra were the only ones on Earth who knew about the raptors. Trudith wasn't sure if she'd scared her teammates, or if they were questioning her sanity.

"Raptor aliens?" Keith asked.

Trudith looked down at her hind paws, footpads splayed on the floor. She clicked her claws a few times against the wooden floor in a soothing rhythm. "Yeah, raptor aliens," she barked, without looking up. "We found out this morning. That cat—" Trudith pointed at the computer screen, where the video of Kipper had so recently played. "She was on one of their ships last night, and now—" Trudith choked up, her voice catching. "Now she's probably fighting them."

The room was utterly silent this time. No movement. Nothing.

"She's my best friend," Trudith said. "And she's fighting raptors to save those cats on Europa. I don't know if I'll ever hear from her again." Trudith hadn't meant to call her scramball team together to hear her talk about how much she missed Kipper. She didn't mean to be crying in front of them. All she wanted to do was convince them of how important it all was. Maybe she wasn't ready to be doing this.

Trudith heard Keith clear his throat and step up from his chair. "Protecting and stewarding the other races is what the First Race would want us to do," he said. "It's what this brave cat is doing, and it's what all dogs are supposed to do too."

Trudith felt weird hearing Keith quote First Race doctrine. The more time she spent with the Brighton cats, the more distanced she felt from those dogmatic beliefs, but he was right. First Race doctrine called for dogs to protect and steward cats— and otters and all the other uplifted species—regardless of whether they were on Earth or up in space. And maybe that's what a traditional dog like Dahlia needed to hear.

"Look," Trudith said, "I wouldn't ask you to even vote for Alistair—even though that's kind of my job, working for him—if it weren't for what's happening in the solar system right now. We need a leader we can trust to carry us through a *war*."

"But a cat???" Dahlia barked, an unnaturally high pitch to her voice.

"It's not about voting for a cat," Trudith said. "It's about making sure our *planet* has a leader you can trust with your whole heart."

Trudith looked straight at Dahlia. One pair of brown eyes staring down another. For a moment, it looked like Dahlia had something more to say, but then she shut her muzzle and looked away.

"I trust Alistair that way," Trudith said. "Are there any politicians that any of you trust like that? With your whole heart?"

Some of the dogs in the room looked excited by Trudith's words; others looked away like Dahlia. None of them offered up any names.

Finally, Keith said, "No, I don't trust any politicians like that, and I work for the one who's most likely to be our next president."

That got an uncomfortable stir from the room, along with a few confused looks. Most of the team probably didn't know who Keith was yet.

"This is Keith," Trudith said, gesturing to him with her paw. "He works for Senator Morrison."

Dahlia's face snapped back, nose pointing at Keith. "What's wrong with Morrison?" she barked. "I vote for Morrison."

"No comment," Keith said, looking supremely uncomfortable. Perhaps he realized that he'd said too much. He did still have a job to look out for.

Dahlia wouldn't let it go, though. She began giving a run down of all Senator Morrison's accomplishments, all the policies he'd written into law, all the good she believed he was doing.

Keith put up his paws. "Hey, hey," he said, barking over Dahlia's tirade. "I didn't say anything about Senator Morrison's policies. I think he's done great work." Dahlia began to simmer down, and Keith continued. "He's a great politician, but he's a politician. And I *don't* trust him with my whole heart. That's all I said."

With a sneer on her muzzle, Dahlia said, "But you trust this *cat?*"

"Actually, I haven't really met Alistair Brighton," Keith said.

Dahlia scoffed, as if Keith has just proved her point for her.

"But," he said, holding up a paw, "I trust Trudith. And I've barely even known her two days." He looked around the room, catching the eyes of every dog he could. "I'm guessing you all know her a lot better."

A lot of eyes turned to stare at Trudith, measuring her up, remembering everything they could about her. Trudith had been a member of this scramball team, on and off, for years. Almost every dog on it had turned to her at one point or another for help through hard times, and they'd all seen the way that she'd changed since she'd met Kipper and begun working for Alistair.

She was a good dog.

And she felt supremely uncomfortable under such scrutiny.

Dahlia narrowed her eyes, but then she sighed. Other dogs looked nervously at her, waiting to see if she had more argument in her. Eventually, Joey hazarded, "If Trudith says this cat she works for is the leader we need right now, then I'm with her."

A couple dogs barked assent. Dahlia wasn't among them, but at least she wasn't arguing any more. Trudith wasn't sure that would be enough. She really needed Dahlia's advertising expertise.

Keith must have picked up on the continued tension between Trudith and Dahlia. He turned to Dahlia and said in a low woof, "We have a responsibility as dogs. A responsibility to the First Race to make sure that their world is here for them, with all their uplifted children, waiting for them when they return." His voice was so serious, it made Trudith's heart flutter. "That means," he said, "supporting the very best leader we can in these dangerous times. Regardless of whether that leader is a dog or a cat."

Dahlia looked abashed.

Hearing Keith say those words with such conviction, Trudith almost believed that the First Race really would return to them some day, and she wouldn't call herself a believer. Dahlia clearly was, and Keith's words had their intended effect on her.

Dahlia's muzzle was tight, but she lowered her head in submission. "What can we do to help?" she said.

CHAPTER 27
JUPITER SYSTEM

While the dogs of Trudith's scramball team worked out their plans to elect a *President* Brighton, the newly minted *Captain* Brighton discovered the terrors of her own command inside the cramped, foreign vessel she could now call her own.

Spinning like a whirligig, the two winged ship *Brighton's Destiny* disembarked from the *Jolly Barracuda's* cargo bay. After a few dizzying swerves, the vessel straightened into a slow arced course for Europa. From inside, Kipper watched the *Jolly Barracuda*, the ship that had been her home for many months now, barrel past on a fast, straight course to the same destination.

Kipper might have felt lonely watching the *Jolly Barracuda* fly into a darkness that surpassed night, but the weight on her shoulders let her know she was not alone.

Captain Brighton's only crew, Emily, clung to her spacesuit clad shoulders. Kipper could see Emily's tentacles through the faceplate of her helmet. Orange-red and muscular, Emily's tentacles waved above her, reaching past her, and fumbled with the alien control panels. Emily wore a spacesuit too, although it clung invisibly to her writhing appendages looking more like a layer of saran wrap than anything that could truly protect her from the ravages of space.

The weight of Emily was substantial on Kipper's back. Although Emily's body was slight, the reverse-SCUBA gear she wore to keep her breathing was quite heavy. Neither captain nor crew was very comfortable. Despite the emptiness of space surrounding them, the small pocket of machinery that transported and protected them felt extremely tight.

Regardless, neither of them looked forward to getting out. That would only mean their friends were busy battling for their lives, while Kipper and Emily needed to begin triage for the colonists of New Persia, deciding who would live and who would be left to fight and possibly die.

Kipper and Emily couldn't see each other's faces, but they could still communicate by signing. A few tests before take-off had shown that Emily could understand Kipper's paws, even muffled as they were by the spacesuit gloves.

Kipper wanted to say something, exchange words of comfort, but she didn't believe anything comforting she could say right now. She doubted Emily had any comfort of her own to offer. Before they'd launched, Emily had fortified herself, replacing her white-skinned pallor of late with the ruddy orange she sported now. The skin between her eyes had tightened in an expression that Kipper understood to mean seriousness and extreme concentration.

Kipper knew Emily was deathly frightened of the raptors. The bravery Emily displayed in agreeing to pilot *Brighton's Destiny* awed and inspired Kipper. She hoped she would be as brave when she found herself face to face with emotionally crippling decisions about which kittens to take on the *Jolly Barracuda* with her and which to leave behind. The prospect of those choices daunted her, making her head feel light and her chest tight.

To stave off the haunting visages of ghost kittens, pleading not to be separated from their mothers, Kipper focused her eyes on the pale face of Europa. Surrounded by glittering stars, the moon's face was white and cracked, smoother than Earth's moon except for the brown lines tracing irregular patterns on its surface. A dirty snowball. It hardly looked like a place to live, let alone a place worth fighting for.

Europa grew larger on the viewscreen, and Kipper began to look for signs of the New Persia colony. She narrowed her eyes, straining to see, but she couldn't make out anything in the shining ice. As they rounded on Europa's night side, the sun rose over the ice, glaring in her eyes and casting the ice a ruddy gray, lit mainly by Jupiter's reflected light. Kipper noticed a dim glow on the horizon.

Movement caught her eye, and Kipper recognized the *Jolly Barracuda's* tiny outline, silhouetted against the moon's surface. Two dark pinecones chased the *Barracuda*. Beyond them, the unnatural lines and lights of colonization shimmered into view, barely visible on the horizon of gray ice.

The *Jolly Barracuda* evaded the pinecone ships, moving faster and changing direction with more agility than they could. Kipper lost sight of the otter ship as it flew away from Europa, but she counted three, four, five more pinecones chasing her. Each of them also disappeared into the darkness.

Kipper drew a deep breath. It came in raggedly between her fangs. Her whiskers tingled. Those ships could have stayed, making her descent on the *Brighton's Destiny* more dangerous. Instead they chased her friends. Kipper supposed that was better? The difference between worse and worst is an intellectual one. Both the idea of facing those raptor ships herself and the idea of them pursuing the *Jolly Barracuda* left her numb.

As *Brighton's Destiny* approached the glow on Europa's horizon, bright specks of light became more visible. They grew until Kipper could make out the shapes of domes and buildings in the pattern of bright and shadow—a city in this bleak landscape of ice, millions of miles from feline-kind's original terrestrial cradle —New Persia, the home of arrogant cats, desperately in need of otter-kind's help.

And Kipper's help.

And Emily's.

At that moment, it was Emily who made all the difference. Kipper couldn't read the controls, but Emily had some ability to read them as the raptor language shared traits with that of the octopus empire, and Emily saw something intriguing on the readouts.

New Persia grew beneath them as their ship barreled toward the icy surface. Kipper tried to make sense of it, but it was strange and small and moving fast. *Brighton's Destiny* leveled out, flying along, above the city and beyond. New Persia passed beneath them as the *Brighton's Destiny* flew straight on past. "What are you doing?" Kipper signed. "Don't you know how to land? Are you looping around?" Kipper twisted her helmeted head about, straining to see Emily, even though she knew she didn't need to.

Emily lowered a pair of tentacles to within Kipper's visual range and signed with their sinuous tips, "New plan. There's something we need to check out."

For being a captain, Kipper didn't feel in control of her vessel. She couldn't read the displays, had no clue what her one crewmember was up to, and could see nothing worth checking out on the bleak beige horizon of cracked ice stretching out ahead of them.

Behind them lay a sparkling city of translucent domes and right-angled sky scrapers. Curves and lines that implied civilization. Shapes that meant *cats are here*. Cats who need help.

The muscles controlling Kipper's claws tightened. She wanted to turn the spaceship around and take it back to New Persia, but she could already see the ground approaching them at an alarming rate. Emily was bringing *Brighton's Destiny* down for a landing in this middle-of-nowhere.

The screeching sensation of metal scraping along ice—like claws on a blackboard—made Kipper cringe. A crack that she felt more than heard sent terror through her body, out to the very tips of her whiskers. Kipper feared for her vessel and herself. She was glad she was wearing a spacesuit. It was not an elegant landing. *Brighton's Destiny* was sliding, uncontrolled, across the ice.

By the time *Brighton's Destiny* reached a full stop, Kipper had to peel herself off the forward control panels. She felt bruised all over, and her body prickled with the sensation of her fluffed out fur. She had grave concerns about whether the spaceship would still be flight worthy. *Was it even in one piece? What had that crack been? If it couldn't take off again, would she and Emily be stranded here?* Kipper didn't know how far they had flown past New Persia, but she was sure it was a lot farther than they could hike back with only the oxygen in their spacesuit air tanks.

Kipper didn't like the idea of being a fool that Captain Cod would have to come rescue, wasting valuable time that could be spent saving kittens from raptors.

With a grumble in her throat, Kipper signed angrily, "What was that?!" Her paws kept gesturing, signing accusatory sentences in a substitute for shouting.

Emily, however, paid no heed. She shifted her weight, lifting off of Kipper's shoulders, and dropping herself in a careful fall to the floor. Tentacles pressed outward, bracing against the walls of the small spaceship hold as her center of weight lowered down. Then, she reached a tentacle back up, twisted a few knobs, pressed a few buttons, and the hatch to the tiny airlock opened.

Kipper had no option but to follow. She didn't know how to work the airlock hatch herself, and she didn't want to get trapped inside, alone.

The first hatch closed behind Kipper, and the exterior hatch opened only moments later, revealing dun colored ice shining dully in the reddish light. Kipper stepped gingerly onto the ice.

Looking up, she saw Jupiter straight above, a gibbous ball of orange and white lace in the black sky. Two other moons, a tiny crescent just above the horizon and a yellowed half-circle near Jupiter, decorated the blackness. Beneath that vault of the heavens, *Brighton's Destiny* lay in a rut of ice, one wing angled at forty-five degrees; the other snapped and dangling from a twisted metal joint.

The whole scene was breathtaking and heartbreaking.

Before Kipper could cry too many tears, though, Emily crawled out onto the ice. Her tentacles flushed crimson, like bloody worms writhing on the ice, pulling her body erratically forward. Kipper had never seen the graceful, elegant Emily move so awkwardly. Although, gravity was light on Europa, her body —without bones or a buoyant liquid atmosphere—was all muscle squashed to the ground. Yet, she still moved strangely quickly, and Kipper found herself fast-walking to keep up.

Kipper wanted to ask where they were going, but Emily wouldn't see her paws. She followed Emily mutely through the desolate landscape, quietly seething over the destruction of her ship and doing everything she could to deny the relief she felt at being saved from facing the harsh reality of cats and kittens dying in New Persia.

The fact that Kipper was stranded in an ice desert out of sight of that destruction didn't make it any less real, but it felt less real. The pit of her stomach, ready to fill with twisting agony and emotion, was grateful for the mere emptiness and confusion she felt here.

In this surreal landscape, Kipper didn't feel like an adult cat with responsibilities and people relying on her. She felt like the tiny tabby kitten she had once been in the cattery at home, too small to shoulder the burdens laid upon her, and merely amazed by the wonder of space yawning above her. *How could this be real?*

How had the years passed in such a way to bring her here, where Jupiter and its moons hung above her? Kipper felt giddy, and she wondered whether she getting enough oxygen from her spacesuit. She hoped that she wasn't growing delirious from oxygen deprivation.

Kipper wasn't practiced with her spacesuit, but she tried to read the life support displays inside her helmet while continuing to trot after Emily at a good clip.

The displays read in the safe levels, but the distraction of looking at them caused Kipper to trip. She slid forward on the ice, front paws flailing to catch herself. When Kipper got herself righted, four paws on the ground, she looked back to see Emily. Had it been Emily's tentacles that had tripped her when the octopus stopped?

Emily pointed her tentacles, like force lines on a magnet diagram, toward a place on the ground between them. Kipper looked down to see that the ground she crouched on was smooth—even smoother than the ice. Darkened by their shadows, it was hard to make out, so Kipper flipped on her helmet light.

Under her paws, a metal plate shone in the pool of light from her helmet. Turning her head to see the extent of the metal, Kipper saw it extended several yards further in all directions. There was a lip of several inches around the edges, tracing out a strange, artificial circle of silver recessed in the natural, dun color of the ice.

Where Emily pointed—in the middle of the metal plate under them—there was a hemisphere of metal, a round dome about the size of a scramball. Its surface was dented with smaller circles, arranged in a swirling pattern, diminishing in size as they curved in toward the center.

It was beautiful and mysterious.

Then Emily curled one of her tentacles, holding it with flared sucker discs, carefully above the hemisphere. The swirling pattern on the hemisphere perfectly matched the curve of her tentacle; the diminishing circles matched her sucker discs—large at the base of her arm, but as tiny as the tip of a claw at her slender tentacle tip.

Kipper saw a quiver in Emily's tentacular arm as she held it there. Kipper didn't know what would happen if she pressed down on that hemisphere, and she suspected Emily didn't know either. It was clearly what had drawn Emily to bring them here. Whatever this was, the displays on *Brighton's Destiny* must have told Emily about it. It must be raptor technology.

"Go ahead," Kipper signed with spacesuited hands.

Emily's yellow eyes with their rectangular pupils stared at her from within the bulb of helmet that fit over Emily's octopus face and bulbous mantle. Their eyes locked together, and Kipper signed the words again, the motions of her paws small as if whispering.

Emily lowered her tentacle into the spiral indentation and pressed down the hemisphere. It receded into the flat metal beneath them, and then the ground began to hum.

CHAPTER 28
EUROPA

n the middle of the Europan ice desert, many miles beyond New Persia and under the watchful eye of Jupiter's great red spot, Kipper and Emily sank into the moon's interior on an old, abandoned elevator. The shaft rose up around them, shrinking the circle of sky they could see. They deeper they sank, the smaller it got. Kipper turned off her helmet light and stared up at the receding stars. Eventually, a metal iris closed above them, sealing them into the darkness.

The vibrating hum beneath Kipper's feet rose and fell in pitch until Kipper's paws grew numb to the sensation. She wondered how long the elevator would descend. She wondered if it would open on raptor guards, holding blaster weapons at the ready in their many mind-controlled tentacles. Could this be a trap or would she and Emily simply find themselves stuck in a relic of technology, enough juice left to start the elevator running but otherwise dead?

The elevator kathunked then stopped humming. Nothing happened for long enough to make Kipper's heart race. She was sure that the elevator had lowered her to an alien grave. No one would come for them. The *Jolly Barracuda* would be unable to find them, and the elevator would never start again.

With her ears flattened inside her helmet, Kipper fumbled to turn on her helmet light. Before she succeeded, the light around her changed, and Kipper felt sure her eyes were playing tricks on her.

A round mouth of lighter gray had opened up before her. Inside that gray, Kipper thought she could see lights moving and dancing. Tiny sparkles dotted her vision, like stars, or maybe only the starbursts that clouded her vision if she closed her eyes, squeezing both layers of eyelids tight.

But her eyes were open, and the lights continued to dance.

Kipper felt movement at her foot, and she looked down to see Emily crawling past. Her eyes had adjusted to the darkness, and there was enough light, barely, to make out the snaky shape of tentacles pulling themselves one over the other. Kipper decided to leave her helmet light off.

Kipper followed Emily out of the elevator, but she had to crouch down. The corridor was too low, even for a cat. Clearly, this was not a raptor base after all. With their greater stature, the raptors wouldn't have fit in these tunnels.

Kipper followed Emily down the tunnel, marveling at the ease with which the octopus pulled herself forward. The rounded, tubular shape of the tunnel leant itself perfectly to her many-armed, radial form.

As Kipper crawled through the tunnel, she realized the dancing lights were embedded in the material of the walls. Wherever she put her paws and wherever Emily's tentacles touched them, the walls blossomed with pinpricks of light.

It was hard to be sure in the low gravity, but Kipper didn't think the tunnel had a level floor. One moment she was crawling uphill; the next moment, the tunnel sloped downward and she strained not to slide forward into Emily.

Between the changing angle of the tunnel and the shape of Emily's body in front of her, Kipper couldn't see to the end of the corridor. She was surprised when Emily's silhouetted shape suddenly disappeared ahead of her. Kipper crawled cautiously forward, thankful that the tunnel was angled uphill here. She slid her paws to make sure they kept solid ground beneath them. When Kipper's forepaws felt the lip of the corridor, she leaned forward.

Kipper strained her eyes to make sense of the varying levels of grayness in front of her. She wanted to taste the space with the vibration of her whiskers and hear it with the turn of her ears. It would have been much easier to understand it that way, but her whiskers were trapped, uselessly inside her space helmet, and the only sounds her ears could hear were the echoes of her own blood rushing through her body and the muteness of her spacesuit radio.

She couldn't talk to Emily over the radio, and she didn't expect to hear from the *Jolly Barracuda* until they'd finished running the raptors a merry chase.

Kipper could feel the temptation of defeatism, but her body was too filled with anxious adrenaline to slump into that kind of depression. There had to be something useful here. Kipper redoubled her efforts to understand the space in front of her. She peered into the grayness looking for Emily. As she stared, vertical and horizontal lines of black resolved. They looked like poles, interlacing a large open space. Kipper was tempted to turn on her helmet light, but it would have only illuminated a small swath of the space, and then her eyes would lose their adjustment to the darkness.

As far as Kipper could tell, the corridor opened near the top of a large room. She thought she could see other openings riddling the walls of that room, so perhaps there were other corridors around it. The poles made no sense to her.

Then she spotted Emily, swinging easily from one pole to the next in the low Europa gravity. Her darkened silhouette gracefully extended tentacles, wrapping half of them around a new pole while the other half still clung to the last one, moving ever downward through the room. The span of her tentacles was marvelous. Kipper never saw Emily stretch out so fully in her little kitchen on the *Jolly Barracuda*. Kipper thought of her as small, and in the tight corridor Emily had been. In this wide space, Emily's long tentacles unfurled to reveal an arm span Kipper had never guessed at.

Emily navigated the poles in this room as fluidly as the otters swam through their artificial rivers on Deep Sky Anchor. It was a beautiful and mesmerizing sight. It left no doubt in Kipper's mind: this space had been built for octopi. Perhaps *by octopi?*

Trusting Emily's octopus instinct in this environment, Kipper crawled forward, extending her torso over the lip of the tunnel, and reached for the nearest pole. She didn't have the arm span necessary to swing between them like Emily. However, Emily headed to the bottom of the room, and Kipper figured she could, at least, slide down a pole. Hopefully, Emily would help her whenever it came time to climb back up. She didn't know if her spacesuited paws would have the grip necessary for that.

Like a firefighter, Kipper grabbed the nearest pole with her forepaws, crisscrossed her hindpaws loosely around it, and slid down. In the low gravity, she drifted rather than plummeted. Her tail only fluffed out a little at the freefall sensation of falling through the dark.

Kipper's paws touched ground, and she looked around at the bottom of this vast room. The ground had an uneven, honeycomb shape. It sloped down into alcoves large enough to hold several cats like her—or perhaps a comfortably stretched out octopus? Between the alcoves, the ground raised into ridges wide enough for her to balance on carefully.

Most of the poles rose out of the ridges, stretching upward from those high points toward the ceiling. Thus, Kipper had touched down at a high point. She squinted into the nearest honeycomb alcove, but she couldn't make out much in the darkness. She would need to get closer. Instead of climbing into the nearest one, though, Kipper decided to continue following Emily.

A dim trail of light in the material of the ground traced the path Emily had followed, over and through the various alcoves. Kipper tried to balance her way along the ridge of high ground between the alcoves, using an occasional pole to steady her, but she ended up finding it easier to climb in and out of the alcoves. A trail of lit up boot prints followed her.

Many of the alcoves in the honeycomb floor that Kipper climbed through seemed to host alien control panels of some sort. Smooth, dark screens, and collections of knobs, switches, and buttons. Kipper didn't stop to look at them closely, but when she caught up with Emily she could tell that Emily had chosen to ensconce herself in the alcove with far and away the most elaborate control panels.

The alcove curved around Emily, and it was indeed the perfect size for her tentacles to comfortably stretch out and reach control panels in every direction around her, all three-hundred-and-sixty degrees. Emily contorted her tentacles, making room for Kipper to climb in beside her.

"Feel at home?" Kipper signed.

Emily's eyes stared at her through the darkness. Yellow and alien. Emily had never seemed so much like an alien entity to Kipper as she did at that moment.

Then she moved her tentacles in the familiar sign language they shared with the otters: "What do you mean?"

Kipper found it comforting to think that Emily might find this sunken base under the surface of Europa as mysterious and alien as she did. Even if it did look like it had built perfectly to the specifications of Emily's tentacled body.

Kipper signed, "I think this place was built by octopi."

Emily blinked. Twice. Then signed, "I can read some of the writing in these computers."

Kipper looked at the panels surrounding them. She hadn't noticed writing on them. They were lit up with moving squiggles. She supposed it could be writing. "Is it octopus writing?"

"Yes," Emily signed. "It's very ancient, but I studied some when I was a mother."

Kipper and Emily had discussed the different meaning of the word "mother" in the octopus culture before. Emily was referring to the time when she was still fertile, before she'd laid her clutch of eggs, done the unthinkable for a female—namely, surviving their maturation—and become an outcast who lived among otters. Perhaps it shouldn't surprise Kipper that Emily didn't feel at home in a world built for octopi. She hadn't felt at home among the octopi living under Earth's oceans either.

"Can you tell what any of these controls do?" Kipper signed.

"I'm a chef," Emily signed. "Not a physicist. And this looks like physics."

Kipper peered at the squiggles. They writhed and danced, little worms of light, playing with her vision. They didn't look like physics, not to her, but, if they did to Emily, then maybe they were. "You're not a pilot either," Kipper signed. "But you got us here. Now, if you can figure out what this place is... Maybe turn on some life support? I dunno, but there are cats dying up there on the surface, and there must be some way we can use this place to help them. Maybe as a bunker to shelter refugees from the raptor attacks?"

The rectangular pupils of Emily's eyes narrowed: a look of determination, recognizable across species. "Aye, captain," she signed, a slightly mirthful writhe in her tentacles at the use of Kipper's newly earned title. Then all eight of her appendages shot into action, reaching around Kipper, working the control panels in every direction. The tendril thin tips of her tentacles traced out delicate squiggles of light, writing her own commands in this octopus language, while the larger sucker discs at the trunks of her arms worked dials and switches. It was amazing and wonderful how much her eight tentacles could do at once.

Kipper had always been impressed by the way that Emily's arms flew into action, wielding knives, kneading dough, cooking an entire meal and several appetizers in the *Jolly Barracuda* kitchen at once. This was the same but with alien computer consoles, and all Kipper could do was stand there and watch, trying not to worry about the kittens in New Persia.

CHAPTER 29
EARTH

I n the hidden base on Europa, the minutes passed like hours, but back on Earth the hours passed like minutes. Trudith's apartment had become the spontaneous headquarters for her scramball team's efforts. Dahlia and several of the other dogs, at Trudith's request, had brought laptop computers with them. Now they crouched around the different computer screens haphazardly arranged on the coffee table. Clips of Kipper played on all the screens.

Trudith had opened up the entire video history of conversations she'd had with Kipper to the team, and they combed through them, scene by scene, looking for snatches of conversations, brief phrases, that could be used in their campaign.

Of course, the crowning jewel of all the clips would still be the clip where Kipper told everyone to "vote for Brighton." Dahlia believed Kipper's word would carry more weight if they came at the end of a longer campaign. Dahlia meant to release a series of short videos to increasingly prominent news sources. The first ones would be leaked to the public, as if they were meant to be kept underground. By the end, top news channels would be clamoring for exclusive first access.

Each video in the series would close on a black screen that

read, *"Kipper Brighton: The Hero of Europa,"* and would feature short snatches of Kipper and Trudith's conversations together. Mere moments. The briefest moments, chosen carefully to leave the viewers wanting more of Kipper, just the way that Trudith always did.

Dahlia meant to make the disenfranchised cats and underdogs of Earth love Kipper. Then, in the last video, Kipper would tell them how to vote, and the final black screen would read,

"Kipper Brighton: The Hero of Europa
Alistair Brighton: The Hero of Earth?"

Trudith didn't know if Dahlia's advertising campaign would work, but it gave her chills to hear Kipper's voice repeating lines of their conversations over and over again from each of the computers. She also noticed as the afternoon progressed into evening, more and more of her teammates asked her questions about Kipper. They wanted to hear the stories about the Hero of Europa.

The most important story about her hadn't ended yet. Trudith began to realize that Kipper wasn't carrying only her own burdens on her shoulders but also the weight of Alistair's election. If Kipper could save all those cats on Europa, she really would be a hero, and Alistair could easily ride the wave of her success into office.

If she didn't...

Trudith shuddered. She couldn't think about her friend not coming home.

CHAPTER 30
EUROPA

For all the responsibility hanging on her shoulders, Kipper stood uselessly in the dark, watching Emily's spacesuit-wrapped tentacles fly around, working the panels. The glowing lights on the panels danced, and Kipper watched their reflections play across the bubble of helmet over Emily's eyes. None of it meant anything to her, but clearly it meant something to Emily.

Kipper's paws itched to sign questions at Emily: *"What are you learning? What does it say? Can we use this base for anything?"* But she kept her paws to herself, endeavoring to stay out of Emily's way and keep from distracting her. It would do her no good to act like an impatient kitten, swatting at anything she saw just to evoke a reaction.

Emily's tentacles slowed to a halt, and she turned her eyes to look at Kipper. There was concern in the creases of her skin. That faceless expanse that nonetheless was her face.

Impatience bubbled out of Kipper, and she signed, "Is there life support? Can you fill this place with some kind of atmosphere?" She still hoped to turn the underground base into a bunker to protect New Persians.

Emily shrugged, a gesture that always looked impressive on

her many-armed body but that was incredibly frustrating to Kipper right now. "There are a lot of controls," Emily signed. "I don't know how long it will take me to understand them."

Kipper sighed. Maybe they could load New Persians into space suits and hide them down here anyway. It wouldn't be comfortable, or a long term solution, but it would be safer than that unprotected city on the surface.

"Kipper," Emily signed, "I'm confused. Everything on these control panels points toward one thing. It's like a big red button in the middle with giant arrows pointing at it. But, I don't know what the button does."

"What do you mean?" Kipper signed. She didn't see anything like a big red button on the smooth panels, laced with intricate glowing squiggles all around them.

"I think this base was built with one big purpose," Emily signed. "Like a nuclear power plant—turn it on, and it will generate nuclear energy. Except, I don't know what *this* base is designed to do. If I turn it on, it will do *something*, but I don't know what."

Kipper thought about that. "Could it be a power plant?"

"Could be," Emily signed. "I don't understand all the physics. I think it generates electro-magnetic waves or a field? Or maybe it's gravity? Some sort of..." She shrugged again.

The roots of Kipper's ears prickled and she felt the tip of her tail start twitching against her leg in the spacesuit. "Could it be a weapon?" *Perhaps something that could shoot down the raptor vessels.*

Emily's expression was unreadable. "If it is, I don't know if I'll be able to control it."

That could be dangerous. If they started up a planetary defense system down here in the dark, might they accidentally shoot down the *Jolly Barracuda*? Would that casualty be worth it if they saved an entire colony of New Persians?

When it came down to it, Kipper realized, she was responsible for the final decision. It was better not to over think it. "Press the red button," she signed.

Emily signed in the affirmative, showing she understood. Then her tentacles flew into a whirl, filling the alcove they shared with writhing motion. The glowing squiggles on the panels began dancing again. Apparently, the metaphorical big red button was pretty metaphorical, because Emily's eight tentacles did something a lot more complicated than pushing a single button.

As Emily worked, the lights embedded in the material of the walls of the giant room brightened. Kipper saw better, but nothing else changed. Nothing Kipper could sense anyway. Eventually Emily stopped.

"Is that it?" Kipper signed. "Did it work?"

"I don't know," Emily signed. Her tentacles drooped, expressing the same disappointment that Kipper felt.

"We can't even tell if it did anything," Kipper signed. She felt a huge temptation to start pawing at the control panels herself, as if her random interference was more likely to produce an interesting result than Emily's careful work.

Kipper jumped in surprise as a robotic voice spoke in her ear. "Jolly Barracuda *to Kipper, this is Jenny. Kipper come in.*"

Kipper's startled jump had sent her sailing in the low gravity. She scrabbled uselessly with her paws in the air trying to catch herself midflight and cried out inarticulately.

"*Kipper?*" the robot said. "*Is that you? Please speak clearly. The voice-to-text translation made complete gobbledygook of your last transmission.*"

Kipper landed several alcoves over from Emily, who was peeking over the top of her alcove to watch Kipper's inelegant flight. Kipper spat at her, ineffectively, and then regained her composure enough to say, "Jenny? You sound like a robot. Please tell me that the raptors haven't turned you all into robots."

The robotic voice replied with an eerie, *"Ha, ha, ha."* It sounded nothing like laughter. *"No, I'm typing messages into a text-to-voice translator for electronic transmission to your spacesuit radio. We're still onboard in oxo-agua."*

Kipper climbed over the honeycomb alcoves back toward Emily. As she climbed, she said for her radio, "Okay, well, things haven't gone as planned here."

Emily signed, "Are you okay?"

Kipper replied with her paws to explain the radio messages. She wondered if Emily's spacesuit was set up with any kind of radio receiver—could she send and receive messages in text form? Kipper found her own otter-spacesuit confusing enough. She had no idea how Emily's octopus-suit worked.

"Look," Kipper said for the radio. "We got kind of side-tracked." She was preparing to explain the underground octopus base and her complete failure to organize the cats of New Persia into refugee groups.

Instead, the robot voice cut in to say, *"Yes, we can tell you've been up to something."*

"What do you mean?" Kipper said, her heart thumping and her tail fluffing. "Are you all okay?" *They wouldn't be calling her on the radio if they'd been shot down by a planetary defense system, right? At least, not unless they'd survived it.*

Out of respect to Emily, Kipper signed her words too as she spoke them; she translated the robotic words into signs for Emily as well.

"We saw the strangest thing happen to a pair of raptor vessels."

Kipper's paws followed along, signing as the robotic voice in her ear continued.

"We'd led the raptor ships away from Europa and then doubled back at full speed. When we got within sight of New Persia again, it turned out that a couple of raptor ships had broken off from chasing us and were already flying toward the surface. As they got close though, it was like they just crunched, like something invisible chewed them up and spat

them out. Before either of the raptor ships could finish their descent, each of them exploded.

"We broke away and have entered a high level orbit."

There was a pause where Kipper and Emily stared at each other wide eyed. What had they turned on?

Kipper said and signed, "We found an underground base—it seems to have been built for and possibly by octopi. We don't know what it does, but we turned it on, hoping it could help the New Persians. So... I guess that was us?"

Static sounds erupted in Kipper's ears. She expected it was the sound of a text-to-voice translator sputtering mashed keys of infuriation. She felt the pit of her stomach twist at the thought of how close she'd come to killing all her friends.

It was cold comfort that the octopus base had in fact done something to protect the New Persians. That had been her goal. She had succeeded. However, she realized, if she could go back in time twenty minutes, she wouldn't have the courage to do it again. It was too much of a risk. It had come too close to having too high a cost.

"Okay," the robotic voice said, *"well, can you turn it back off to let us in?"*

Emily signed to Kipper, "I think so."

"Yeah," Kipper relayed back to the radio in her helmet. "But, can you send some sort of test objects through before going through yourselves? 'Cause, I really don't want this to go wrong."

"No kidding," the robotic voice replied. *"We don't either."* After a moment of silence, the voice continued, *"Felix says we can shoot crates of empty fish tins ahead of us to see how they fare."*

Turning off the newly powered up base turned out to be harder than turning it on. Emily's tentacles whirled around Kipper, working their magic on the glowing squiggles. Nonetheless, one crate of fish tins after another crunched into a ball of scrap metal on the *Jolly Barracuda's* viewscreen. On one paw, this meant the New Persians were safe from the raptors. On the other, the *Jolly Barracuda* was trapped on the raptor side of a powerful force field, and the longer it took to let them in, the more raptors there would be ready to follow them.

One by one, the raptor ships returned to Europa. The first few threw themselves unwittingly against the standing gravity wave that now surrounded Europa a couple hundred miles above the surface. They crunched and exploded like the fish tins. The rest of the raptor ships wised up fast.

The *Jolly Barracuda* led the raptors in a complicated game of chase, hide and seek, and the occasional round of dodge ball at a high orbit. All the while, Felix kept hopefully lobbing empty fish tins toward the moon, and Emily tinkered with the mysterious glowing control panels.

The robotic voice in Kipper's ear couldn't convey frustration in its tone, but Kipper could hear it in her own voice. She knew the tension on the *Jolly Barracuda* must be rising when the robotic voice switched from Jenny's matter of fact updates to the enigmatic though flatly delivered line, *"One fish short of a mackerel! Can't you two move any faster? We're a flamingo without a leg to stand on up here!"*

"Captain Cod?" Kipper asked.

"Sorry, that was the captain, but this is Felix. There are enough raptors up here that I don't think you should shut down the force field for us even if you can."

Kipper swore under her breath. "What are you going to do? Fly away and leave us here?" She and Emily didn't have the resources to make it to New Persia on their own.

"Maybe, but I have an idea first. Since we can't shut down the whole field anyway, let's see if we can cancel out one part of it. That way, the Barracuda *could fly through without all the raptors following us."*

Unlike Emily and Kipper, Felix *was* an expert on physics, but he was trying to understand physics equations written in a language he didn't understand, on a console he couldn't see, translated into Swimmer's Sign by an octopus, relayed by a cat whose speech was being converted to text by the *Jolly Barracuda's* computer. It was not ideal. Not at all.

Nonetheless, Felix and Emily figured out how to send a directed gravity wave to cancel out a small part of the planet-wide wave, effectively creating a temporary opening. The *Jolly Barracuda* slipped through the opening. Several raptors vessels tried to follow the *Jolly Barracuda*, but Emily closed the field, crunching them, before they made it through.

Kipper's body flooded with relief when the robotic voice said, *"We've landed next to* Brighton's Destiny.*"* She hadn't realized all her fur was fluffed out against her spacesuit until she felt the prickly sensation of it smoothing down.

"Emily sure did a number on the Destiny, *but the captain says we'll put a team on repair duty, see if we can't fix that broken wing for you. This is Jenny again, by the way. We're also going to send a team to investigate the octopus base. Felix wants an up close look at those control panels."*

"What about New Persia?" Kipper asked. Now that her friends were safe, he mind turned to all the cats and kittens who'd been scared and wounded by the raptor attacks. "They probably need medical aid. And, even after we get this base figured out, I bet a few of them will still want to go home. Force field or not, Earth is a lot safer than anywhere in Jupiter System right now."

The voice in Kipper's ear was quiet. As she waited to hear the captain's plan for dealing with New Persia, she found herself formulating her own plans. If there were too many cats who wanted to leave New Persia right away, there would need to be a hierarchy assigned to their level of need and perhaps a lottery to maintain fairness when the level of need was unclear or approximately equal. She'd never had so much power over so many people's lives before.

The next voice Kipper heard through her space helmet was

Captain Cod's, buoyant and flamboyant, a huge contrast to the robotic monotone of the text-to-voice translator. The oxo-agua must have finished draining from his captain's quarters. "Skippy sandpipers, Kipper! Congratulations on a job well done! Now, I know you were planning to decommission, but before you do, I hope you'll accept a promotion."

Kipper's ears twisted uncomfortably against the otter-shaped ears on her spacesuit helmet. "A promotion?"

"I'm going to need some help sorting out the New Persians," Captain Cod said. "And I'll need your help. I'd like to promote you from Ship's Spy to Diplomatic Ambassador to Independent Cat Nations."

Kipper's ears burned with pride. It was a silly title, but she loved it.

"Of course, you'll be free to leave the crew and return to Earth after this whole Persian situation is sorted out—"

Kipper cut the captain off. "Never mind about that." Certainly, she would want to go home and see her littermates, but Kipper was beginning to think that it would only be a visit. Her place was up here, having adventures with these crazy otters. "I accept."

CHAPTER 31
THE SOLAR SYSTEM

The first of the *Kipper Brighton: The Hero of Europa* videos hit the sketchier parts of the interwebs before Kipper's friends and family even knew if she'd survived the rescue mission to Europa. No one in the rest of the Solar System knew what was happening in orbit of Jupiter. Had the *Jolly Barracuda* succeeded? How many had they rescued? Or was the *Jolly Barracuda* just another ship smashed to pieces by the raptors?

Otters, cats, and dogs alike—on Earth and in space—waited with bated breath for the next transmission from Jupiter.

Shortly after the second *Kipper Brighton: The Hero of Europa* video appeared in a small-time webzine of questionable repute, Kipper's family received a personal message from her, letting them know she was safe.

Before the third video could be released, information about New Persia and the octopus base on Europa had exploded all over the web-o-sphere. Every animal and her littermate had an opinion. Trudith was assaulted on a daily basis by cats who wanted to thank her for being such a great friend to the Brightons or by dogs who, well, the reactions of dogs were more mixed.

Some dogs laughed at Trudith, taunted her, called her a cat herself and said she should shape up—"start acting like a real dog." Because real dogs don't have such intimate friendships with cats. Real dogs don't let cats "boss them around."

Sure, being loyal and obedient to your alpha is a wonderful thing, *if your alpha is a dog*. An alpha cat though? No such thing. Any cat in a leadership position must only have weaklings for followers. Therefore, logically, Trudith was a weak, sniveling, pathetic cat-worshipper.

Not all dogs reacted that way. Trudith's scramball team stood by her, and so did Keith. As the weeks passed, dogs were more likely to seek her out with questions—"Is Kipper really as brave and good as the videos make her out to be?" "Is she really your best friend?" And, "what's it like to work for a Brighton?" All the kinds of questions that Keith had asked her, back during their first date in the ice cream shop.

Trudith gave the same answers, staying steadfast and true to her cat family.

Shortly after the third *Kipper Brighton: The Hero of Europa* video was released amid much anticipation, the colony of New Persia released a news video of their own. A yellow-furred, snub-faced cat with a delicate gold crown balanced in the fluff of fur between her ears introduced herself as the empress of New Persia. She declared her colony's undying gratitude to all the crew of the *Jolly Barracuda*, and announced that Kipper, who truly was a hero, had been welcomed as an honorary citizen of their colony.

Two days later, with much less fanfare, Kipper's honorary citizenship was revoked when the empress of New Persia learned what the octopus base was doing to her planet.

The standing gravity wave above the surface was mirrored by a gravity wave in Europa's core—one of the waves provided a force field, crushing ships that tried to approach the planet; the other caused turmoil and friction deep inside Europa's heart, slowly melting the ice. As the ice melted, Europa began to grow oceans, and the water from the oceans evaporated. The gravity wave that functioned like a force field held in the gases that evaporated from the oceans—Europa was growing herself an atmosphere, but she was also melting.

In a matter of months, New Persia would sink. The octopus base, on the other tentacle, had been designed to float. Working together, Emily, Felix, and Ordol were able to translate enough of the information in the octopus base's computers to establish that more bases would be revealed under the oceans as the planet melted. It was enough information to throw doubt on the idea that raptors had uplifted octopuses to become slaves for them. In fact, it was beginning to look much more likely that octopi had uplifted raptors. Then, the raptors had turned on them.

Regardless, the New Persian empire was not pleased to learn that it would soon find itself sinking into a worldwide ocean. Cats are not fans of water. They certainly didn't like the idea of living on a water world. However, if the gravity wave was turned off, then New Persia would find itself at the mercy of the raptors again.

Amidst much protest, the New Persian colony evacuated. Some of the cats were invited, at least temporarily, to join Siamhalla, the cat colony on Mars. Others moved back to Earth. A few maintained their refugee status, settling into life on one or another of the otter space stations.

The future of Europa became a huge question mark. The otter ships that came to evacuate New Persian cats brought otters to inhabit and study the octopus base. However, the octopus empire on Earth declared itself unequivocally interested in those proceedings. Octopus delegates were sent to take part, and Ordol, the freed raptor slave, argued eloquently that the octopus base should, in fact, belong to the octopi of Jupiter. As soon as they could escape from the raptors' talons.

Regardless of who controlled the octopus base, it was clear that it would play an important role in the possible war with the raptors to come. The raptors had responded to the Europan shield by backing off on their attacks. For now. It wasn't clear how long that would last, and the octopus base on Europa provided an important foothold in the Jupiter system for otter and octopus kind.

As for the *Jolly Barracuda*, her crew split ways. Emily, Felix, Ordol, Jenny, and about half of the rest of the crew stayed behind to man the octopus station. Kipper left her own ship, *Brighton's Destiny*, under Jenny's command. Under the haphazard piratical law of the otters in deep space, Captain Cod felt that the octopus base was his—as long as he kept his paws on it, by leaving his own officers there to run it. Kipper wasn't sure that would work with so many conflicting interests in the base. On the other paw, by the time anyone else arrived, the Barracuders would be far more fluent in using the ancient octopus technology than the newcomers.

The rest of the *Jolly Barracuda* crew—including Captain Cod himself, Trugger, and Kipper—carried a distraught vessel full of New Persian refugees back to Earth. Watching the New Persians flounder in the oxo-agua atmosphere gave Kipper a whole new view on how awkward and silly she must have seemed to the otters when she first joined their crew. It also gave her a whole new idea of how adept at swimming she'd become. Around the otters, she felt clumsy as a newborn kitten. Around the New Persians? She felt like a bona fide otter.

Kipper followed the politics on Earth through transmissions from her brother, sister, and Trudith as the *Jolly Barracuda* flew across the solar system back home. It confused her to see the image of herself created for, reflected and distorted by the media. *She was brave. She was important. She was a hero.* She felt the same as she'd always felt, but most of her life the world had ignored her. Now that she was gone from Earth, she looked back and saw that a reflection of her had grown large. It was very strange.

However, Kipper loved seeing the videos of Alistair on his campaign trail. His running mate, Morrison, was overbearing and frightening as always. Alistair, though, was reasonable, insightful, and mellow. Too good to be a politician. Yet, there he was—running for vice president. Kipper wasn't sure if she should root for him or not though. Whatever good he could do, wouldn't it be offset by the damage that Morrison could do as president?

Trudith, Keith, and the scramball team had held their cards close, so not even Kipper knew what to expect from the final *Kipper Brighton: The Hero of Europa* videos. In fact, Trudith had convinced Keith to spread quiet rumors about the "harmless, silly cats running that ad campaign" among Morrison's agents. Until the last video, Morrison himself was quite happy with the *Hero of Europa* videos. They bought political goodwill for his running mate, and he thought that meant political goodwill for himself.

When the last video ran, the political scene on Earth exploded. With only days until the election, all the polls were suddenly rendered meaningless. All bets were off.

CHAPTER 32
EARTH

The *Jolly Barracuda* docked at Deep Sky Anchor for the first time since Kipper had joined the crew. She watched the gray metal habitat rings of the rotating station approach on the main bridge's viewscreen, and she remembered all the times she'd watched space fly by through one of the porthole windows elsewhere on the ship instead. She was sure that those windows were all crowded full of the pug faces of miserably wet Persians now, but she wasn't among them. She was on the bridge, manning one of the stations. She had come a long way.

With the *Jolly Barracuda* crew diminished by half after leaving so many crewmen on Europa, Kipper had been needed to help take up the slack. She now worked Jenny's bridge console. It seemed a fair trade—Jenny took care of Kipper's ship, *Brighton's Destiny* on Europa, and Kipper took care of Jenny's station on the *Jolly Barracuda*. It made Kipper feel like her friend wasn't quite as far away.

Besides, Kipper and Jenny had stayed in close contact by video transmission. Kipper had accrued quite the set of pen pals —Jenny on Europa, Josh the Siamese tomcat on Mars, and, of course, her brother, sister, and Trudith on Earth. It made her feel extremely cosmopolitan; she was a cat with connections on many worlds.

Once the *Jolly Barracuda* finished her docking procedures, Kipper felt her old impatience flare up: like all the cats onboard, she couldn't wait for the oxo-agua to drain away. This time, though, it wasn't because she hated the stuff. (Although, of course, she still did.) No, Kipper felt how close she was to home, and she could hardly hold her paws still or keep her tail from twitching. She wanted to put her paws down, all four of them, and run as fast as she could through Deep Sky Anchor for the elevator down to Earth.

Her tickets were all lined up: a ride down the space elevator, the ferry to Ecuador, and then a flight straight to New LA. Trugger had agreed to accompany her. They would arrive at Papa Fido's T-Bone Steakery just in time for the big Morrison/Brighton Election Night Party. Only eighteen hours and about 30,000 miles away! That was nothing compared to the rest of her journey that had already passed.

Once the oxo-agua finished draining, Kipper washed out the gummy residue left in her fur with a quick shower. She packed all her belongings—which were limited—into the purple duffel bag that she'd first brought onboard with her.

Then Kipper made snippy, sarcastic comments while Trugger indecisively packed, unpacked, and repacked his own bag. By the time the two of them were ready to disembark, she was seething and felt strangely tempted to slash his broad otter's nose with her claws when he asked if they'd have time to stop at a fur tattooist before their elevator ride.

"I thought blue swirls would be a good look for this Election party." Trugger gestured with his right paw at his left arm and then reversed the gesture for his other arm. "You know, blue swirls like ocean waves. It'd look very otterly."

Kipper skewed an ear and said, "You already look otterly. How much more otterly can you get? Is there even such a thing as more otterly than *being an otter?*" She slung her duffel bag over a shoulder to free up both paws and readied herself to actually start pushing Trugger down the hall toward the *Jolly Barracuda's* airlock.

Before their relative strengths were put to the test—a test that Kipper feared she would lose given Trugger's stocky swimmer's build—Captain Cod came strolling down the corridor with an amber wine bottle in his paws.

Trugger jumped to attention. He raised a paw to his forehead in a perfectly serious salute. Kipper followed suit, somewhat less energetically.

"At ease," the captain said. "I know you must be in a hurry—"

Kipper glared at Trugger who hadn't seemed to be in a hurry at all.

"—but," the captain continued, "I wanted to see you off and give you this gift for your family." Captain Cod held out the amber bottle. Kipper accepted it and turned it in her paws so she could read the label. "It's an aged sardine scotch. The sardines came from the Strait of Gibraltar. Very good stuff."

"Thank you," Kipper said, genuinely touched. "We'll open it at the election party. Win or lose." She looked at Trugger and added in a hiss under her breath, "*If we get there in time.* Come on, let's go."

The elevator ride down to Earth's surface was spectacular. The panoramic view of the planet's curve grew until that crescent of oceans, clouds, and continents flattened into a world that contained them, large and all encompassing. With them inside it. Instead of large but separate. Earth became the world that Kipper was on, rather than the planet she was above and looking at.

All the other passengers on the ride seemed strangely blasé, but Kipper was in raptures. She was probably the only passenger who had never seen the view before, as her only other ride on the space elevator had been spent hiding in the cargo hold.

The airplane from Guayaquil to New LA had videos for the passengers to watch, but none of them were live. Sure, Kipper could watch glossy action films or the latest puppy heart-throb rom-coms, but she was completely cut off from what was happening right now on election day.

Trugger watched several movies starring a Springer Spaniel with curly brown ears and soulful eyes who kept falling in love with big dogs who were bad for her, always to find that it was her best friend—a loveable mutt or zany terrier—who she was really meant to be with. Kipper tried to sleep and not think about the election.

Bleary eyed and rumple furred, Kipper and Trugger arrived in New LA. They staggered off the plane to find themselves in an airport swamped with media. Newscaster cats and dogs shoved microphones at their muzzles while shouting questions. Lights flashed. It was terribly confusing, and there was no way to hide. While Kipper could have disappeared into the crowd fairly easily —despite her fame, she was still one of many small gray tabbies —Trugger was the only otter in sight.

The horde of reporters parted, and a retinue of lanky Grey-hounds wearing crisp suits and wires in their ears stepped forward to surround Kipper and Trugger. One of them held out a paw to Kipper and said, "I work for Mr. Morrison. My name is Keith, and I've been sent to bring you to the Morrison/Brighton Election Party."

Kipper looked up at the Greyhound towering above her and nodded dumbly.

He smiled, parting his long, slender muzzle. "By the way, I'm also a friend of Trudith's, and, may I say, it is *an honor* to meet you." The Greyhounds escorted Kipper and Trugger to a limo. Their first stop was at Trudith's empty apartment where Keith supplied Kipper with a fancy, green brocade tunic and pants that

Petra had picked out for her. There were no special clothes for Trugger, but he did try to dye his fur with some red vinegar in Trudith's kitchen before they left. It didn't work.

The next stop before Papa Fido's was at the local public library where, amidst a complete media circus, the Greyhounds ushered Kipper into a curtained stall to vote for Alistair with the "little curvy arrow" that she and Trudith had made famous. Kipper hadn't expected a chance to vote for her brother. In all seriousness, she wasn't even sure she was still registered after her year of adventures in deep space. She didn't mention that to anyone, and none of the volunteers running the polling station gave her any trouble.

After the noise and hubbub of the library, Keith brought Kipper and Trugger to the relative quiet of Papa Fido's T-Bone Steakery. The whole restaurant was reserved for the Morrison/Brighton election event. It was a big place with high ceilings and dim lights hanging down in lanterns. Lots of atmosphere. The whole place was decorated with streamers and colorful paper fans and stars. Dogs and cats crowded around video screens in all the corners to watch live footage of exit pollsters and news anchors arguing over competing predictions.

It was a lot to take in for a cat who hadn't been home in over a year and who had only stepped off the airplane an hour ago. Trugger was enthralled. His head kept bobbing, and Kipper avoided looking at him to keep herself from feeling seasick.

"Your littermates are this way," Keith said, continuing to guide Kipper. He took her to a private back room with a glassed in door.

Trugger split off to find his own way, saying that "Like a seagull," he wanted to mingle. Kipper just wanted to see her family.

CHAPTER 33
PAPA FIDO'S T-BONE STEAKERY

Through the glass of the door, Kipper saw the pointy ears and orange fur of her brother and sister. They faced the other way, seated at a table and watching a television screen on the wall. The screen showed a pug dog gesticulating wildly. Trudith and Lucky also sat at the table, but they seemed preoccupied with something Kipper couldn't see.

Kipper opened the door quietly. Keith stood behind her. Before going in, Kipper stayed in the doorway and simply listened to the voices of these people she loved and hadn't seen in so long.

"You really think this is funny?" Trudith woofed.

"Are you kidding?!" Petra meowed between hysterics of laughter. "Topher Brooke is a genius!"

Kipper recognized the pug dog on the screen now—a comedian who mocked anti-feline dogs by pretending to hate cats in the most outrageous ways.

"I don't get it," Trudith woofed. "He's saying that it'll be the worst thing in the world if Alistair wins, and you think that's funny?"

"He's being ironic," Lucky said. "Or sarcastic. I think? It's subtle. It's a cat thing."

A tiny meouwl wailed out from the floor; Kipper's ears perked up in curiosity. Was that—*a kitten?* More tiny meouwls followed, and Kipper stepped forward into the room to see better.

Spread out on the floor by the table was an old cattery blanket that Kipper and her littermates had grown up sleeping under. It was worn and patched. Three kittens dressed in tiny kitten-sized fancy tunics were toddling about on it, batting at each other with clawful paws.

Kipper's head tilted and her ears skewed. As she watched, Trudith and Lucky worked to separate the three kittens—two orange and one gray—from each other. Each of the dogs earned several scratches in the process, but the kittens eventually settled down into clawing a set of plush spaceships toys instead of each other.

Keith cleared his throat pointedly, and all the heads in the room turned to see Kipper standing in the doorway.

"Kipper!" Trudith shouted. She nearly knocked over three chairs on her way to engulf Kipper in the canine version of a bear hug.

Alistair and Petra played it cooler, but Kipper saw the sparkles in their eyes.

"Welcome back, Space Cat," Alistair said.

Petra twisted one ear around provocatively and said, "I hear you melted Cat Haven."

Kipper felt overwhelmed by emotion, but she didn't want to be the first cat to show it. She said, "What's up with the kittens?"

"Campaign ploy," Petra quipped. "If we don't win, Alistair will threaten to abandon them in a burning building until Morrison hands over the presidency. It's Trudith's idea."

"I don't think Morrison would care a fig's worth about a litter of three adopted cattery kittens," Alistair said drily. Petra and Alistair began arguing over the finer points of Morrison's personal sense of ethics—or lack thereof.

Lucky, however, stepped forward and held out a paw to Kipper. The last time they'd seen each other, they'd been mere office mates, barely acquaintances. Now they were brother- and sister-in-law. Kipper held her paw out in return. Lucky clasped it warmly. Kipper felt the roughness of his paw pads, the wiry quality of his fur, and the dullness of his blunt dog's claws.

"You're an aunt now," Lucky said. "Petra and I officially adopted Allison, Peter, and Robin shortly after the battle of Europa, but she wanted to wait and tell you in person." Lucky looked at his wife, who was still deep in argument with her brother, and said, "I guess she wanted you to find out in person."

Kipper knelt beside the cattery blanket and watched the three kittens. She had two nephews, the orange kits in little black and white tunics, and a gray-furred niece, dressed in a green brocade tunic much like a miniature of Kipper's own. Lucky and Trudith both crouched on the floor with her, and she began telling them about her travels.

As Kipper and Trudith caught up with each other, excitement rose in the restaurant around them. Every few minutes, a dog or cat poked a head in to their back room to announce the results from a new district.

One district after another elected Alistair Brighton president —beating out both the competition and his own running mate. On the television screen, Petra and Alistair watched Topher Brooke's faux misery escalate. He claimed he'd rather die than live in a country run by a cat and tried, ineffectively, to kill himself by eating his chair. Petra rolled on the floor with laughter. Alistair, however, looked increasingly serious and sober.

"This is good news," Lucky said. "You want to be the president, right?"

Alistair nodded, but he didn't say anything.

"Don't worry about him," Petra said, pulling herself together enough to climb back into her chair. "He's just worried about the legal battle that Morrison has threatened us with if he wins."

"I'm not worried about that," Alistair said testily. His tail twitched irritably under the table. "I just feel bad letting down so many people when I decline."

"WHAT?" Petra exploded.

"You can't decline!" Trudith woofed.

Everyone barked and meowed at once. Everyone except Alistair, who waited calmly until the rest of them quieted down before he would speak.

"I will not tear this country apart with a drawn out legal battle." His whiskers were set at a determined angle, and his gaze steady as he looked at each of his compatriots in turn. "I appreciate everything that has been done for me, and I appreciate what it means to those who have voted for me. But I don't have the resources to defeat Mr. Morrison in the courts of law. If I step down gracefully, however, I may still be able to work with him as vice president. That was always my plan. Through this whole campaign, that has been my plan. No matter what the rest of you may have secretly had in mind."

Each of them weighed Alistair's words, a silence settling heavily over them. However, they heard through the walls as the rest of the restaurant exploded in caterwauls, barks of glee, and howls of anger. Kipper recognized Mr. Morrison's voice rising above the rest, but she couldn't make out his words.

"Has Morrison been out there all along?" she asked Trudith.

"Yeah," Trudith said. "He and Alistair have kept their distance from each other for the last few days, ever since the final *Hero of Europa* video came out—as much as possible, anyway, given all their joint political commitments. That's why we're in here. Out of sight, you know."

"Who's been making those videos?" Kipper asked, and

suddenly Trudith looked like she would burst with pride. "Ah," Kipper said. "That explains how they got all that footage of us."

"Are you really going to decline?" Trudith asked Alistair with a look of disappointment in her brown dog's eyes that could haunt the most hardened, cynical cat to the end of his days.

Alistair was neither hardened nor cynical, but he managed to nod his assent. "I have to," he said. "It's the right thing to do."

In the awkward silence that ensued, Trugger finally found it suitable to make his way into their back room and begin introducing himself to the glum group of Kipper's friends and family he found there. He began regaling them with stories about the *Jolly Barracuda*.

Trugger started with a retelling of Captain Cod's highly fictionalized version of how Kipper had joined their crew. He followed that with a completely factual explanation of how he'd found Ordol the octopus slave hiding in the *Jolly Barracuda's* kitchen, squeezed into a drawer of spatulas to avoid piloting *Brighton's Destiny* into the battle of Europa. Octopi are strange enough that stories about them don't need any embellishment. However, neither story elicited much encouragement from his audience, and Trugger seemingly realized something was up.

"Gosh, you're a quiet bunch," he said. "All the cats and dogs out there are a lot more worked up over the election results."

"Is it over then?" Alistair asked, looking surprised.

Petra began arguing vociferously in favor of Alistair fighting for his presidency, but Trudith stood up and stared her down. "Let him do what he thinks is right. That's why we all voted for him." Then one of the kittens started mewling, and Trudith was suddenly busy calming a tiny orange feline. Trudith was good at soothing angry orange cats.

"The scuttlebutt out there," Trugger said, rocking on his paw pads, "is that Alistair wouldn't have won today if it weren't for all the media excitement about us—" Trugger pointed over at Kipper and then back at himself, "—travelling down to this shindig. A show of support from the heroes of Europa and all that. Good timing, eh? The early bird wins the election."

Alistair and Petra looked like they were actually trying to understand Trugger's bird metaphor, so Kipper tried to save them a headache and said, "Don't think too hard about it."

"Look," Alistair said, after giving his head a good shake to get the bird metaphor out, "if all the polls are in and I've won, then I need to get out there and make my speech stepping down. The longer I put it off, the more turmoil there will be." Alistair's whiskers drooped, but his eyes looked determined.

All around the room, ears sank to half mast and tails hung limply that had earlier wagged in happiness. Then a voice that none of them expected broke into the room.

"Like hell you will," said Morrison standing in the door.

Keith stood beside Morrison and said, "I think you all need to take a closer look at the results." Keith pointed at the television screen they'd all been ignoring.

The comedian Topher Brooke was drawing floppy ears and a lolling tongue on a picture of Alistair, but, more importantly, the marquis scrolling along the bottom of the screen showed the exact breakdown of the election.

Brighton/Morrison had won at 39%. Followed by Jankowski/Dorowitz at 37%. The final 24% went to Morrison/Brighton.

"My legal aides tell me," Morrison said, "that I could easily make the case that the votes for you should be thrown out, and you wouldn't have the resources to fight me." Morrison ran his paws over the fluff of mane that burst out of the collar of his suit. He looked ruffled and unhappy. "Apparently, it would be much harder to make the case that they should be counted as votes for me."

Alistair's posture changed subtly. He looked more lively, more alert. "You mean..."

"I mean," Morrison huffed, "if I fight you, I get nothing. If I throw my support behind you, well..." His voice thickened into a gruff grumble. "I would be honored to be your vice president, sir." Morrison held out a paw, and Alistair didn't hesitate to take it.

Around the room, tails wagged and ears stood tall. Trudith handed the orange kitten she'd been coddling to Lucky and stood up to join Alistair. It was time to be Alistair's guard not Petra's nanny.

Keith led the way out, staying close to Morrison. Trudith followed, clearing the way as she led her alpha cat toward the stage set up in the back of the restaurant to make his speech. She'd never looked prouder or like she felt more important. She was a good dog working for a good cat, who was about to become the president of their country. He would be everyone's alpha cat now.

ABOUT THE AUTHOR

Mary E. Lowd is a prolific science-fiction and furry writer in Oregon. She's had more than 200 short stories and a dozen novels published, always with more on the way. Her work has won three Ursa Major Awards, ten Leo Literary Awards, and four Cóyotl Awards. She edited FurPlanet's ROAR anthology series for five years, and she is now the editor and founder of the furry e-zine *Zooscape*. She lives in a crashed spaceship, disguised as a house and hidden behind a rose garden, with an extensive menagerie of animals, some real and some imaginary.

For more information:
marylowd.com

To read Mary's short stories:
deepskyanchor.com

ALSO BY MARY E. LOWD

Otters In Space

Otters In Space

Otters In Space 2: Jupiter, Deadly

Otters In Space 3: Octopus Ascending

Otters In Space 4: First Moustronaut

Otters In Space Spinoffs

In a Dog's World

When A Cat Loves A Dog

Jove Deadly's Lunar Detective Agency (with Garrett Marco)

The Entangled Universe

Entanglement Bound

The Entropy Fountain

Starwhal in Flight

Entangled Universe Spinoffs

You're Cordially Invited to Crossroads Station

Welcome to Wespirtech

Beyond Wespirtech

Brunch at the All Alien Cafe

Xeno-Spectre

Hell Moon

The Ancient Egg

The Celestial Fragments (A Labyrinth of Souls Trilogy)

The Snake's Song

The Bee's Waltz

The Otter's Wings

Tri-Galactic Trek

Nexus Nine

Commander Annie and Other Adventures

The Necromouser and Other Magical Cats

The Opposite of Memory

Queen Hazel and Beloved Beverly

Some Words Burn Brightly: An Illuminated Collection of Poetry

Furry Fiction Is Everywhere (with Ian Madison Keller)

www.ingramcontent.com/pod-product-compliance
Lightning Source LLC
Chambersburg PA
CBHW061336160726
47995CB00001B/46